MURDER WITH
CINNAMON SCONES

This Large Print Book carries the
Seal of Approval of N.A.V.H.

A DAISY'S TEA GARDEN MYSTERY

MURDER WITH CINNAMON SCONES

KAREN ROSE SMITH

WHEELER PUBLISHING
A part of Gale, a Cengage Company

Farmington Hills, Mich • San Francisco • New York • Waterville, Maine
Meriden, Conn • Mason, Ohio • Chicago

LIBRARY OF CONGRESS CIP DATA ON FILE.
CATALOGUING IN PUBLICATION FOR THIS BOOK
IS AVAILABLE FROM THE LIBRARY OF CONGRESS

ISBN-13: 978-1-4328-5453-9 (softcover)

Published in 2018 by arrangement with Kensington Books, an imprint
of Kensington Publishing Corp.

Printed in Mexico
1 2 3 4 5 6 7 22 21 20 19 18

To my son, Ken . . .
and the good times we had
baking and cooking together

ACKNOWLEDGMENTS

I would like to thank Officer Greg Berry, my law enforcement consultant, who so patiently answers all my questions. His input is invaluable.

CHAPTER ONE

The Victorian house with its gray siding and white gingerbread trim loomed in front of Daisy Swanson as she and Tessa Miller approached it. The January darkness had wrapped around the town of Willow Creek, Pennsylvania, early tonight with a cloudy pewter sky before sunset and the prediction of snow later. Daisy wasn't sure she should have let Tessa talk her into coming here to Revelations Art Gallery with her after hours. But Tessa was the chef and kitchen manager at Daisy's Tea Garden and Daisy's best friend. They'd been confidantes since high school. Still . . .

Daisy voiced her concern as a gust of wind blew her wavy shoulder-length blond hair across her cheek. She brushed it behind her ear, thinking she should have worn her hat. The temperature was below freezing. "I don't know if I should have come with you."

Walking along the side of the house to the

back door of Revelations, Tessa assured her, "I'm just going to pick up my sketchbook and leave your cinnamon scones on Reese's desk."

Tessa had been dating Reese Masemer, the owner of Revelations Art Gallery, since her show in October. She'd left her sketchbook there when she'd stopped in to have lunch with him.

Tessa went on, "You know you want to see the quilt display Reese set up. Quilt Lovers Weekend is coming up in a little over three weeks. I'm sure Reese won't mind you being in the gallery with me. He knows you and I are close friends."

Without hesitation, Tessa turned the key in the lock, stepped inside, and pressed in a security code. The long braid that kept her caramel-colored hair relatively confined swished across the back of her purple down jacket as she switched on a light. "He trusts me with the key and the code now."

And Daisy knew why. Often Tessa spent the night with Reese in his apartment upstairs.

Even in the dim light, Daisy could see Tessa blush a little. Her friend's relationship with Reese was fairly new, and Daisy wasn't sure what to think about it yet.

She stepped inside with Tessa and looked

10

around at the office. It was business-messy with a few paintings positioned on easels and art books spread across a large maple desk. Papers — invoices and such — were scattered over the surface of the desk too. A computer station sat at the far wall and the computer was off. At least it looked as if it was off but it could have just been sleeping, Daisy supposed. Tessa's sketchbook rested on the corner.

"I'm surprised you and Reese aren't out on a date tonight," Daisy said. Reese and Tessa had been spending most evenings together.

Approaching the desk, Tessa set the foil-wrapped package of cinnamon scones there and picked up her sketchbook. "He has a meeting with a client tonight in York and he said he won't be back until late."

Willow Creek, in the heart of Lancaster County, was close to Lancaster as well as York, making it an ideal small town with other accessible services close by.

"I *am* interested in the quilts display." Daisy unzipped the first few inches of her fleece jacket patterned with cats. "Especially if Reese has any Album quilts. But then I want to get home."

"Vi only has a few more days at home before returning to college, doesn't she?"

Tessa asked.

Her friend knew how much Daisy had missed her older daughter. "Yes, and I want to spend as much time with her as I can. And Jazzi —"

Her fifteen-year-old had had a lot on her plate the past six months. Not only had she missed her sister, Violet, who had gone off to college, but as an adoptee, Jazzi had decided to search for her birth parents. After weeks of silent secretive behavior in the fall, Jazzi had finally confided in Daisy. She knew her girls missed their father, who had died three years ago, and Jazzi particularly had been close to Ryan. Putting her own feelings about the search aside, she'd aided Jazzi's efforts to find her birth mother. Now Daisy wanted to be available to her younger daughter because Jazzi had an upcoming visit planned for this Sunday with Portia Smith Harding. Jazzi might want to talk about it. Although her daughter had spoken with Portia on the phone, she hadn't seen her face-to-face since their first meeting in October.

"Come on," Tessa said, disrupting Daisy's thoughts. Crossing to the doorway that led into the other rooms of the gallery, Tessa paused.

When Reese had bought the old Victorian

to use for the art gallery, he'd kept its charm and only done renovations that would help show off work in the gallery. Now Tessa guided Daisy through a dark room into a larger one where ambient light glowed from a track along the ceiling.

"I have to find the light switch," Tessa said.

Daisy stayed perfectly still so she didn't inadvertently knock an elbow into an art piece. Most of the work Reese carried was from new artists, but some of it was still valuable.

There was an eerie quality about the Victorian that manifested in several ways. A light mustiness always floated in the air. Did that come from the house being over a hundred-fifty years old? Possibly. Or perhaps from the antiques that Reese used for display tables. The floorboards, although they had been refinished to their original character, creaked. It was hard to find one that didn't.

She and Tessa stood in one of the rooms toward the back of the house. As she peered through the duskiness to the front room, it looked as if shadows appeared to be waving in the streetlights. Those were tree branches swaying in front of the huge bay window.

When there was a bump and swish as if a branch had brushed against the side of the house, Daisy jumped. She wasn't a nervous person, only anxious when she had concerns for her daughters. But this gallery, devoid of patrons, was giving her the creeps.

Finally Tessa found the light switch. An overhead light glowed mildly over the room. Daisy knew Reese didn't want glaring illumination to disturb the atmosphere of his displays or damage any of the works.

"Over there." Tessa pointed to a corner where Daisy could see quilt stands and several quilts folded over chairs. Another was spread across a table. The array drew her to it as she forgot all about the eeriness of the Victorian house. She went straight for one of the quilt stands where she recognized an Album quilt. It *was* beautiful. The tag on the quilt read BALTIMORE ALBUM QUILT.

"Isn't this gorgeous?" she whispered.

Tessa came up beside her. "Reese said that one's worth about fourteen thousand dollars."

"Just look at this fine needlework."

"It's hard to believe it's from the nineteenth century. I can't imagine anyone sewing so evenly with those tiny stitches."

"This is appliqué and reverse appliqué, embroidery, and more padded appliqué that makes up the three-dimensional blocks. I really should learn to quilt. Rachel Fisher

14

teaches it." Rachel and Levi Fisher, friends of Daisy's, owned Quilts and Notions. They not only sold quilts but cloth and sewing supplies, too.

"Reese believes the Quilt Lovers Weekend will bring in the most business for Rachel and Levi."

Daisy knew the Amish family well. Although she'd moved away from Willow Creek after college, she remembered her childhood as if it was yesterday. Rachel's parents had grown shrubs and trees for Daisy's mom and dad to sell at their nursery, Gallagher's Garden Corner. So Daisy had spent time on that farm. She admired the family and their Amish way of life.

Reluctantly, she moved away from the Baltimore Album quilt to study another.

Suddenly she heard a noise coming from another room. It didn't emanate from the office or the front gallery. If she remembered the downstairs layout correctly, it was coming from the stairs that led to the second floor.

"Someone else can't be here," Tessa murmured, stepping toward a sculpture of an old man sitting on a tree stump. She picked it up as if she intended to hit someone with it.

Daisy held her breath, unsure what Tessa

would do next.

Tessa hadn't yet taken a step when Reese appeared in the doorway!

They were as surprised as he was.

Reese Masemer wasn't quite six feet tall, but he was fit and lean. At forty-something, his hair was sandy brown, thick, and long. It shaggily splayed over his denim shirt collar. His dark brown eyes landed on Daisy and Tessa. His face, which had seemed too pale, showed a little more color.

Tessa spoke first. "What are you doing here? I thought you had dinner and a meeting with a client."

Appearing a bit shaken, Reese shrugged. Then he smiled. "I thought I had intruders. I'm glad to see it's the two of you. I was worried I might have to invest in a new alarm system."

Crossing to Tessa, he wrapped his arm around her waist. "My client cancelled so I was spending the evening working on my laptop upstairs. I have a lot to catch up on — invoices to input from the sales over the holidays." He wiggled his brows at Tessa. "Including two of your paintings that sold. I'm ready for you to bring more to the gallery."

Daisy's woman's intuition told her that Reese was trying to distract Tessa from the fact that he was still here and hadn't told her.

Her friend, a bit besotted by her relationship with him, let him do it. "I came over to bring some of those cinnamon scones you like so much and pick up my sketchbook. The scones are on your desk. I asked Daisy along because I knew she'd like to see the quilts before we had to scramble through people to view them. They're going to be a big draw."

"I suspect they will be," he agreed. "Those Album quilts are a real find. But that's another reason I'm concerned about security."

He did seem troubled, Daisy thought. But did his concern really have to do with the Album quilts?

Reese gave Tessa another squeeze. "Remember, we're going to have a candlelit dinner in York on Saturday evening. Is that still good for you?"

"It is. But I hope we can spend some time together before that. Are we still on for dinner tomorrow evening?"

"We are."

With Reese and Tessa gazing into each other's eyes, Daisy felt like the proverbial fifth wheel. This was Wednesday. She imagined Tessa would be staying overnight again

17

before Saturday. "I'll let you and Tessa say a proper good-night." Crossing the room, she headed for the office and the outside back door.

It wasn't long before Tessa joined her, rosy-cheeked and looking just-kissed. However, she was quiet as they left the gallery and closed the door. Once outside, she glanced up at the apartment on the second floor where all the blinds were drawn. No light escaped. Had Reese really been working up there?

A cold wind buffeted them. Daisy pulled the zipper on her jacket up to her neck and turned toward the tea garden where her car was parked.

Tessa took a few quick steps to keep up and asked, "Do you think Reese rushed us out?"

In spite of the wind, Daisy stopped. "What's on your mind?"

"Reese's assistant, Chloie Laird, flirts with him constantly. What if she's been doing more than flirting? What if she was upstairs with him?"

Daisy watched as Tessa took another look up at the second floor. "Are you saying you don't trust Reese?"

"You know it's hard for me to trust anyone."

Daisy *did* know that. But before they could delve into that subject, Tessa changed it. "We're going to be passing Woods. We could stop in and say hi to Jonas."

Tessa was aware that Daisy and Jonas Groft had spent time together. Daisy enjoyed his company and, if she had to admit it, more than enjoyed it. However, Jonas had closed his shop from Christmas to New Year's and gone to Philadelphia to spend the holidays with good friends. They'd spent New Year's Eve together, though, with her girls. That was a few days ago. Since then, she hadn't heard from him. She wasn't sure she should visit Woods because she didn't want to push.

Because of his background as a former Philadelphia detective, Jonas had gotten pulled into her life to help Jazzi search for her birth mother. It was quite possible he didn't want a serious relationship. To be honest, she wasn't sure *she* did.

Still, Tessa caught her arm and pulled her along, saying, "Come on. You've got to take risks in your life. You don't very often."

"Opening the tea garden with my aunt was a risk." After her husband had died, she'd returned to her hometown to start over. She and her aunt Iris had bought a house to establish Daisy's Tea Garden, and

Daisy had also renovated an old barn where she and the girls now lived.

"Your aunt knows more about tea than Wikipedia. And the two of you created a place where everybody comes to chat and relax, eat good food, and drink the best tea. How could it have missed?"

"It still could. You know the track record with small businesses."

"I do. But we're growing. We hired more help."

"When you become a rich and famous artist, you won't want to be my kitchen manager."

With a frown, Tessa studied Daisy. "If I ever do become rich and famous, I'll still be your best friend. And if I have to quit my job, I would find you the best kitchen manager on the face of the earth."

"Now that reassures me," Daisy said wryly as they stood in front of Woods.

"Come on," Tessa urged again, opening the door and pulling Daisy inside. "At least we'll get warm for a few minutes."

Daisy just shook her head and gave in to the inevitable enthusiasm Tessa usually exhibited. However, to her relief, Jonas was nowhere in sight within the store. Elijah Beiler was. He was an Amish woodworker who sold furniture through Jonas's shop. In his forties, Elijah wore black pants with suspenders and a dark blue shirt. His beard signified he was married.

"Good evening, ladies," Elijah said with a broad, welcoming smile.

"Evening, Elijah. Is Jonas around?" Daisy asked.

"No. He went searching for reclaimed wood. He's thinking about adding a line of furniture created from it."

"I've seen furniture crafted from reclaimed wood on those building shows on the Home & Garden channel," Daisy recalled. "They're beautiful."

Elijah went to the counter in the back of the store and reached underneath. After he brought out a few sketches, he carried them to Daisy and Tessa. "Would you like to look at these? They're what Jonas has in mind."

When Daisy had renovated the old barn that she now called *home,* she'd included an island in her kitchen. She'd examined many in her search for the best one for her use and was familiar with the styles. She admired the plans for islands that Jonas had designed, as well as those for a sideboard table and a practical desk.

"You and Jonas are both very talented," Daisy said, meaning it.

A humble man like most Amish, Elijah

21

reddened at her praise. "Like me, Jonas takes pleasure in bringing the real nature of wood to life."

"I'm looking forward to seeing what the two of you come up with," Daisy assured him. She glanced at Tessa. "We'd better go. I want to get home to the girls."

"I'll tell Jonas you stopped in," Elijah assured them.

Daisy wasn't certain she wanted him to do that, but she kept silent. After a round of good-byes, she and Tessa left Woods.

They walked briskly up the street. In front of Daisy's Tea Garden, they paused and glanced at *their* Victorian. The tea garden took up the first floor. Tessa lived in the second-floor apartment and used the attic for painting.

A light that came on at dusk and went off at dawn glowed on the front porch. It illuminated the pale green exterior with its white and yellow trim. On the first floor Daisy and her aunt had furnished the be-served or buy-it-to-go room with oak, glass-top tables. She'd painted the walls the palest green. A second tea room on the first floor was a spillover area. It was also the room they used when they took reservations and served afternoon tea by appointment. That room's walls were the palest yellow.

Daisy's office was located to the rear of the tea room and the kitchen spread behind the walk-in room. They also had a side patio where they served customers outside, weather permitting. A private parking area for Daisy's, her aunt's, and Tessa's vehicles ran in back of the Victorian.

"Business is still good," Tessa reminded her. "Even though it's early January and the tourist season has slowed down. That means the community is embracing Daisy's and the tea garden is an integral part of the area."

"I hope that's what it means. The uptick in business could still be from the notoriety of the murder that happened here."

Daisy's Tea Garden had been the scene of a murder in the fall, and there had been publicity from that with local TV coverage as well as discussions on online blogs.

"Foster has really helped to spread the word about Daisy's Tea Garden on social media too," Tessa added. "You have to give him credit for that."

Foster Cranshaw was a college student Daisy had taken on when they'd gotten busier. He and Violet dated when she was home, and Daisy had mixed feelings about that. Yes, she wanted Violet involved in relationships so eventually she could find a permanent life partner. Daisy was sure marriage and vows would mean as much to her daughters as they had to her and Ryan. On the other hand, Violet was still young and she hoped her oldest and Foster weren't too serious.

"Foster has been a huge help," Daisy agreed. "I don't know what we'd do without him. He has a way with customers, and his tech skills are a godsend."

They were walking along the lane that led to the private parking lot when a shrieking alarm pierced the silence of the night.

Tessa spun around toward the direction from which they'd come. "That sounds like it's coming from Revelations."

The alarm was so loud and piercing that Daisy supposed it could have come from any of the businesses along their street. But she followed Tessa as she raced down the sidewalk. Daisy wasn't going to abandon her friend now.

As Tessa streaked past a candle shop, an insurance office, a store that sold hand-sewn purses and travel bags, as well as Woods, Daisy kept up with her pace. Elijah had come out of Woods and was staring down the street too.

Tessa ran by him and so did Daisy, realizing now that Tessa had been right. It was the alarm from Revelations that had sounded. Running along the side of the building to the back entrance, Tessa didn't hesitate to go inside when she saw the door was opened.

Daisy called after her. "Tessa, wait! We don't know what's happened. It could be a fire . . . or *anything.*"

But Tessa didn't wait. And when Daisy ran inside and caught up with her, she saw Tessa holding up Reese, who leaned heavily on her. There was blood on his forehead and down the side of his face.

Daisy pulled out her phone to call 9-1-1.

Reese saw her do it and held up his hand. "You don't need to call anyone. The alarm alerted the PD. They'll be here."

Tessa led Reese to a wooden captain's chair and he flopped into it.

"What happened?" Daisy asked. Certainly, Reese didn't do that to himself. Could someone still be in the gallery?

"An intruder got in before I reset the alarm. He hit me and escaped. I managed to smack one of the panic buttons."

Reese had definitely been hurt by someone. Papers from the desk were strewn across the floor. But something about his story didn't seem to ring true. How could anyone have known the alarm was off? Why hadn't Reese reset the alarm after she and Tessa had left? Had a break-in really occurred?

Or had something else happened that Reese didn't want anyone to know about?

CHAPTER TWO

Daisy had a logical mind, barring emotions getting in the way. After all, she was a mom. She ran a business. She used self-talk to convince herself that her mother didn't like her sister best. Therefore, she had a pretty good women's intuition meter when it came to separating a lie from the truth. Reese's story didn't make sense.

Reese was a business owner and somewhat influential in Willow Creek. Daisy had attended Chamber of Commerce meetings where Reese had gotten things done.

His story just didn't ring true. Not only patrol officers arrived on the scene. No, the chief had sent Detective Rappaport to investigate whatever had happened. Morris Rappaport and Daisy had crossed paths before. He wasn't especially fond of her or her aunt, though the three of them had made a type of peace at the conclusion of his last murder investigation. But tonight he looked as grumpy as usual and not at all happy to see Daisy. He'd questioned Reese and now he approached her and Tessa. He looked from one of them to the other as if he thought about separating them to question them.

Daisy said amiably, "Detective Rappaport. It's good to see you again."

"Is it?" he asked, running his hand through his thick blond-gray hair. "I was off duty when the chief called me in. This doesn't seem worthy of my time."

Already Daisy could sense Tessa's outrage. "Reese was hurt. What do you mean, it's not worth your time? Someone could have killed him."

In his fifties, Rappaport had grooves along his mouth and deep lines on his face. He gave Tessa a steady look. "Tell me, Miss Miller, what you and Mrs. Swanson have to do with all of this."

"We told the patrol officers why we were here earlier and why we're here now," Tessa said, crossing her arms across her chest.

Rappaport studied his notebook. "Indeed you did, something about bringing cinnamon scones to Mr. Masemer. It seems an odd reason to be here, don't you think? Does Daisy's Tea Garden now have delivery service?"

In her dealings with Detective Rappaport in the past, she'd learned it didn't do any good for them to antagonize him. She laid her hand on Tessa's arm hoping to quiet her. "Tessa and Reese are dating," she said calmly, looking Rappaport in the eye. "Tessa knows he likes my scones and she suspected I'd like to see the quilt display. She'd also forgotten her sketchbook here and wanted to retrieve that."

"Quilt display?" Rappaport's eyebrows arched as he focused on that part of her explanation.

"Reese is displaying antique quilts in preparation for Quilt Lovers Weekend in three weeks. He felt it would help draw in business. The Baltimore Album quilt, especially, is very valuable."

"I know Amish quilts run up a good sum of money," the detective said. "But just how valuable could a quilt be?"

Tessa's hackles were up again. She pointed toward the quilt stands in the other room. "One of those quilts in there is worth close to fourteen thousand dollars. That's probably why an intruder broke in."

Rappaport looked to Daisy. "Is she right about that?"

"Tessa knows more about it than I do. She helped Reese with the display. If you ask him, he can tell you what they're worth. But, yes, a Baltimore Album quilt like the one he has displayed can be worth thousands of dollars."

"You grew up in Willow Creek, didn't you?" Rappaport asked Daisy.

Remembering what Jonas Groft had advised her last time she'd dealt with the Willow Creek Police Department, she answered with as little explanation as possible. "I did."

"So you've been around the quilts and Amish all your life."

"I have."

He looked a little perturbed at her short answers. They had been through this before when she'd had a lawyer advising her.

Rappaport cut his gaze toward Tessa again. "So how long have you and Masemer been dating?"

"What does that have to do with someone hitting him on the head?" Tessa asked tersely.

"*I'm* asking the questions," Rappaport reminded her imperiously.

Daisy tried to communicate to Tessa without words that she'd be better off just answering the detective's questions. She must have gotten through to her telepathically because Tessa said, "We got to know each other when he showed my work here in the fall. Afterward we began dating."

"A few months then," Rappaport said, summing it up.

"That's right," Tessa answered.

"So let me get this straight. Kravitz over there told me you have a key to this place, that you unlocked the door, pressed in the security code to disarm the alarm, and then what? Give me a play-by-play."

Because they'd gone through this with the patrol officers, Tessa answered a little impatiently. "I put the scones on Reese's desk, picked up my sketchbook, and then Daisy and I went to look at the quilts. While we were admiring them, we heard a noise. I didn't expect Reese to be here because he said he was having a meeting with a client. It turns out his client cancelled and he was working upstairs. So when he heard us down here, he came down."

"And he found the two of you with the quilts?"

Daisy found herself feeling a little huffy too. He made it sound as if they'd been doing something sinister.

"We were admiring the workmanship on the quilts," Daisy explained. "That's when we heard Reese come down. But we didn't know it was him."

31

"So what did you do?" Rappaport asked.

"I picked up that sculpture over there in case there was an intruder," Tessa said. "But then Reese stood in the doorway and we saw it was him. That was it. After he and I talked about dinner plans, Daisy and I left."

"But you came back," Rappaport said almost accusingly.

Now Daisy *was* getting impatient. "We came running back when we heard the alarm go off. We didn't know what had happened."

"Why would you come running back here when a robbery could have been in progress?"

"Don't be so dense," Tessa said. "I love . . ." She stopped. "I care about Reese. I didn't know what might have happened. It could have been a fire. He could have hit a panic button by mistake —"

"Panic button?"

"It's an art gallery, Detective. He brings in valuable work. There's an alarm button in every room," Daisy informed him.

"I see. And you know this how?"

"Because we're friends," Daisy said with some exasperation. "Tessa has shown her work here. I know Reese, not well, but I do know him. We're business owners. We're on the Quilt Lovers Weekend committee together. We go to the same Chamber of Commerce meetings. Willow Creek is a small town, Detective."

"Don't I know it," he mumbled. "Every day I'm here I'm reminded again how different it is from big-city life. That's why this break-in is a little out of character. And to tell the truth, I'm having a little trouble with the whole scenario."

"What does that mean?" Tessa asked.

"Mr. Masemer insists he didn't recognize the intruder. If the intruder was close enough to do him harm, and if Mr. Masemer had enough time to push a panic button, I have to wonder —"

"Detective!" the patrol officer suddenly called to him.

Her gaze targeting where the patrol officer and Reese were standing, Daisy spotted Reese put his hand to his forehead. He looked incredibly pale and shaken, and suddenly he took an unsteady step forward and the patrol officer had to catch him and lower him to a chair.

Tessa ran over to him. "Reese. What's wrong?"

"Just a little dizzy," he said.

Tessa had her phone in hand. "I'm calling the paramedics."

But Reese waved his hand at her. "No. I

33

don't want any more commotion."

"Then let me take you to the urgent care center," Tessa said. She rounded on the detective. "You have to let him be taken care of. You can't question him under these conditions. He's not even fit to know what he's saying."

Detective Rappaport was silent for a few moments, and then he nodded to the patrol officers. "I agree that you need to be treated," he said to Reese. "But answer me one question, Mr. Masemer. Did the intruder touch anything that you're aware of?"

Reese took a bolstering breath. "He was headed toward the quilt stand when I came upon him, but I surprised him. So I don't think he had a chance to touch anything. And now that I think about it, his hands glowed white in the dark like he was wearing gloves. He was also wearing a ski mask."

The detective studied Reese for a long moment. "Well then," he said, "I don't suppose fingerprint dust is going to do us much good. And even if we tried to get prints, I imagine you have enough of a crowd coming through here from week to week to make elimination of prints almost impossible. Tell me again where he hit you."

Reese looked down for a moment, then back up at the detective. "In my office. I startled him. He ran. I ran after him, and he turned around and slugged me."

"And why did you run after him?"

"I wasn't sure if he'd stolen anything or not."

"Did you run after him before or after you hit the panic button?"

Reese didn't miss a beat. "Before. After he hit me, I stumbled back and fell. That's when he ran out. That's when I hit the panic button."

"I'm going to get my car," Tessa decided, cutting off the questioning. "Reese, don't move. I'll be back in five minutes. Detective, I thought you were going to wait to question him further."

"Yes, I was, wasn't I? I'll give you a call tomorrow, Mr. Masemer, to see how you're feeling. And we can set up a time for you to come to the station. We'll go over your story again there and get a full report. And then you can sign your statement."

Daisy had the feeling that Detective Morris Rappaport would be going over Reese's story more than one more time. He obviously didn't think Reese was telling the truth.

The chatter at Daisy's Tea Garden the next morning was thicker, faster, and more vigorous than usual, not only among Daisy's customers but amidst her staff, too. In a small town, the gossip mill could be faster than cell phone service, and Willow Creek was no exception. Her aunt Iris, her ash-brown short curls bouncing, had come up to her more than once during the morning, leaned close, and exclaimed, "I can't believe you found Reese Masemer after the break-in."

Daisy sighed inwardly and tried to keep her mind on what she was doing — putting together an order for a dozen cinnamon scones for a customer having tea at one of the tables. She glanced across the room to see if her customer was still involved in sipping her Darjeeling tea. She was.

Usually Daisy loved the tea room atmosphere. She and her aunt had decided not to make the tea room fussy, though they did have a subtle flower theme. They wanted both men and women to feel comfortable here. They wanted both casual tourists and professionals from town and Lancaster stopping in. So when Daisy had decorated the front Green Room with glass-topped tables and mismatched antique oak hand-carved chairs, she felt everyone would be comfortable there. A yellow bud vase adorned each table. After the holidays, she'd decorated each with dried lavender and rosemary tied by a yellow ribbon.

Aunt Iris didn't wait for Daisy to respond, but rather she said, "I have to check on that group that came on the bus from Harrisburg. They had the big table for six."

Her aunt nodded toward the spillover room where they took reservations for and served afternoon tea on specified days. That room reflected the best qualities of the Victorian with a bay window, window seats, crown molding, and diamond-cut glass. There the room was the palest yellow. White tables and chairs always looked fresh and wore seat cushions in blue, yellow, and green pinstripes.

At that moment, Tessa came from the kitchen to stand with Daisy at the counter as her aunt bustled away. She checked the case. "The cinnamon scones are selling out. I have another batch in the oven, but we might need four or five more batches today."

Tessa was age thirty-seven like Daisy. Today she wore her medium-brown hair braided. Her colorful, flowy tops and skirts weren't hidden by an apron as Daisy and Aunt Iris's were, but rather she wore smocks. Her smock today was swirls of brilliant turquoise, fuchsia, and gold. However, her eyes had blue circles under them. The creases around her mouth seemed deeper and she wasn't wearing her usual brilliant smile.

The front door to the tea room opened, letting in frosty January wind along with Russ Windom, one of their regular customers. He was a retired schoolteacher who came in almost every morning for one of their baked goods and a cup of tea. He was a widower with time on his hands, and he enjoyed chatting with other customers as well as Daisy and her staff. He unzipped his brown corduroy parka as he came to the counter and smiled at them. His gray hair had been ruffled by the wind, and he fingered through it trying to put it in order. He had a high forehead, bushy white brows, and titanium black-framed glasses that made him look like the schoolteacher he'd once been.

"Hi, Russ," Daisy said genially. "What would you like today?"

"How about a cup of lemon crunch tea and one of those cinnamon scones?"

"Coming right up," Tessa said, and she was headed back into the kitchen. But Russ stopped her.

"I heard you two were questioned by the police last night."

Daisy and Tessa exchanged a look, and

almost with resignation, Tessa said, "We were."

"What happened?"

They certainly didn't want to add to the gossip, but Daisy knew one way or another, what had happened would leak out. Still, she kept her response simple. "Apparently, someone tried to break into Revelations."

While they'd been talking to Russ, the door had dinged and now Chloie, Reese's assistant at the gallery, stood beside him at the counter.

Chloie was a twenty-seven-year-old bleached blonde who was model-tall. Almost belligerently, she said, "Reese was a hero. He beat off the intruder, and the man fled. Who else do you know who would do that kind of thing?"

Daisy knew one person who would — Jonas Groft — but then with his police training, no one would blink an eye at that.

However, the fact that Chloie was calling Reese a hero was a bit of a stretch.

"Do the police know what the thief wanted to steal?" Russ asked. "A night deposit or an artist's piece in the gallery?"

Again Chloie was the one who answered. "The detective on the case thinks the intruder was after an antique quilt. It's quite valuable, and it was on display. That really only makes sense. After all, lots of the pieces in the gallery are new artists who don't bring in much income." Chloie shot Tessa a look, and Daisy could see Tessa glare back. Tessa obviously didn't like Reese's assistant, who knew how to push Tessa's buttons. Daisy had heard either from Tessa or gossip at a Chamber of Commerce meeting that Chloie had worked in a museum in Philadelphia right out of college and her knowledge of art was invaluable to Reese. She'd been working for him over a year now.

Although tension was thick between Tessa and Chloie, Daisy knew Tessa probably had a question she wanted to ask yet wouldn't, so Daisy asked it for her. "How is Reese?"

"That cut on his head was nasty and needed stitches. But don't worry. He'll be at the committee meeting here this afternoon. He's all gung-ho for Quilt Lovers Weekend. This bump on the road won't slow him down. In fact, just to keep up his energy, I thought I'd buy him some of those cinnamon scones he likes so much. How about a half dozen?"

Daisy watched Tessa try not to react. She was sure her friend was remembering their excursion to the gallery last night and leaving the scones on Reese's desk.

Apparently, Tessa couldn't help herself

because she jumped into the conversation. "I suppose Reese ate the scones I took him last night."

Chloie's face clouded. "Maybe. But if he didn't, they're stale this morning and he could use some fresh ones."

The timer in the kitchen beeped and Tessa said, "I'm just taking a tray out of the oven now. I'll put the package together for you to give to Reese. They'll still be warm." With that she hurried into the kitchen.

Chloie looked after her, her hazel eyes shooting sharp little daggers. Daisy had the feeling that if Chloie had her way, Tessa wouldn't even touch the scones. Daisy said to Russ, "Have a seat and I'll bring you your tea and a warm scone."

He smiled at her. "You know coming here every morning has added some structure to my life since I retired. I always find a smile or two here and it's a great way to start the day."

Comments like that always warmed Daisy's heart. "I'm glad you're a part of our tea-sipping family."

As Russ walked away, Chloie mumbled, "I don't know what Reese sees in Tessa's scones. It seems to me a chocolate muffin would put a bigger smile on his face."

"It must be the secret ingredient Tessa

41

puts in the scones," Daisy said. "I'll be right back with them in a minute."

When she entered the kitchen, she saw that Eva Connor, her dishwasher and girl Friday, was spooning tea into an infuser inside a porcelain pot for Russ. "Ready soon," she said. "I'll brew it for five minutes, then bring it out."

Daisy nodded.

Tessa had arranged the six scones in one of their boxes made for half a dozen. She was writing on a sheet of paper torn from the pad on the refrigerator where they often jotted down their to-do lists. She folded the paper, put it into the box on top of the scones, and then shut the lid. She inserted the box in a waxy bag.

"Did you include more than scones?" Daisy asked with a smile.

"You bet I did. I refrained from writing on the piece of paper, 'You should fire Chloie.' Instead I just wrote, 'Thinking of you,' and added a little heart with my name."

"You should probably have a talk with Reese about Chloie," Daisy said in a low voice. "Especially if she bothers you so much."

"We haven't been dating long enough," Tessa said. "I don't want to seem clingy and possessive."

"You're not clingy and possessive. You're not the type."

"Then why am I jealous?" Tessa whispered.

"Because you don't know where you stand. When I've seen Chloie and Reese together, she might flirt with him sometimes, but I haven't seen him flirt back. Talk to Reese and leave Chloie out of it. Just have a chat about where your relationship stands."

"You make it sound so simple."

Daisy merely lifted her brow.

"I'll see him tonight and maybe we'll talk about it, but for right now . . ." Slipping on a latex glove, she plucked a warm scone from the cookie sheet and set it on a china plate that was painted with pink and blue roses with a gold trim.

"Here's Russ's scone. He's the kind of customer I like to serve. I'll take the box out to Chloie. It will give me satisfaction to hand it to her knowing there's a love note inside, and she doesn't know it's there."

Daisy's eyes met Eva's and they both just shook their heads. Tessa could see for herself how Reese was feeling when he attended the committee meeting this afternoon.

The committee planning Quilt Lovers Weekend had decided to have their next meeting around three PM in the tea garden's spillover room. Three o'clock was a slow time for most businesses, especially in January. During the week in winter, the shops in Willow Creek were usually open until five.

The committee wandered in, one by one. Daisy first brewed tea for Amelia Wiseman, who owned the Covered Bridge Bed-and-Breakfast, not far from Daisy's barn home. Daisy greeted Amelia herself and brewed her a pot of China white tea with a touch of cranberry and rosebuds.

As Daisy brought the pot to Amelia, who was sitting at a large table by the bay window, Amelia said, "I hope Quilt Lovers Weekend really brings in the customers. We've been especially slow this year."

Amelia, in her mid-forties, wore her dark brown hair layered around her face in a straight cut. She'd inherited the bed-and-breakfast from her parents. She and her husband, Phillip, poured their energy into the Colonial almost-mansion that had been in the family for generations.

"Have you done as much advertising as

44

you usually do?" Daisy asked.

"I have, but advertising that reaches the right audience is getting more and more difficult."

Just then Foster Cranshaw approached the table with a three-tiered plate of goodies for all of the members of the committee to enjoy. He set it down with a smile. "Good afternoon, Mrs. Wiseman."

"Hello, Foster," she said pleasantly. "How are your studies?"

"Getting back into the groove after the holidays."

Amelia said, "Keep those grades up even though you enjoy brewing tea. Everyone now should have two or three career back-ups."

Daisy decided to share her good fortune in hiring Foster. "Amelia, do you have a social media page?"

"Goodness no," Amelia said. "I don't know anything about it."

Glancing at Foster, hoping he knew what she was thinking, he gave a little nod and Daisy realized he did. "I didn't know anything about it either, at least not more than what the girls do on there. But Foster set up a business page for me, and we're getting more Likes every day. That means those are people who want to know about Daisy's

Tea Garden. You could do the same thing for the bed-and-breakfast . . . and maybe set up a website. That could help business."

"I wouldn't know where to start," Amelia murmured.

"Foster makes a great virtual assistant. He keeps track of the pages for me and posts things for me. He keeps a time sheet so I can pay him an hourly wage for what he does." She wouldn't expect Foster to give his services free to Amelia.

The bed-and-breakfast owner studied Foster and then Daisy. "Let me look at my bottom line for the month. If Phillip says I can afford you, we can start out small and maybe get a page set up before Quilt Lovers Weekend. Do you have time for that?"

"I can make time. As you said, it's good to have one or more backup careers," Foster said.

They all laughed.

Daisy heard the ding of the front doorbell and Reese Masemer walked in along with Rachel Fisher from Quilts and Notions. They stopped at the counter where Iris chatted with them. She was learning what tea they liked to drink during their meeting. She noticed Reese took a step or two toward the kitchen, realizing Tessa was there. Reese and Tessa talked for a few moments, and then he headed Daisy's way along with Rachel.

As they were all seated at the table, Rachel and Amelia avoided the obvious conversation about what had happened to Reese the night before. Instead they enjoyed the cookies on the table, the scones with clotted cream, the mini smoked salmon sandwiches. After Aunt Iris brought Rachel a Japanese sencha green tea that tasted of almonds and coconut and a rooibos tea blended with cinnamon and blackberry for Reese, talk turned to the promotion plans for the Quilt Lovers Weekend. The four of them had been the only ones in their Chamber of Commerce group to volunteer to coordinate the weekend.

Reese opened his electronic tablet and studied a list on it. He nodded to Daisy. "So you've placed ads on quilting sites and in quilting newsletters, correct?"

"I actually had Foster research quilting sites and check out which ones had the most traffic. He's put comments on their blogs and taken ads. I think they'll be hitting a good audience there."

Reese nodded. "And, Amelia, you're going to display hand-fashioned quilts from this area on all the beds in the bed-and-breakfast? Is that correct?"

"We surely are. We're also going to display two that are in a raffle over the staircase railings."

Next Reese looked at Rachel. "That display should help you."

"I'm sure it will. We'll begin selling the raffle tickets a week before. So will the other participating businesses." The strings of Rachel's *kapp* floated down over her black apron. Today her dress was a dark royal blue. Her blond hair was pulled away from her face into a bun under her *kapp.*

Her blue eyes sparkled with helpfulness as she further explained, "I've already made out the schedule for our shop. We'll have local women actually working on quilts on Friday and Saturday. Customers can bring their questions and even their problems for us to solve. Amelia and Daisy, along with Jonas Groft at Woods and a few of the gift shops, will offer our hand-quilted potholders, placemats, and smaller wall hangings for sale. Everyone seems eager to be involved. They just didn't want to plan the weekend."

"Or put their money into the pot for ads or any expenses we might have," Reese said. "I admire the three of you for doing that. I think in the long run you'll get it back fourfold."

"As long as the weather cooperates," Amelia decided. "A sudden snowstorm could derail all of our plans."

"God willing, the weather will be *gut,* ain't so?" Rachel said. "It wonders me how everything usually works out."

Living in Willow Creek, Daisy was used to the Pennsylvania Dutch phrasing and manner of speaking. Amish children learned Pennsylvania Dutch before English. Rachel and Levi were New Order Amish. Their district had their own school, separate from the public school. Amish didn't believe in advanced learning because that could be prideful. However, they found trades that suited their talents, including owning a business like Quilts and Notions.

Suddenly a sound came from Reese's flannel shirt pocket, like a low buzzing. "I have my phone on vibrate. Let me see who this is. If it's not important, I'll let it go to voice mail."

Pulling the phone from his pocket, he checked the screen. When he frowned and a concerned look came into his eyes, Daisy knew he was going to take the call.

"Please excuse me a few minutes," he said, standing. "I have to take this." Then he went to the far side of the tea room to have a bit of privacy. He turned his back to them and

49

kept his voice low.

Daisy wondered if an important client of Reese's was calling. Could it be the police with more questions? Or could it be someone who had something to do with what had happened to Reese? Daisy still doubted his story about what had happened last night. If he cared about Tessa, would he confide in her?

Maybe after he and Tessa talked, Daisy could find out.

CHAPTER THREE

After the committee for the Quilt Lovers Weekend left, Daisy and Iris enjoyed a cup of tea. Daisy filled her aunt in on everything that had been discussed. In the main tea room, Tessa, Foster, and Cora Sue were serving end-of-the-day customers.

Glancing toward Tessa, Daisy told Iris, "After the initial part of the meeting when Reese went down his list, he seemed distracted."

"Maybe he was distracted by Tessa," Iris suggested. "You know when people are in love, they can't think of anything but each other."

"That's possible," Daisy said. "But it didn't seem like a happy distraction. Do you know what I mean?"

"Sure, I do. More like something was on his mind. The break-in?"

"Possibly. I just wonder if he's as serious about Tessa as she is about him."

"You can't protect the world, honey," Iris said, patting Daisy's hand.

"I know," Daisy agreed with a smile. "Maybe we can just serve the whole world tea."

As Iris chuckled and took another sip of her orange pekoe, Foster came into the room and approached their table. "I have a favor to ask," he said to Daisy when he reached them.

Iris started to rise to her feet. "I'll let you two have some privacy."

He shook his head. "It's not necessary, Iris, really. I talked to Vi on my break," he said. "I know you don't have many more nights with her before she goes back to college on Monday. But she and I —" He stopped. "We haven't had much time to ourselves this week with my classes starting up and my hours here."

"Do you want to cut your hours?" Iris asked.

"Oh, no, nothing like that. But I just wondered — do you mind if Violet and I go out tomorrow night? The indie bookstore is having an indie musician play. I thought it would be a nice change of pace for both of us."

"You don't have to ask my permission to take Violet out," Daisy said. "You're both over eighteen."

"I know, but it's a little sticky dating the boss's daughter."

Daisy laughed. "I hadn't quite thought of it like that."

"And I know you miss her when she's gone, and she and Jazzi like to spend time together, and we kind of all know each other here since we work together."

"I suppose we do," Daisy agreed, liking Foster more and more each day. "I don't mind if you and Vi go out, as long as that's what she wants to do."

Foster looked greatly relieved. "I just wanted to check it out with you. I'll call her as soon as we close."

The bell on the front entrance dinged and Foster looked over his shoulder. "I'd better get back in there and help Tessa. Thanks, Mrs. Swanson."

"He's a nice boy," Iris said. "It's just a shame he and Vi are so young. What are the chances it will last?"

"What are the chances *any* relationship will last?" Daisy found herself asking.

"You haven't seen Jonas since New Year's Eve, have you?" Aunt Iris asked with a probing look.

"No, I haven't. We've both been busy."

"Have you spoken to him since then?"

Daisy shook her head.

"Texted?" Iris questioned.

Daisy shook her head again.

Iris gave a little nod. "I see."

"What do you see?"

"I see two people with a lot of stuff they're using to protect themselves. Why don't you call him?"

"Because he might not want to talk to me."

Iris rolled her eyes. "What an excuse. That sounds like one of your mother's directives from when you were a teenager. Don't make the first move. Don't unsettle anybody in any way."

Daisy's mom and her aunt didn't always get along. They loved each other but, in many ways, Iris was much more forward-looking, much more open-minded. Daisy supposed that rules and regulations as well as values that her mother had instilled in her sometimes got in her way. But she didn't want to talk about that. "Have you talked to Mom this week?"

"She and your dad seemed to be enjoying themselves in Tampa. They needed a vacation, but I'm sure they'll be glad to get home next week."

The front door chime dinged again and Iris and Daisy exchanged a look. Iris said,

"I suppose we'd better start inventorying the case and the refrigerator. Apple bread for a special tomorrow?"

"That sounds good." Daisy pushed her chair back and rose to her feet. She and Iris carried their cups and saucers into the main tea room. Seeing them there, Foster said, "I'll take those for you," gathered their cups and saucers, and carried them to the kitchen.

Daisy recognized the customer who had just come in. It was Dutch Pickel from Dutch's Deli down the other side of the street. He wasn't a tall man, about five-eight. His hair was white blond and ran in a ring around his balding head. His mustache was the same light blond. He moved in quick jerky movements that said he was a busy man. He hadn't even worn a coat to run over to the tea garden . . . just a sweater and jeans.

He said to her, "How about a cinnamon scone and Darjeeling?"

"Take a seat. I'll bring it right over." She liked to keep up good relations with the other shopkeepers. She and Dutch didn't compete against each other. He sold sandwiches and hoagies, both hot and cold. She carried soup and he didn't. He sold basic salads where Tessa created specialty ones for the tea garden. He sold chips and sweet and sour pickles made by a local Amish man. She sold tea and her menu revolved around the types of tea and baked goods.

Five minutes later, she brought him his scone and tea. He pulled the scone in front of him, tore off a bite, and popped it into his mouth. He sighed. "This is good. I don't know how you keep coming up with different recipes, but I like them all." He sighed again.

"Busy day?" she asked.

"I wish it were busier. I hope the Quilt Lovers Weekend gets us some attention from those new offices in Lancaster. We're not so far away that they couldn't stop here for a sandwich and a scone, right?"

"Not so far away," she agreed, "for a lunchtime jaunt, and if they want a change of scene. The Quilt Lovers Weekend committee met today and we're hoping the ads that we did place pay off."

"I wish I could have helped with the promotion, but I just couldn't afford the added expenses right now. I'm really trying to save for retirement."

"I understand. Running any business is tough these days. We're hoping the cross promotions will pay off for all the shopkeepers."

"I have posters up already, and I'm inserting flyers in every customer's bag. I'm hoping every tourist who comes into town will grab lunch at my deli, so the least I can do is help any way I can." Dutch looked up at Daisy. "You know, I think I'll take another scone. Do you have any more left?"

Looking over at the case, Daisy saw there were a few more on the daily special tray. "I'll get you one. More tea?"

But Dutch waved his hand over the cup of tea. "No, I'm fine. Maybe I'll take that scone to go."

It had only taken Daisy a minute to package up the scone for Dutch when the door dinged again. She thought they might have an early closing, but not today.

As she carried the bag with the scone to Dutch's table, she saw who had just walked in. Cade Bankert. She and Cade had gone to high school together. He was a real estate agent who had sold her and her aunt the house for the tea garden and also her property where she had refurbished the barn. She'd gone out with Cade a few months before. He hadn't followed up with another date, and then she and Jonas had seemed to grow closer.

When Daisy brought Dutch's scone, she laid his bill on the table. Standing, he picked it up and went to the counter where Aunt Iris was at the register.

"Are you serving the competition now?" Cade asked Daisy.

"Dutch isn't really competition. Actually, we help each other. We were just talking about cross-promoting the Quilt Lovers Weekend."

"I can only hope that weekend will bring in clients for me, too. I have more time on my hands than usual with the market slowing down over the winter. Keep your ear out if anybody wants a property in the area."

"I certainly will. You know I'd send them to you if anyone asks."

Cade had dark brown hair and brown eyes, and a smile that helped him win clients and sell houses. He gave her one of those smiles now. "We small-town businesses have to stick together."

"Yes, we do."

Tessa came out from the kitchen and was at the counter talking with Dutch and Aunt Iris. Cade noticed her and asked, "Is Tessa upset about what happened to Reese?"

She and Cade and Tessa had all been classmates together and had remained friends. So it was quite in keeping for Cade to ask.

"She was shaken up, that's for sure. She

58

went with him to urgent care."

"I heard he had stitches from the assault."

Daisy just nodded. "That's true. He seems okay today, though. I just wish we really knew what the assault was all about."

"You mean, what the intruder wanted to steal?"

Daisy wasn't sure that was exactly what she meant, but she didn't say anything differently to Cade.

Cade studied her for a few seconds and then asked, "Do you find Reese to be a closemouthed kind of guy?"

Daisy thought about it. She hadn't known Reese long or well. "He readily states his opinion." She remembered their committee meetings.

"Oh, I don't mean in general," Cade said. "I mean about himself and his past."

She considered that, and then admitted, "I don't know anything about him or his past, really. Tessa hasn't mentioned it either, and that did seem unusual since she's dating the man. Would you like a cup of tea and a snack?"

"That's why I'm here," Cade said. "You know my favorite, orange pekoe, and one of those cinnamon scones if you have any left. I heard through the grapevine they were a hit today."

She laughed. "Let's hope they'll be a hit the next time we make them too." She motioned to the mostly empty tables. "Have a seat. I'll brew the tea and be right there."

Once she brought Cade his tea and scone, he motioned to the chair across from him. "Do you have a few minutes?"

"For you I do."

He took a bite of the scone, then picked up the cup with the tea and took a whiff. "Just what I need at the end of a winter day." He set it down again without taking a sip. "I know better than to try it before it cools a little." He glanced at Tessa again, who was now cleaning out the case of baked goods. "I know Tessa's an artist and all, but Reese doesn't really seem like her type."

"What do you think her type is?"

"I don't know. Someone with a bit more pizzazz than Reese. I mean, he doesn't even dress like one of those artist types — all in black."

Daisy couldn't help but laugh. "You mean because he wears flannel shirts and jeans he can't be an artist type?"

Cade shrugged. "He's indecisive, too, and I can't see Tessa liking that in a man."

"Indecisive about what?"

"Reese came to me in the fall looking at properties to buy, but nothing seemed to suit and he couldn't commit. I took him around to about five different properties. He didn't want to go ahead with loan pre-approval, which seemed odd if he really wanted to buy a house." Now Cade did take a sip of the tea and peered at her over his cup. "I probably shouldn't have told you that."

"Don't worry. I'll keep it to myself."

After another bite of scone, Cade surprised her by asking, "Are you dating Jonas Groft?"

She wasn't exactly sure how to answer that, but she decided to be as truthful as she could be. "We've spent some time together, including New Year's Eve."

"But?" Cade asked, prompting her.

"But . . . I haven't heard from him since, so I don't really know where we stand."

Cade looked serious as he commented, "Then you're not dating exclusively."

She admitted, "We haven't discussed it."

A small smile played over Cade's lips. "Then how would you like to have lunch with me? You don't have to call it a date. We can meet at Sarah Jane's Diner."

Old high school classmates, business owners in the same town, and friends. That's what she considered Cade to be. "It would have to be a day we don't serve afternoon tea. The tea garden needs all hands on deck those days. But I'd like to have lunch with you."

Cade gave a nod and smiled again. "I'll call you."

How often did a man say he was going to call and then not call?

But this was Cade. If a lunch with him was meant to be, then it would be.

On Friday evening, Daisy was free. Since Violet was going out to dinner with Foster tonight, and Jazzi had gone home from school with a friend to work on a debate team preparation, Daisy decided to visit Levi and Rachel Fisher's farm.

After going home to change and give her two felines attention, she ate a light supper while Marjoram, a dark tortie, and Pepper, a black cat with a white chest, enjoyed theirs. They gave her thank-you affection around her ankles, then settled on a rug in the living room to wash themselves. As Daisy set the alarm, Pepper meowed a good-bye. Marjoram just blinked at her, her golden eyes narrowing as if telling Daisy not to stay out too late.

Fifteen minutes later, Daisy drove down a slushy lane and pulled into the parking area behind the Fisher house. Visits here reminded her so much of her childhood days.

She'd rambled through the cornstalks with Rachel. They'd laid on their backs in sweet grass, imagining pictures in the clouds. Although Rachel Esh had dressed differently than Daisy had, although their lifestyles were very different, they'd become fast friends.

Rachel's family didn't have electricity. They hung their wash on a clothesline that reached from the house to the barn. And they traveled in a horse and buggy. However, despite all that, Daisy's family's values and the Eshes' values seemed to be very much alike. Hard work was a core tenet. Daisy's parents had taught her that while running their nursery. Rachel's parents had taught her that while running their farm. Where Rachel's faith was strong, so was Daisy's. Daisy had loved visiting the Esh farm because Rachel's family was boisterous — she'd had four brothers and two sisters. Daisy had appreciated the deep family bonds and sought to be part of them. When Rachel had married Levi Fisher, Daisy had realized her friend would continue to nourish all the bonds in her life.

Now as Daisy knocked on the back door that led into the Fishers' mudroom, she considered the Amish way of life. Rachel's oldest brother and his wife lived and farmed on the Esh property, the farm next door. In this house, Levi's *maam* — his grandmother — lived with him, Rachel, and their children.

The back door swung open and Rachel wore a broad smile. "It's so *gut* to see you. Come in. Have dessert with us. Some shoofly pie and tea."

"I don't mean to intrude."

"Don't be silly." Rachel took Daisy's arm and led her into the kitchen, which was warm with delicious smells. A gas light shone overhead. There were smiles all around the table from Rachel and Levi's three children — who ranged from sixteen to twenty — and Levi's *maam.*

It looked as if the children had just finished up their dessert. Levi stood and nodded to Daisy. "We'll busy ourselves in the living room." He looked to his wife. "You visit." He patted his stomach. "I already had two pieces of shoofly pie."

Levi's *maam,* whose name was Mary, nodded approvingly. "*Ya.* You'll need it when you have to start shoveling snow again. I heard it's coming and my bones agree."

Maam was already cutting Daisy a slice of shoofly pie. She scooped a generous dollop of whipped cream onto the top.

Rachel brought a teakettle from the gas stove to the table. Taking a teacup and saucer from a beautifully fashioned handmade hutch in the corner, she set it on the table and poured Daisy tea. "I have a whole stack of potholders that *Maam* made that you can sell in your shop."

"They'll go fast when the tourists start coming in," Daisy assured her.

"I'll have placemats, too," Mary said. "Maybe even sets. I still have three weeks."

"Do what you can," Daisy advised her. "But don't wear yourself out."

Mary helped any way she could on the farm but she also spelled Rachel at the shop now and then. She was still active and vibrant and didn't show her years. She wore her gray hair the same way Rachel did, parted down the center and pulled back tightly on both sides under her *kapp*.

While Levi and the children sat in the living room, Daisy, Mary, and Rachel caught up on what was happening on the farm and at the tea garden.

"Your parents are enjoying Florida, ain't so?" Rachel asked.

"They are, but I think they miss Willow Creek, too. Dad's enjoying the pool. Mom wants him to join a gym when they get back so he can swim if he'd like. But he says he doesn't have time for that back here."

"A swim in a pool isn't quite like our dips in the pond, are they?" Rachel asked with a twinkle in her eyes.

"No, not at all. I think about those days when the tea garden gets really busy. Life seemed so much simpler."

"Was it?" Mary asked. "Or did it just seem so because you were children?"

Mary imparted wisdom and Daisy knew Rachel went to her for advice. Daisy wished she could go to her own mother that way more often, but Aunt Iris was easier to speak to, discuss with, hash out problems with. Her mother was more judgmental. Maybe that's why she admired Mary so. She didn't judge.

Daisy dug into her shoofly pie. The sweet gooey dessert with the luscious whipped cream on top was just what she needed with a cup of tea to fortify her for the weekend. She didn't know what would happen when Jazzi's birth mother arrived on Sunday for an overnight visit.

Talk in the Fishers' kitchen soon turned to the committee meeting that Rachel had attended with Daisy. "Plans seem to be going smoothly for the Quilt Lovers Weekend, but Mr. Masemer just didn't seem quite himself," Rachel observed.

So she wasn't the only one who had noticed. "I think someone breaking into the gallery really shook him. Tessa told me the doctor checked him out thoroughly. But that doesn't mean he's not having ill effects."

Levi had wandered back into the kitchen, gone to the cupboard, and pulled out a glass. Then he filled it with water. "Mr. Masemer is lucky he wasn't hurt worse."

"I think he knows that," Daisy agreed. "Maybe that's what's shaking him up, too, that he could have been hurt more seriously. He didn't want the doctors to stitch him up. Tessa said he kept arguing that he just needed a bandage. But the doctor on duty convinced him he needed stitches."

Levi took a few sips of his water, and then he set his glass on the counter. "Mr. Masemer can be difficult at times."

Daisy looked from Levi to Rachel to Mary. "Difficult? I didn't know you'd had dealings with him."

"Not usually," Levi answered. "He wanted to buy my *grootmother*'s Album quilt, but we didn't want to sell it."

"So one of the quilts he has on display is yours?"

"It belonged to Levi's great-grandmother," Rachel explained. "It not

67

only holds memories but history. We want to hand it down to our oldest daughter."

"I can understand that," Daisy responded.

Levi shook his head. "Mr. Masemer didn't want to take *no* for an answer. I bet he came here three times to try to convince us."

"But?" Daisy prompted.

"Levi convinced *him*," Mary said. "He could put it on display to hopefully draw tourists into his gallery. But he had to be very careful with it, protect it, and bring it back in as good a condition as we gave it to him."

"And Reese agreed?"

"*Ya,* he did. He had to agree if he wanted to show it in his gallery," Rachel said.

Daisy wondered if Reese was simply like that in business or in his personal life, too. Would he take no for an answer?

"I can only imagine the hours and hours that are put into Album quilts. I'd like to learn to quilt but I don't know if I have the time," Daisy admitted.

Levi went back into the living room with the children.

Rachel said, "Quilting shouldn't be about finishing. It's about putting your heart into each stitch and just relaxing and doing your best in that moment."

Daisy thought about that. "I still have

dresses and slacks from when the girls were little. I'd love to sew those into a quilt."

"Then you must come to the store on a quilting day," Rachel said, not for the first time.

"I'll seriously think about it."

"How are your girls?"

"They're good. Vi is enjoying college, I can tell. She's coming home more often than she thought she would, to date Foster as well as to see me. But that's okay. As long as her mind stays on her studies, I'm okay with her having a beau."

"And Jazzi?" Mary asked.

Both women knew about Jazzi's search for her birth mother.

"She's excited about Portia coming to visit us again. I'd like to encourage her excitement but I don't want her to be disappointed. The fact that Portia hasn't seen her since October might mean she's not ready to have Jazzi in her life. I don't know if Jazzi can accept that. We've talked about it some but Jazzi's still very idealistic. I think she expects us all to be one big happy family at some point."

"It *is* possible," Mary said, "if it's what everyone wants."

But was it what everyone wanted?

Suddenly Daisy's phone played from her

pocket, making a tuba sound. A little embarrassed, she waved her hand at it, knowing phones ringing weren't common in an Amish household. Amish businesses might have a phone, but many families used phones with answering machines in sheds that served more than one family. "I'll just let it go to voice mail," Daisy said.

But Rachel shook her head. "Nonsense. Even Amish teenagers during their *rumspringa* have cell phones now."

Rumspringa was a time in an Amish teenager's life when he or she decided whether or not they wanted to join the church and remain Amish. They got to taste the English world, including driving cars, attending parties, stretching their wings.

"I can take it outside," Daisy offered.

But Mary said, "See who's calling, then decide what you want to do."

Daisy smiled at Mary's practical advice and took it from her pocket. As her phone played again, she saw Tessa's picture on the screen. "It's Tessa," she murmured. "Maybe I should take this."

She stood and, out of respect for the family and their beliefs, she walked out to the mudroom. She still had reception there. "Tessa, hi. What is it? I'm at Rachel's."

"Daisy, you won't believe what's hap-

70

pened. I don't know what to do."

"What's happened?"

Daisy could hear Tessa crying now. Actually sobbing.

"Tessa, take a deep breath. What's wrong?"

Somehow Tessa managed to say shakily, "A body was found in the woods near the covered bridge. Reese was murdered."

CHAPTER FOUR

"Are you all right?" Daisy asked.

"I don't know," Tessa mumbled. "I'm at the police station."

"At the police station? Why?"

"Because Detective Rappaport asked me to come down here. He has loads of questions. We're taking a break."

Daisy wondered if Tessa should be talking to a lawyer instead of to her. "How can I help?"

"You can't. I think he's almost done with me. He went to get us something to drink."

"Do you want me to come down there?"

"No, I don't want you involved. Besides, as soon as he lets me go and I go home, I'm crashing. I'm going to have a glass of wine or two and go to bed. I don't even want to think."

Her friend might not want to think, but she had to, or she could become a suspect. It sounded as if she already might be.

"Tell me what happened," Daisy prompted.

"I was supposed to meet Reese at his place but he never showed up. I was mad so I left and came home. But then Detective Rappaport came to my door and asked me to go to the police station with him."

"He couldn't talk to you at your apartment?"

"He recorded our interview. I guess he didn't want to do that there."

"Why did he come to you?"

"Apparently, they'd gotten a warrant to search Reese's place and the gallery, and they found my things there."

Daisy didn't want to make things worse for Tessa, but she asked, "When did they find Reese?"

"Apparently, they found him this morning . . . or rather someone from the bed-and-breakfast did. I guess they didn't find anybody else's things but mine in his apartment."

"Did you really expect them to?"

"I don't know. Chloie has this way about her that makes it sound as if she and Reese have a tight relationship."

"But that doesn't mean they've been intimate, and you've never seen any signs of

it. If the police didn't find anything there
—"

"Or Chloie could have cleaned up Reese's apartment really well," Tessa said with a sigh in her voice. "I guess it doesn't matter now. I just don't want them to blame me for what happened to Reese. I loved him."

"Do the questions Detective Rappaport is asking sound as if he's blaming you?"

"I don't know. He wants to know every-thing — like what nights I stayed there, how many nights I've stayed there, when we started dating, do I know anybody who would hurt him. No, I don't know anybody who'd hurt him. This is Reese, for good-ness' sake. He gets along with everybody."

"You should call Marshall Thompson." Marshall was a criminal defense attorney who had helped Daisy and her aunt stay out of trouble when the murder had oc-curred at the tea garden.

"I don't want to look guilty."

"Maybe, but I don't think you should be talking as much as you are. I know Marshall would tell you just to give them minimal information."

"But that will make me look guilty," she wailed again.

"Tessa."

Her friend's voice lowered. "Rappaport's

coming back in. I gotta go. I'll see you at the tea garden tomorrow. I'll be there. Promise." The line went dead.

Daisy stared at the phone, not knowing exactly what to do. She couldn't just leave without saying anything to Rachel and Levi. They deserved to know what was going on. The north boundary of their farm wasn't that far from the Covered Bridge Bed-and-Breakfast.

Daisy climbed out of her purple PT Cruiser Saturday morning along with Vi and Jazzi. As they rounded the nose of the car and headed to the back entrance of the tea garden, Daisy said, "You two really didn't have to come along with me today if you wanted to hang out together."

The two sisters exchanged a look. Vi pulled her knit beret from her honey-blond hair. Her golden brown eyes were sincere as she explained, "In the two years we've been back in Willow Creek, Tessa has become like a favorite aunt. We're worried about her too. Besides, what are we going to do at home other than do our nails? And . . . Foster will be coming in this afternoon."

The wind tossed Jazzi's long straight black hair across her face. "And I could use the extra money."

75

"So your motives aren't altogether altruistic," Daisy prompted as she opened the door.

"Not altogether," Jazzi agreed, her dark brown gaze honest. "But we want to help."

Inside the tea garden, the aroma of baking scones and cookies filled the two rooms. Iris was at the counter arranging the display case. When Vi and Jazzi went to Daisy's office to hang up their jackets, Daisy stopped by Iris. "Did you sleep last night?" Daisy had called her aunt on the way home from Rachel and Levi's farm to tell her what had happened.

"Not much. I just kept thinking about Tessa. And when I came in this morning, she looked like she hadn't slept a wink. While we cut the scone dough, we talked. But I don't know if she should be here, Daisy. She doesn't look good."

"I'll talk to her," Daisy assured her aunt. "Could you take over as kitchen manager for the day if she leaves?"

"Of course I can. If we need more baked goods, I'll whip up apple bread in between brewing tea and chopping up veggies for soup. I can always call Karina if we need her." Karina Post was their go-to person for short notice. With her fuchsia hair, she was twenty and she and her two-year-old lived

76

with her mom. She worked in her mom's leather goods shop but could almost always get away to help Daisy because her mom was available to babysit.

"I checked my weather app before I came in. The temperature is dropping into bitter cold today. Either we'll have tourists on planned bus tours that come in just to keep warm, or we'll have a very light day."

"Go talk to Tessa," Iris encouraged. "She's already burned herself twice. We don't need a major accident in the kitchen today."

As Daisy entered the kitchen, Tessa was lifting scones from a cooling rack onto a serving tray. Daisy greeted Eva, then turned to Tessa. "How are you doing?"

"I'm fine," Tessa mumbled.

She didn't look fine. Her hair was escaping its braid. Today she was wearing a tea garden apron with a daisy emblazoned on the front instead of her usual smock. Her tunic sweater with its cowl-neck was dusted with flour above her apron as if the flour had puffed up from the mixer. She was pale and wore no lipstick. Again, that wasn't like Tessa. And her eyes — they were red-rimmed and puffy with black circles beneath them.

Daisy felt so sorry for her. She enveloped her in a big hug. At first Tessa resisted, but then she leaned into Daisy, and Daisy could feel her sobs.

"You shouldn't be here. Let's go to your apartment. I'll make us both a cup of tea there and we can talk."

"There's nothing to talk about," Tessa sniffled. "Reese is dead. How can that be?"

"I know how you feel," Daisy said simply.

At that, Tessa leaned away and gazed into Daisy's eyes. "Now I understand how you felt when you lost Ryan — like the bottom had dropped out of your world."

"Exactly. Come on. Get your coat."

Tessa followed Daisy's instructions, not even taking off the apron. She walked like a robot to Daisy's office, grabbed her multicolored poncho with faux fur trim, and followed Daisy out the back door. They didn't talk as they went to the door to Tessa's apartment.

Daisy noticed Tessa had trouble putting her key in the lock. Finally she got it, turned the deadbolt, then unlocked the door. They climbed the interior stairway to the apartment. As they stepped inside, Daisy remembered all over again how very different her taste was from Tessa's.

Her friend's bohemian sensibilities about fashion were present in her apartment too. Her sofa was kidney-shaped with throw pillows along its back. The colors of the pillows went from vibrant red to patterns in blue, orange, and wine. The sofa itself wore a fabric patterned with diamonds and chevrons in the same colors as the throw pillows. A low coffee table in front of it was covered with a scarf in bright colors too. The vase with dried flowers, including lavender, was positioned at one end along with a wood candlestick holding a pillar candle. There was a platform rocker with wooden arms and burnt orange fabric.

Daisy's glance went to bookshelves along a wall. Multicolored scarf valances in burnt orange, red, and yellow were draped over rods on the front windows. An antique corner shelf along with prints framed in walnut, pine, and white distressed wood decorated the walls. Daisy knew Tessa's bedroom was just as colorful. A crazy quilt with patches from velvet to gingham to stripes was the focal point.

When Daisy and her aunt had redone the kitchen, they'd replaced the old cabinets with birch. Tessa had picked the backsplash, a multicolored blue tile. Her teapot was blue too, and sat on the stovetop. Crocks on the counter held kitchen utensils, flour, sugar, and tea. Tessa had definitely made the place her own.

"Let me make you a cup of tea," Daisy offered.

Tessa wandered into her living room and sank down on the couch. "Okay," she murmured. "You know where the tea is."

Yes, Daisy did. She let Tessa settle a bit as she filled the teapot with water, set it on the stove, and turned on the burner. Taking one of Tessa's bone china teapots from a cupboard, Daisy opened a canister on the counter, spooned what smelled like peach tea into the infuser, and went into the living room to wait for the water to heat.

"I really think you should let me call Marshall Thompson."

Tessa looked up at her. "Not Jonas?"

Jonas Groft did have contacts at the Willow Creek Police Department, but Daisy was feeling awkward about their friendship. She simply said, "I think it would be better to call Marshall. I still have him on speed dial."

Tessa's eyes seemed to glaze with her thoughts for a moment, but then she nodded.

Daisy didn't waste any time because she didn't want her friend to change her mind. She dialed Marshall, hoping he'd pick up. He did. He was a regular customer at the tea garden and they often chatted . . . or rather he often chatted with her aunt Iris.

"Daisy, hi. Is something wrong?"

"I'm sorry to bother you on Saturday."

"Nonsense, I work every day. How can I help?"

She explained the situation.

"Tell him I'll pay him an hourly fee," Tessa said.

"I heard that," Marshall told her. "Let's not worry about a fee yet. I'll see what I can find out and get back to you."

The teakettle whistled and Daisy quickly took it off the heat, poured water into the teapot, waited a few minutes to let the tea steep, and then poured two cups. She brought them both in and set them on the coffee table. "Do you want anything with this? I can make you breakfast."

Tessa shook her head. "I'm not hungry. I'm not . . . anything. I feel numb."

"And shocked over what happened. You're still trying to absorb it."

"I just can't. It's not just Reese. It's the gallery, too. What will happen to it?"

"I don't know. It depends on Reese's estate, on who the executor is. Do you know if he had a will?"

Tessa shook her head. "We never talked about anything like that."

"Do you know if he has family who needs

to be notified?"

"He never mentioned any. The detective asked me the same thing. He got very snooty about it. He said if Reese and I were involved, shouldn't I know something like that? Yes, we were involved, but we talked about art, painting, my work, the quilts, new artists. We went to plays and concerts in Hershey and Harrisburg and York and Philly. We didn't get into personal stuff. You know I don't like to talk about my background, and apparently Reese didn't either. So we let it be."

Daisy understood that, just as she understood that Reese and Tessa had lived in the now. They hadn't been serious enough long enough to delve into the past or project into the future. Certainly, the detective could see that.

Daisy's phone played its tuba sound. It was the only ringtone she could hear and decipher when she was busy at the tea garden. The caller was Marshall.

Without preamble, he said, "I found out a few things. First of all, Rappaport wants to get the crime scene tied down and handled before snow moves in tonight. Once snow falls, there won't be any evidence to gather."

Daisy lowered her voice. "So the body was found near the covered bridge?"

"Looks that way. Blunt force trauma killed Reese Masemer, but there are oddities about the crime scene."

"What kind of oddities?"

"Rappaport wouldn't say. I couldn't find out more than what I told you, but it does seem as if the police are looking at Tessa for the murder. She doesn't have an alibi."

Daisy thought of something. She looked at Tessa and asked, "Were you on your computer last night?"

Tessa shook her head. "No, I was painting."

"Did you hear that?" she asked Marshall.

"I did. It doesn't look good. If the police call her in for questioning again, she needs to call me and I need to go with her. Does she want me to represent her?"

Daisy handed her phone to Tessa. "You need to talk to him and make this official."

So Tessa did.

As Daisy lifted her cup to take a sip of tea, Tessa's doorbell chimed. When Tessa looked stricken, as if the police had come to the door again, Daisy said, "I'll get it. Finish your call with Marshall."

To her surprise, when she opened the door, she found Jonas Groft. He looked just as surprised to see her.

"I heard what happened and that Tessa

83

was taken down to the station. I thought I could help."

"That's why I'm here," Daisy answered, ignoring the twinge of attraction she usually felt around Jonas. He was tall and fit with thick black hair. "I called Marshall." She motioned Jonas inside.

Still near the door, he said, "Elijah told me you and Tessa stopped in at the store this week. Did you want anything in particular?"

At a loss, Daisy couldn't find any words. What could she say? *I wanted to know why I hadn't heard from you.* No, she couldn't say that. So she murmured, "Nothing in particular."

However, one thing Jonas was good at was reading people. His green eyes gave her a probing look. "We should talk after I see Tessa."

Without waiting for her answer, he strode up the stairs into Tessa's living room where she was now seated on the sofa looking dejected.

Daisy wasn't sure she wanted to have that conversation with Jonas, but she'd deal with that after Tessa's crisis. Jonas motioned to the cushion beside Tessa on the sofa and asked, "Do you mind?"

She shook her head.

He gave her a reassuring half-smile. "The person closest to the victim is always the best and probably the first suspect."

Daisy's friend remained silent.

"I heard you don't have an alibi."

"How did you hear that?" Daisy asked.

"I have a contact at the station. I called there. I got filled in as much as they'd let anybody know, probably the same thing with Marshall if he called."

"I don't have an alibi," Tessa said tersely.

"Let's go a little further than that," he suggested. "Have you been anywhere near the covered bridge lately?"

"Yes," Tessa admitted, surprising Daisy.

Jonas waited for more. His silence pushed Tessa to give him more. "I've been sketching there in the early morning before I go to the tea garden. I'm painting a *Morning Has Broken* series."

Jonas's frown was deep, cutting lines on his cheeks and around his eyes. Those lines must have come from his police work, not from laughter, Daisy thought.

"Did you tell Rappaport that?" Jonas inquired.

"He didn't ask."

"The fact that you've been there recently is proof that you know the area. Did anyone see you there?"

"Sure. I've been doing it for a few weeks. Guests from the bed-and-breakfast who go on early morning walks could see me. I don't hide. I even set up my easel."

"How can you sketch or paint when it's so cold?" he asked.

"I do it quickly, probably no more than half an hour at a time. I have leather gloves that fit like a second skin. But I can sketch and charcoal with those on."

"Don't tell Rappaport about the gloves," he murmured. "I wouldn't be surprised if the police ask for a warrant to search your apartment. But they need cause before they can do it. You don't want to give them cause."

"Marshall already told me not to say more than I have to, and if I have to go in again, I'm supposed to call him."

"Heed his advice." Jonas gave Daisy a look. "I'm still surprised you didn't call me before you called Marshall."

Usually Daisy tried to communicate her feelings, but this case could be an exception. She just gave a little shrug.

"Do you want to come to my shop with me so we can have the privacy to talk?"

"Not right now. I don't want to leave Tessa."

"Are you avoiding me?"

"Are you avoiding *me*?" she asked back.

Seeming to come out of the daze she'd been in, Tessa looked from one of them to the other. "Why don't you two go up to my studio in the attic? You can have some privacy there. I promise not to listen unless you shout."

Daisy felt her cheeks growing a little red. "It's really not necessary right now."

Tessa motioned to her attic steps. "Go on. Yes, I'd like you to stay here with me, but I could use a few minutes to think about all this. Go on and talk to Jonas. You know you should."

No, she didn't know she should. But he was looking at her as if he expected her to want to talk to him. Men.

When Daisy had renovated the attic of the tea garden, she'd made sure it was heated and also had air-conditioning like the rest of the house. As she and Jonas went up the stairs located in the spare bedroom, she realized the temperature was a little cooler than on the second floor. But Tessa had said she didn't mind that.

Sunlight poured in from the pair of double pane windows at both ends of the space. Paintings were propped everywhere. Tessa painted realistic scenes and enjoyed doing animals. There were several of cats in yards and on porches with flowerpots, and some of dogs, too. Their furry faces and eyes were filled with expression. Many of the propped works were landscapes of the Lancaster countryside. There wasn't much furniture up here — a purple brocade love seat, a floor lamp with a beaded, fringed shade. There was a craft light, too, so Tessa could aim light wherever she wanted it. She'd set a drop cloth under an easel and it was obvious that that painting was her work in progress.

Two finished paintings were propped against the wall, and it was apparent they had the theme *Morning Has Broken.* The first painting was the morning winter sky, gold and orange and fuchsia with purple breaking the other colors. A horse and buggy were depicted with a misty shadow as part of the scene. The second painting depicted a half-risen sun gleaming across the fir trees in that area. Only a corner of the covered bridge was evident. The third painting that Tessa was obviously working on showed the covered bridge at its best in full sunlight. About half of it was finished. She was working on laying in the covered bridge amidst the other colors of sunrise.

Studying the paintings, Jonas frowned. "We can only hope Rappaport doesn't get a warrant and come up here to see these."

"Just because she painted the area doesn't mean she killed Reese there."

"Why did you call Marshall instead of me?" Jonas asked in a low voice.

Since all of her relationships were built on honesty, she admitted, "I didn't know if you'd want me to call you. I hadn't heard from you since New Year's Eve. Even after Tessa and I stopped in at the shop, you didn't call . . . or text."

Hurt must have sounded in her voice. Jonas's expression softened and he motioned to the purple love seat. She went over to it and sat. A folding wooden chair was propped against the wall. He took hold of it and dragged it to the love seat and opened it.

Sitting across from her, almost knees to knees, he confessed, "I didn't call but I've been thinking about you a lot. I've enjoyed the time we've spent together."

Uh-oh. She heard the underlying message there. A very big "but" was coming. "You've enjoyed the time we've spent together. Does that mean we're not going to enjoy any more time together?"

After all, she wanted to be clear about this. After her husband's death, she'd been hurt, lonely, angry, filled with pain so deep even when she cried it wouldn't come out. After she'd been able to breathe again, take stock again, made the decision to come to Willow Creek, she'd also made several resolutions. She would not need a man to make her life full. She would not depend on a man again to fill any need. She would protect herself and her girls from caring for anyone who could love them and then leave. She wasn't sure how she intended to do that, but it was one of the reasons she hadn't dated since Ryan had died. Jonas had been the first man she *wanted* to date. She wasn't sure how to tell him all that.

He leaned forward a bit. "I came to a re-alization on New Year's Eve when I spent the evening with you and Vi and Jazzi."

"Do I want to hear this?" she asked.

"I don't know. But I can only be honest about what I was feeling. I realized that night you deserve more than I can give. I let a woman down once before and I don't want to do it again. The stakes are even higher now with your girls involved."

Because she was still smarting from not knowing where she stood, she bristled and leaned back. "If you don't want to date me or even be friends, that's fine. I'm not asking anything of you."

Because she knew she'd started caring

about Jonas, because she didn't want to take their discussion any further, she rose to her feet, turned, and said, "I have to get back to Tessa," and went downstairs.

Why did she feel as if they'd broken up when they'd never really been together?

That was easy. Because they were often on the same wavelength. Because Jonas had been respectful and kind and compassionate with her. Because he'd seemed to care.

In the living room, Daisy found Tessa sitting on the sofa, staring into space. She heard Jonas's footsteps coming down the stairs, and then on the hardwood floors following her to the living room. He looked pained as if he'd wanted to say more and she hadn't given him the chance. Why should she?

Jonas looked from Tessa to Daisy, then ran his hand through his hair. "I'll see if I can collect more information for you. Tessa, if I learn anything else, I'll call you. Make sure you phone Marsh if Rappaport calls you."

After a glance at Daisy, he said, "I can let myself out."

As he left Tessa's apartment, Daisy felt her breath hitch and her throat constrict a little.

"What happened up there?" Tessa asked her.

"Nothing happened. Jonas has his life and I have mine. I'm going to concentrate on the Quilt Lovers Weekend and help you stay out of trouble. I don't need any romance in my life."

Tessa's expression said she didn't believe a word of what Daisy had just said, but Daisy was determined she was going to put Jonas Groft right out of her mind . . . and her heart, too.

CHAPTER FIVE

On Sunday, Daisy moved around the kitchen and dining area quickly, readying everything for dinner. The huge wagon-wheel chandelier cast a mellow glow over the area. Daisy had started a fire in the floor-to-ceiling stone fireplace that was a focal point on the east wall. The blue and rust braided rugs woven by a local Amish woman added another artistic touch with the furniture upholstered in blue and cream with a touch of green.

Daisy had to admit she felt awkward around Portia Smith Harding and that's why she'd invited her aunt Iris to join them tonight. Iris was always a good buffer between Daisy and her mom, so she thought her aunt would be a good buffer today too. In addition, Vi had asked Daisy if Foster could join them since she'd be leaving for college the next day and it would be her last chance to spend time with him.

Of course, Daisy couldn't refuse. She'd decided on a sit-down meal this evening because that seemed more conducive to conversation and getting-to-know-you time.

Vi and Foster had their heads together over the mixer bowl. They were murmuring in low conversation when the mixer wasn't running to mash the potatoes. Daisy worried about their relationship. How could she help it? They were so young. On the other hand, she and Vi had had all the talks they were supposed to have. She was over eighteen now. The rest was up to Vi unless she came to Daisy for advice. Daisy knew full well how too much motherly concern could push a daughter away. Her own mother had done that with her. Aunt Iris, on the other hand, had just always been there to give advice when it was asked for. Daisy still appreciated that quality about her aunt.

As her aunt took broccoli from a steamer, then pulled a bowl from a knotty pine upper cupboard, Daisy mixed flour and water with a hand blender. She'd stir it into beef broth to make a gravy.

While Foster held a bowl for Vi to spoon the potatoes into, Vi said to Daisy, "I'm going to leave early tomorrow morning, Mom. Bad weather is supposed to move in around noon. I'd like to get back before it does. I imagine Portia will want to do the same."

The last snow prediction had only amounted to about four inches. But tomorrow's forecast could be a different story. Winter in Pennsylvania was like that. "I'll talk to her about it tonight before she turns in," Daisy assured Vi. She was giving Portia her downstairs bedroom and Daisy would sleep on the pull-out sofa bed in the living room.

Vi looked toward the living room where Portia and Jazzi were seated on the sofa paging through a photograph album Daisy had made. Pepper's head and front paws were in Jazzi's lap. Marjoram sat in a bread loaf position on the back of the sofa. "Portia and Jazzi seem to be getting along okay. Doesn't that bother you?"

Daisy looked that way too. Portia's hair was black like Jazzi's. She wore it in a short stylish cut. At thirty-two, she was younger than Daisy. "I'm not sure how I feel about it, honey," Daisy said honestly. "Part of me is glad for Jazzi. She once told me she has a bit of a hole that needs to be filled up simply because she didn't know who her parents were — her biological parents. And since your dad died, I imagine that hole feels even deeper. So if Portia can help fill her up again, I'm glad about that."

As Aunt Iris frowned, Foster said, "That's an admirable attitude, Mrs. Swanson."

She lowered her voice. "Nothing admirable about it, Foster, because, on the other hand, I'm worried that Jazzi could get closer to Portia than she is to me."

"That will never happen, Mom," Vi said loyally.

Giving her a wan smile, Daisy said, "You never know what will happen when the heart's involved."

Foster and Vi exchanged an intimate look, a look that said they were more than dating — they were involved.

Daisy shoved her pangs of worry about Vi aside to concentrate on making the meal go well. She'd baked a recipe for brownies that she'd created for Valentine's Day at the tea garden. She, Aunt Iris, and Tessa had taste-tested them many times. But this would be their first public appearance along with tea and flavored coffee. She was hoping for a long meal with lots of conversation. Maybe she'd have a better handle on Portia's personality by the time dinner was over.

Foster and Vi took the bowl of mashed potatoes to the round pedestal oak table with distressed wood. Daisy had bought the antique chairs at a flea market and refinished them herself. That had been part of her starting-over process.

Iris broke into Daisy's thoughts. "It's a shame Tessa couldn't join us."

"When I invited her, she seemed torn," Daisy responded. "She offered to stay at the tea garden all day and close tonight. I'll call her later to make sure she's okay."

Once everyone was seated at the table, the conversation revolved around the food. Foster grinned at Daisy. "That pot roast smells delicious. You have to tell me how you make it."

"If you have a Crock-Pot, it's easy," Daisy told him.

"Easy is good. I can put it on before class and we can have it for supper. Dad isn't much on cooking. I mean he does it, but it's because he has to. So burgers and tater tots are a big part of our menu."

Foster and his brother and sister had lost their mom. His father was doing the best he could on his own, and Daisy admired him for it. It wasn't easy raising kids as the only parent. She was lucky she'd had her parents and Aunt Iris to help her transition to single parenthood when she'd returned to Willow Creek with her daughters.

Jazzi took a forkful of mashed potatoes. "We should have these more often, Mom."

Portia looked Daisy's way and gave her a

knowing mother's smile. Maybe they were more alike than they were different. After all, Portia had two children of her own.

In the middle of the meal, Portia said to Daisy, "Jazzi tells me you want to give me your bed tonight. Really, the couch is okay for me."

Daisy shook her head. "I want you to have my room and privacy. I'll be fine on the couch."

Iris had been fairly quiet up until now, which wasn't like her. They were almost finished with their main course when she turned to Portia and asked, "What's your family doing today?"

Daisy tried to give her aunt a warning look. She did manage to give her a hand signal that told her she wanted to cut off that conversation, but Iris ignored that with a little shake of her head. She was telling her niece she wasn't going to back down and she wanted an answer.

Silence reigned around the table as Portia's cheeks turned red out of obvious embarrassment. But she didn't say it wasn't any of Iris's business. She responded, "My husband, Colton, is out of town on business. That's why this weekend was good for me to come up here. And my kids are with my sister today and tomorrow. The nice thing about working at home for myself is that I can take a day off whenever I like."

Daisy thought about working at home. Portia was a graphic artist who could probably do her work anywhere as long as she had a laptop with her. Daisy would miss the interaction with other people and knew she preferred conversation and friendly faces.

Still ignoring Daisy's signals, Iris followed up one awkward question with another. "Does your family know you're here?"

Portia hesitated and shook her head. "No, they don't. My husband and my sister think I'm seeing college friends."

It was obvious that Jazzi was embarrassed for Portia, and Daisy hoped Iris could see that too. She quickly jumped in. "Vi, why don't you tell Iris about your course load for the new semester. What's your favorite class going to be?"

On the same wavelength as Daisy, Vi answered immediately. "I know it doesn't seem to fit with all the business administration courses, but I'm looking forward to Nineteenth-Century English Poets. They've been a favorite for a long time." She glanced at Foster, who was sitting next to her. "They're so romantic."

He just gave her a grin and Daisy almost wanted to groan.

In a lower voice, Vi admitted, "It's going to be hard going back after the break. My time won't be my own again."

Daisy didn't believe Vi was worried about her time. More than anything, she sensed her daughter didn't want to leave Foster. But Daisy saw both of them returning to class as a very good thing. They needed to have their minds on something other than each other.

As Daisy peered out the kitchen window later that evening, she could see the lights of Foster's car in the drive in front of the detached garage. Violet had grabbed her coat and gone outside to say good-bye to him in private. Daisy understood the need for privacy. She remembered young love, and hopefully, with the temperature below freezing, Vi and Foster wouldn't be doing more than saying good-bye and kissing.

She heard the sound of slippers on the stairs and suspected that was Portia coming down after saying good night to Jazzi. When Daisy had renovated the barn, the upstairs bedrooms with a bathroom had been perfect for her daughters.

Daisy went through the dining area into the living room knowing it would be better if she made up the sofa bed and turned in too. Violet would be in shortly and they could all get some sleep.

But first she needed to see if Portia wanted anything before bed. When the woman reached the bottom of the open stairway at the rear of the living room, she turned toward Daisy with a smile.

"Would you like a cup of tea or hot chocolate before bed?" Daisy asked.

"If it's not too much trouble, a cup of tea would be good. I can make it myself."

Daisy studied Portia again. She was wearing a high-collared velour zippered robe in a beautiful shade of green. Her slippers matched and Daisy wondered if she'd bought the outfit just for this visit. Maybe she wanted to make a good impression, though Daisy didn't consider the visit about impressions. It was about getting to know each other.

She said, "I could use a cup of chamomile myself. How about if I mix a little peach in with it?"

"Sounds good," Portia agreed, and both women went to the kitchen. Daisy filled her copper teakettle and set it on the burner. She was grateful for the filtered water system in her house. The type of water anyone used for tea could make a difference in the taste.

She motioned to the eat-at island and asked Portia, "How about another brownie?"

Portia gave her a conspiratorial grin. "Sounds good. I don't usually indulge. It feels as if I've been watching my weight forever but this seems like a good occasion to forget about calories."

Going to the corner hutch in the dining area, Daisy removed a James Sadler teapot, cream colored with pink roses. Taking it to the kitchen, she slipped her tea infuser into it and filled it with three-quarters chamomile tea and a quarter of the peach mixture. Then she went to the island to sit with Portia to wait for the kettle on the stove to whistle. The brownies were stored in a can on the island. Daisy opened the decorative lid and pushed the tin toward Portia. Portia took out a brownie and pulled a napkin from a holder. However, she set it on the napkin without taking a bite.

After a moment's hesitation, she said, "You've done a wonderful job with Jazzi. She's so bright. She has so many interests, and she seems —" Portia hunted for the right word and finally found it. "Balanced."

"I hope that's true," Daisy said. "She had a tough time after Ryan died. Vi talked to me more about her feelings, but Jazzi kept a lot inside until she told me about her search for you."

Portia plucked off a corner of the brownie, popped it into her mouth, and ate it. The teakettle whistled and Daisy went to it and removed it from the burner. Then she poured the water into the teapot and waited for the tea to steep.

Portia raised her head and her dark brown eyes made contact with Daisy. "I wish I had as much courage as you do."

"I don't understand."

"I hear the admiration in Jazzi's voice when she talks about you. She told me how you continued on after your husband died, how you moved here with them and started the tea garden." She motioned to the barn home. "How you bought this and renovated it. All the ideas to do it were yours. But mostly I admire how you're raising the girls on your own."

"I don't see any of it as particularly courageous," Daisy protested. "I try to roll with what life has given me. At times it isn't easy. But I have my family and I have the motivation to keep going for Violet and Jazzi. If I'd been alone, maybe I wouldn't have had that motivation."

"You're the type of woman who sees what she wants and goes and gets it," Portia concluded. "Me?" She shrugged. "I didn't want to be alone. I think I married and had a family to make up for the child I gave up."

Daisy wasn't sure what to say to that. So many questions floated through her mind. Didn't Portia love her husband? Did she regret marriage and having more children?

She asked the one question she thought was appropriate. "So you regret giving up Jazzi for adoption?"

"I regret it personally for me. Yet I know it was the best thing to do for Jazzi. I was so young and had only my family's disapproval and no funds to raise her. How could I have kept her? I've told Jazzi that. But deep down I know she believes if I had loved her enough I would have found a way. Maybe I believe that too. Just because something's hard doesn't mean you shouldn't do it."

Portia's own comment led Daisy to the next question. "When are you going to tell your family about Jazzi?" After all, that was one of those hard things that had to be done, wasn't it? Just how long could Portia keep this secret?

"I don't know," she admitted. "I'm afraid. I'm afraid Colton will see it all as a betrayal, that he won't want to accept Jazzi, that I might have to give her up when I just found her."

"Would you give her up again?" Daisy wanted to know.

Portia shook her head vehemently. "I don't know. I hope not. But if I have to make a choice —"

"You don't know what you'd choose," Daisy said in a low voice, trying to understand Portia's dilemma.

She took two teacups from the cupboard, one painted with violets, the other with hydrangeas. She set them on the island in front of her place and Portia's. She was glad she had something to do as they both contemplated their conversation. Taking the infuser from the teapot, she set it in the sink and poured tea into both of their cups.

Finally she took her seat and looked at Portia. "You have to tell your husband and tell him soon."

"I know," Portia agreed.

"Secrets and lies only make a problem worse."

"I know that, too," Portia said.

Daisy reached for a brownie as Portia ate hers. Maybe chocolate and tea would help a little. But not very much.

All was quiet in the house. Vi had come in and gone upstairs after saying good night. She'd looked both sad and happy — happy she was dating Foster, but sad she would be leaving him. Daisy just hoped the idea of school and a future would be more important than a boyfriend.

The fold-out bed wasn't the most comfortable, and Daisy knew it would probably be a while until she fell asleep. She'd laid her phone on the coffee table and now she picked it up. Eleven-thirty. Sometimes Tessa stayed up late painting. Now, however, she might be curled up in bed with the covers pulled up over her. It was hard to know.

But old habits died hard and Tessa was a late-night woman. She didn't need as much sleep as Daisy did, at least not usually. If Daisy texted her, she'd disturb her if her friend had her phone on. So she might as well just try to call her.

Tessa picked up on the second ring.

"Had you turned in for the night?" Daisy asked.

"Are you kidding? Who can sleep? My mind is buzzing in so many directions, I can't keep track of even one."

"You're painting?"

"Yes. At least with that, I can focus for a few minutes at a time." She hesitated. "But I can't work on my painting in progress."

"One of your *Morning Has Broken* series?"

"You saw them when you were up here?"

"I did. They're good."

"If I work on that, it just reminds me of what happened. I imagine Reese's body there at the covered bridge —" Her voice broke and she stopped.

"Don't imagine it."

"That's what I do, Daisy. That's how I paint. I imagine pictures in my mind and then I stroke them onto the canvas."

"What are you working on?"

"I have a commission for a calico cat on a porch. But my heart's not in it."

"I'm going to suggest something and I don't want you to freak out."

"I'm done freaking out. I have to stay cool or Rappaport is going to think I did it."

"He might think that whether you're cool or not. Suspects who don't react cause as much speculation as those who do. You have to watch that you don't fly off the handle at him, but other than that, take Marshall's advice."

"I will," Tessa said in a small voice that wasn't like her at all. "What's your suggestion?"

"You've done a few portraits."

"I have. It's not my forte, but I do okay."

"Why don't you try a portrait of Reese?"

Silence met Daisy at her suggestion. Daisy didn't know if Tessa was offended or not.

Then her friend admitted, "I never thought of that."

"I thought of it because after Ryan died, I created collages of the good times we'd had together. They're hanging in my bedroom. There's one in Jazzi's room, and one in Violet's room. Just the process of doing it helped me. Yes, I cried, and I remembered. But it was a way to wade through my grief and sense of loss. You have a gift, Tessa. Maybe if you use it to paint a portrait of Reese, that will help you forge through your loss."

"I *will* think about it," Tessa said. "I don't know if I'm ready to do that yet."

"If you're not ready for a portrait, how about painting the outside of the gallery, or someplace the two of you went together? Just a thought."

"I wish I'd hear something from Marshall. Or even Jonas. Jonas's contact in the police department is reliable, isn't he? Jonas could also learn something from the coroner. But I haven't heard from him. Have you?"

"No, I haven't."

"Daisy, the two of you need to talk."

"We did when we were in your attic. Remember?"

"I remember, but you weren't up there long enough to have a decent discussion. I know you like him."

"This isn't about me liking him. He mentioned something about —" She stopped. Did she really want to share everything with Tessa?

"What did he say?"

Jonas hadn't been specific. There wouldn't be anything wrong with sharing this with Tessa. "He said he let a woman down before and he wouldn't do it again."

"What does that mean?"

"I don't know. Too much responsibility, I guess, for me and Violet and Jazzi. Not that he'd have to take any. I'm fine on my own."

"Yes, but if you were together he'd want to share some of that. He seems like that kind of man."

"What he is is the kind of man who doesn't want the responsibility."

"You don't know the whole story. Everybody has one."

Daisy knew how true that was. Jonas knew *her* story. He knew that she and Ryan had married and she had Violet. But they'd wanted more children and she couldn't have them. Their marriage had gone through a very rough patch, but then they'd decided to adopt Jazzi. She and Ryan had been so compatible in some ways . . . in most ways. Compatible and comfortable. After they had

Jazzi to focus on, along with Violet, their marriage had gone on like any normal marriage. Daisy had wondered sometimes if marriage shouldn't be more intense, more passionate. She'd loved Ryan with all her heart. But it hadn't been a giddy kind of love. It had been sensible. But often she'd wondered if love was supposed to be sensible.

"I don't think Jonas was finished talking to you," Tessa offered. "I think you cut him off. I could tell from his attitude when he returned to the living room. And you rushed down here much too fast. I don't think you gave him a chance to finish. So think about that when he calls or when you see him again."

When Daisy didn't respond, Tessa asked, "Daisy? Are you still there?"

"I'm here. We both have a lot to think about."

"I still don't know if Reese was cheating on me."

"You can't think about that, not until you know differently. Paint, Tessa. Pour your feelings out onto the canvas, even if you do it in an abstract."

"I don't do abstracts."

Daisy had to smile a little at that. No, Tessa didn't do abstracts. "You can always burn it," she suggested.

"I'm wondering if I should burn my *Morning Has Broken* series. But I've put too much heart and soul into those paintings, and I won't do it just because they might cast suspicion on me."

"The police have no cause to ask for a search warrant."

After a few beats of silence, Tessa sighed. "So Portia's there with you?"

"She's sleeping. She's leaving in the morning before the snow moves in."

"I'll be at work in the morning," Tessa said. "I need to work as much as I need to paint."

"I'm worried about you."

"I know you are, and I thank you for it. You're the only person in my life I can really depend upon. Good night, Daisy. I'll see you tomorrow."

Daisy hoped Detective Rappaport already had a lead on whoever had killed Reese because she wanted her friend to be free of suspicion.

"Drive safely," Daisy said to Vi as she hugged her on the gravel drive outside of the garage the next morning. The garage had once been a large equipment shed and had an unfinished second floor. It now matched the house in red siding with white and black trim. It could house two cars comfortably.

"I always drive safely," Vi told her mom. "I made you that promise when you got me this car."

The car was a blue Chevy Malibu. After Vi had decided to go to Lehigh to college, Daisy knew they wouldn't want to depend on carpooling for her to get to and from. Fortunately, an elderly customer who came into the tea garden with her daughter revealed she was turning in her keys and the daughter was selling her car. The car was five years old but in wonderful condition and they'd gotten a tremendous bargain on it. It was one of the serendipitous events Daisy knew they had to take advantage of.

After Jazzi hugged her sister, and Portia also said good-bye, Daisy felt misty as Vi settled in the driver's seat, started up the car, and drove down the lane that led to the rural road. Daisy watched her taillights as her daughter stopped at the end of the lane and then headed back to college.

Portia said to Daisy, "I imagine it's always hard to see her leave."

"Always," Daisy confirmed with a look at Jazzi.

Jazzi said, "I thought I'd be glad when she

went to college. You know, I could even use her room if I wanted to. But I miss her. Talking to Marjoram and Pepper just isn't the same thing as talking to Vi."

They all smiled at that as Jazzi meant them to.

"And now I have to be leaving too." Portia picked up her traveling case that she'd set on the gravel.

Jazzi and Daisy walked her to her car. It was an expensive compact SUV with all the bells and whistles.

"This is such a sweet car," Jazzi noted.

Portia nodded. "It is. It's my husband's. When he's out of town, I use it."

Daisy was thinking, *And he doesn't know how you're using it . . . or why.*

Portia tossed her bag into the back seat of the vehicle and then she turned to Jazzi. "This has been a lovely visit."

"When am I going to see you again?" Jazzi asked.

A troubled expression crossed Portia's face. "I don't know. It's not always easy to get away."

Daisy wanted to say, *Without telling your husband where you're going.* But she didn't.

Portia's gaze met Daisy's. "I have to figure things out."

"You will call, though, right?" Jazzi

sounded hopeful.

"Of course, I'll call, maybe even Skype. I can download the app onto my phone. I'll text you when it's a good time."

Daisy knew what that meant. Portia had to make sure no one else was around who would see her or hear her. That was no way to live.

As Daisy stood a little distance away, Jazzi and Portia hugged. She could see the bond that was forming between the two of them. Did she regret helping Jazzi find her birth mother? Only time would tell. She just hoped her daughter wouldn't get hurt.

CHAPTER SIX

Daisy was still thinking about Portia and Jazzi, as well as Vi and Foster, when she decided to take her lunch break by stopping at Quilts and Notions. The covered bridge where Reese was found was right near the border of the Fishers' farm. She wanted to find out what Rachel had to say about it. Rachel didn't gossip, but Daisy was sure she'd be concerned about what happened there and might need a listening ear.

When Daisy walked into Quilts and Notions, in spite of her serious errand, she had to smile. It was a cozy, bright shop with colorful quilts hanging from racks. Potholders fanned out on two other shelves along with placemats. There was also an area with bolts of cloth, threads, and buttons. A spinning corner rack held books on subjects from quilts to the historic nature of Lancaster County.

Rachel was pulling a bolt of material, yellow gingham, as Daisy walked in and the bell above the door jingled. The shopkeeper glanced over her shoulder. "*Wilkom, Daisy.*"

She carried the material to the cutting table and Daisy joined her there. "I came to see how you were faring after what happened," Daisy said, unzipping her jacket.

The strings on Rachel's *kapp* floated forward as she shook her head. "We can't think about much else. What a terrible thing to happen."

"Did the police come calling?"

Rachel's brow furrowed. "They did, and you know what we think about that."

The Amish didn't like to involve the police. They settled grievances and problems on their own within their community. But this was different. Daisy suspected the Amish way of life could be somewhat foreign to Detective Rappaport. She just hoped he understood that the Amish believed in peaceful resistance and nonviolence. It was more than a philosophy for them — it was a way of life.

"A Detective Rappaport came and seemed so uncomfortable. I offered him a cup of tea and shoofly pie but he acted as if he'd never seen that kind of pie before."

"Detective Rappaport is a very focused man," Daisy explained, knowing it was true from her own experience with him.

"He asked us questions about where we were Thursday and Friday. Mostly Levi was on the farm tending to chores and I was here. In the evening, we were all together."

"Did the detective seem satisfied with what you told him?"

"He did, but he said he might be back to ask more questions. It's winter with snow and mud and ice on the ground. Even the *kinner* don't go hiking across the field toward the covered bridge in this weather. Come spring, they'll be sure to do that, but for now they stay closer to home or stick to the well-worn paths between farms."

"It's too cold to go hiking, that's for sure," Daisy agreed.

Rachel unfolded the bolt of cloth, ready to cut it. "Have you heard anything else about what happened to Mr. Masemer? I mean, how he came to be there?"

"No. But Jonas Groft talked to a contact at the police station. I got the feeling that whatever happened didn't happen at the covered bridge."

"You mean, he was killed elsewhere?"

"I don't know. It was just something Jonas said about unusual circumstances that gave me that impression."

117

Rachel stopped her work to ask, "How is Tessa?"

"I told her to take as much time off as she needs, but she insists on working."

Rachel nodded as if she understood. She studied the material before her for a few moments and Daisy knew her friend looked too serious to only be thinking about cutting the cloth. "What's the matter?" she asked.

"One of my customers told me something this morning that might get back to the police."

"What did you hear?"

"It's about Tessa."

"Truth or rumor?" Daisy asked.

"Do you know Colleen Wolf?"

A soccer mom with dark auburn hair came to mind. "Yes, I do. She often stops in at the tea garden."

"Then you know she wouldn't say something that wasn't true."

No, Colleen wouldn't. She and Colleen had often had conversations about raising children and what they wanted for their future. She wasn't the type to spread rumors. "What did she say?"

"I think this was on her mind and she didn't know whether she should tell the police or not. She said she was at the gal-

118

lery looking at the antique quilts last week when she overheard an argument between Mr. Masemer and Tessa that became quite loud. Apparently, Tessa stormed out. Colleen said she wasn't the only one who overheard so even if she doesn't tell Detective Rappaport, someone else might."

That information was indeed worrisome. "I'll talk to Tessa about it. Maybe she already told the detective about the argument."

After speaking to Rachel a bit more about Quilt Lovers Weekend, Daisy left the shop and crossed the street. The gray sky had begun letting loose intermittent snowflakes. As she opened the door to the tea garden, she forgot about the snow. She was too worried about Tessa to consider snow accumulation.

At the counter, Aunt Iris nodded to her and then at the kitchen. Daisy knew that was her aunt's way of saying that Tessa was baking. Good. They needed to have a talk.

Aunt Iris was adding up a customer's order at the cash register. Mrs. Pallermo, who lived by herself about two blocks off the main street, smiled at Daisy and waved at the two containers of soup and the bag of baked goods on the counter. "This should keep me going for a couple of days. I won't have to come out in this cold weather."

"Mrs. Pallermo, I'd be glad to drop off some soup for you if you can't get out." An idea came to Daisy. Maybe they should think about a delivery service for their elderly clients. That might be something to talk to Foster about. He was good with new ideas.

Mrs. Pallermo waved Daisy's words away. "My dear, I will walk here myself as long as I'm able. When the time comes that I can't, I suppose I'll have to have help. But that time isn't here yet. Did you hear about the senior center the town is thinking about adding on to the fire hall?"

"No, I didn't," Daisy said. She'd been so tied up with the tea garden and Quilt Lovers Weekend, she hadn't kept up.

"It's not a reality yet," Mrs. Pallermo explained. "There is money to be raised and council members to coax onto the right side. But it's a possibility. Just think, I could play bingo at my church *and* at a senior center."

Daisy smiled. "Then I hope it comes to pass. You enjoy your soup and goodies."

Iris was putting the older woman's purchase into a shopping bag as Daisy went into the kitchen. Eva was washing a few teapots and Tessa was standing at the window looking out at the back. Daisy went over to her, then laid her hand on her friend's arm. "Hey, Tessa. Can you come into my office with me for a minute?"

Tessa studied her as if she'd been someplace far away. Then the present took over once again. "Sure, I can. Is there a problem?"

Daisy began walking toward her office, removing her jacket. When they were inside, she closed the door. After she hung her jacket on the clothes rack, she pulled her desk chair around to the front of the desk so she was facing Tessa.

"There's something we need to talk about."

"What? I know I'm a bit distracted, but I promise, I'll get the baked goods out in the case."

"It's not that," Daisy assured her. "I told you if you need time off, just let me know. I'll increase Karina's hours."

"I feel better working," Tessa assured her.

"Okay. That's fine. But I was just over at Quilts and Notions."

"Are you going to join the quilting circle?"

"Maybe, but Rachel told me something that troubled me."

"What?"

"She said that one of her customers told

her about an argument you had with Reese at the gallery, and other people overheard it. What was that about?"

Tessa shook her head. "It had nothing to do with what happened to him."

"The fact that others overheard it makes it relevant because any one of them could tell Detective Rappaport you were fighting with Reese."

"I was upset with him. We were getting closer, spending more time together, but he wouldn't tell me about his background."

"What made you ask?"

"How do you know something made me ask?"

Daisy shrugged. "Usually something happens and that changes the discussion between two people."

"Something *did* happen," Tessa admitted. "Reese had a teenage visitor over the holidays — the son of a friend. Reese spent two days with him, too busy to include me. I didn't mind at the time because I wanted to paint. If you remember, I also spent extra hours here. But when I asked him, Reese just wouldn't talk about it. That didn't make any sense to me."

"You don't like to talk about *your* past," Daisy reminded her.

"No, I don't. But both my parents are

dead. I don't have any family. Why wouldn't Reese talk about a friend and his or her son?"

"I've known Jonas as long as you've known Reese. Granted, we weren't seriously dating the way you two were, but Jonas has been closemouthed about his past too. Do you think that means he has something to hide? It might be nothing to hide at all. He might just not be ready to share it with me."

"But Reese and I — *you* know. I was spending nights there. I never just wanted a fling."

"Did he know that?"

Tessa groaned. "I don't know. Maybe he didn't. Maybe that's all I was. Why does communication with the opposite sex have to be so hard?"

"I don't know if it's so hard. I do know that sometimes we're afraid to push."

"Did you push with Jonas? Is that why you two argued?"

"We didn't argue exactly. And maybe I did push because I wanted to know where I stood."

"You can't find out if you don't talk to him again."

"Enough about me and Jonas. You need to ask Marshall if you should tell Detective Rappaport about that argument."

Tessa was thinking about that when suddenly there was a rap on the office door. Daisy could see Iris through the glass. She motioned to her aunt to come in.

"I'm sorry to interrupt you two, but someone's here who wanted to give Tessa his condolences. Should I just tell him another time?"

Already Tessa was rising to her feet. "No, of course not. I'll come out."

When Daisy followed Tessa into the tea room, she recognized the man waiting for her friend. George Beck often stopped in for a cup of tea and a scone. He was in his late forties with light brown hair laced with gray. His goatee, a little darker than his hair, seemed unusual for an accountant. Many of the small businesses in the community used his services. He and Reese had come in together more than once. So she assumed they had been friends, maybe even good friends. He was the one person she remembered seeing Reese with in a casual way, joking and talking.

George stepped right up to Tessa and took her hand. "I'm so sorry, Tessa," he said. "Reese spoke of you often and I know you meant a lot to him."

Tessa's eyes misted over and she nodded. Daisy felt as if she should stay by her friend

124

in case Tessa needed her, though the conversation was personal.

"How long were you friends?" Tessa asked George.

"Not too long, but we got along well from our first meeting. I bought my wife a painting for her birthday last fall."

"Tell me something, if you can. Do you know where Reese was from?" Tessa asked George.

He looked perplexed for a moment and then he said, "Not exactly. Reese mentioned more than once that he moved to Willow Creek for a slower lifestyle. So I guess I assumed he was from a big city. He traveled to New York often to visit galleries. It's possible he was from there."

"I'm asking," Tessa said, "because I didn't know if there were relatives I should contact. A friend's son visited him over the holidays but I don't know anything about him or how to get in touch with him."

George shook his head. "Reese never mentioned him. Actually I haven't seen Reese much lately. My wife and I were visiting her sister in Scranton over the holidays. I was going to call Reese to see if he wanted to meet here, or to go get a beer," he said with a quirk of his brow.

Tessa smiled. "He did like his lager."

"Yes, he did." George patted Tessa's arm. "Again, I'm sorry. If there's anything I can do to help, please let me know. My wife, Tanya, will be in touch soon to invite you to dinner. Would you like that?"

Tessa nodded. "It would be good to talk to someone else who knew Reese. He had many customers who said *hi* when we were walking down the street, but I got the feeling he didn't have that many friends."

"I'm just glad I was one of them," George said. "I think I'll buy one of those apple bran loaves to take with me. Tanya would like that. Now don't forget, if you need anything call us."

Tessa nodded.

Daisy had altogether lost track of the time. Foster had come in for his shift and he was motioning her to the spillover tea room. When she crossed to him, he said, "You have an appointment to meet that reporter, Trevor Lundquist."

"Oh, my gosh. How did I forget?"

"A murder seems to trump everything else," Foster said grimly. "I brewed him tea and gave him a scone. He's waiting for you."

Daisy gave Foster a smile. "Thank you. You're making yourself irreplaceable around here, do you know that?"

"I'm trying," Foster joked.

As Daisy spotted Trevor, she hurried to his table. Foster had set a cup of tea there for her, too. Yes, Violet was dating a good guy.

Trevor looked as dapper as usual. His brown hair was stylishly long. He'd hung his down jacket across the back of his chair. He was wearing a cream-colored oxford button-down shirt and khaki cargo pants. He stood until she sat down and then he sat too, motioning to the half of the cinnamon scone still on his plate. "They're good."

"I'm glad you like them. Thank you for doing the story on the Quilt Lovers Weekend. We need all the publicity we can get. It will be good for the whole town."

"I know shopkeepers are counting on it to bring tourists in. I just hope they're right."

"If we get the word out, it will happen." She wanted to be as positive about this as she could be.

"So tell me about everyone who's involved in this," he suggested, "and how businesses will be participating."

She took a folded sheet of paper from her pocket and opened it. "I wrote them all down so I didn't forget anyone." She related who was on the committee, then handed over the list she'd made so he could see all the businesses that were participating.

"And just what can the weekend offer tourists?" he asked.

"There will be so much to do."

"In spite of Revelations being closed. Wasn't the gallery supposed to have a quilt exhibit?"

"Yes, it was. But from what I understand, those quilts will now be displayed at Quilts and Notions. Rachel and some of the women there will be giving quilting instructions, and anyone who has a problem with their quilt can bring it in for a consultation."

"That sounds nice. What else?"

"The book store ordered books on every aspect of quilting. Most of those are paperback and they'll be available too. The Art Society is having a hands-on event where anyone can draw their own quilt patterns. The Covered Bridge Bed-and-Breakfast will be displaying many quilts in the bedrooms. Two of the quilts will be raffle prizes. Tourists can buy raffle tickets at any participating shop. I'll announce the winners at afternoon tea on Saturday. I'm almost fully booked. The history of quilting will be presented at Willow Creek High School in the cafeteria. Students from each grade had a period to concentrate on their project. So that should be interesting too."

"You're making it quite clear to enjoy this weekend I have to be involved in quilting or quilts."

"Maybe. It's a popular pastime. But there might be couples who just want to get away for the weekend and enjoy something different. And shoppers are always looking for bargains. Coupons will do that. We have enough specialty shops here to make just strolling down the street fun. From what I hear, the children's clothing store, Pinafores, will have a toy section with quilted toys as well as pillows and wall hangings for children's rooms."

"Besides notifying me, have you sent out press releases?"

"I have. I sent to the York, Harrisburg, Hanover, and Gettysburg papers."

"I know someone who works on the *Philadelphia Inquirer* digital edition, as well as the *Pittsburgh City Paper.* I'll contact them to see if they can get your press release to the top of the pile. Can you e-mail it to me?"

"Of course I can. That's exactly the kind of PR I was hoping for."

"Then I guess we're finished," Trevor concluded with a smile that told her he wasn't quite done. His gaze went to the main tea room where Tessa was at the counter talking with Iris.

"Don't even think about interviewing her," Daisy warned Trevor.

"Are you going to get involved in solving this murder? You did pretty well with the last one."

"I have no plans to stick my nose into this one," she assured him.

"I'll let everything play out a little, but in a week or so I might be back asking questions of you and Tessa. Let's face it. If I get you additional publicity for the Quilt Lovers Weekend, an exclusive now, or even when the murder investigation is completed, is the least the two of you can do."

Daisy had made a similar bargain with Trevor before. She felt as if she were making a deal with the devil. But it had worked out for both of them the last time. "In a day or two, I'll talk to Tessa about it," she said. "But I don't want you badgering her."

He raised his hands in surrender. "No badgering." Then he lowered his voice. "Just probative questions."

Daisy shook her head. She wasn't going to let Trevor anywhere near Tessa, not until the murderer was found and the case closed.

As Daisy followed Trevor into the tea room, Iris beckoned her into her office.

"What's up?" Daisy asked.

"I'm going to give Tessa a hand and start

the chocolate scone batter for tomorrow. Do you want chocolate chips in it?"

"That sounds good."

"You're going to have to call the tea supplier. We're low on the green tea blends."

Daisy picked up the electronic tablet from her desk and made a note for herself. "Okay. Anything special you want to add to that order?"

Iris thought about it. "How about pomegranate black tea? The white teas are holding because their price is higher. Everyone wants a bargain, and our daily special doesn't include the white tea."

"No, it doesn't. Maybe we should have one day a week when the special *does* include white tea. That way customers will drink it, enjoy it, and order it the next time they come in."

Iris knocked her forefinger against her temple. "Now why didn't I think of that?"

"Because two heads are better than one."

This collaboration was just one of the reasons that Daisy enjoyed working with her aunt. For probably the millionth time, she wondered why she couldn't have this easy relationship with her mother. But her mother's personality was very different from Iris's.

"One more thing," Iris said, "then I'll let

you get back to whatever you were going to do. I'm glad you and Foster deal with that computer. It's beyond me."

"You just have to understand how it thinks," Daisy kidded.

"That's something I never want to learn," Iris said. "I just wanted to remind you that Thursday is your birthday."

Daisy wrinkled her nose. "I don't think I have to be reminded. Another year older and all that."

Iris laughed. "You still look twenty-five and you know it."

Daisy didn't bother commenting.

"Anyway," her aunt went on. "How about you and Jazzi come over for dinner on Thursday? I'd like to celebrate with you."

"I don't know how much we'll be celebrating," Daisy joked. "But I'd like that. I'll ask Jazzi and see if she's free."

"Your mom and dad should be back soon."

"I don't think they're coming back until the weekend, but I'm sure we'll know when Mom's back."

Iris gave Daisy a knowing smile. "I'm sure we will. I'll see if anyone needs tea refills before I help Tessa. She seems to be doing okay today. I'll let you know if there's a problem."

"Thanks," Daisy told her aunt as Iris left the office.

Daisy wished she could solve Tessa's problems for her, but she knew that was unlikely. Yes, she'd helped solve a murder in the fall, but that had been a onetime occurrence. She was sure of it.

CHAPTER SEVEN

The morning crowd on Tuesday was becoming a trickle when Tessa's phone rang. She and Daisy exchanged a look. Every call now seemed to be more of a stressor, whether it was a reporter, a friend, or someone more ominous.

Daisy saw Tessa's eyes go wide and she realized this was one of the ominous calls. She heard Tessa say, "I'll be bringing Marshall Thompson with me. I have to call him and see when he's available."

When she spoke again, she assured whoever was on the other end of the call, "Yes, we'll try to make it this afternoon. I'll call you."

Tessa closed her eyes as she ended the call and turned to Daisy. "The police want to question me again." Her voice caught. "I'm going to phone Marshall. I just hope he's available."

Fortunately, she reached the receptionist

in his office. He called her back ten minutes later. He would meet her at the police station at one.

For the remainder of the morning, Daisy was glad they had a steady stream of customers. Tessa needed to be busy so she didn't think. Just what had happened? Did the police have more evidence? Had forensic reports come in? It would take longer for tox screens. She was beginning to know more than she wanted to know about murder investigations.

Marshall picked up Tessa at twelve forty-five. After the two of them left, Daisy kept busy. When she wasn't helping out front, she made a batch of apple-raisin bread in the kitchen. It helped her pass the time. Eva gave her empathetic glances as she stacked clean dishes.

Two hours later, Marshall and Tessa returned, both of them looking grim.

Iris said, "Karina and I can take care of the front. Tessa, why don't you go into Daisy's office?"

Daisy motioned Marshall there and asked if they'd like tea. Tessa looked absolutely pale and shaky. Marshall just appeared worried.

"That would be good," Marshall agreed. "We both need to slow our heart rates."

"I have an orange-cinnamon green tea that you might like," Daisy offered.

Tessa was staring into space, and Daisy knew she didn't even hear her. But Marshall nodded.

Ten minutes later Daisy had prepared a tray with a teapot, teacups, and a dish of warm apple-raisin bread. When Tessa took the teacup in her hand, it shook.

She set it on the desk and looked up at Daisy with wide, scared eyes. "Apparently, the police found cinnamon scone crumbs on Reese's shirt. They asked if I knew anything about that."

Marshall cut in. "Tessa had told me Detective Rappaport already knew about the cinnamon scones she took to Reese on the night of the break-in. So I let her explain that she'd also sent some with his assistant on Thursday."

Tessa clasped her hands together. "Rappaport was sarcastic about Reese's sweet tooth . . . wondered how a man could eat that many scones. I could have punched him," she blurted out, with some of the fear gone, replaced by anger.

"But you didn't," Daisy guessed.

"No, I didn't and that's why I'm so angry now. He's such a bully." Her face took on color as she proclaimed it.

"He's trying to get answers," Daisy tried to soothe.

"Well, maybe he should get them from the *right* person instead of me." Tessa was on a roll and her cheeks pinkened further.

Marshall placed a hand on her shoulder and she suddenly deflated.

To Daisy she explained, "You were right about others hearing my argument with Reese. Detective Rappaport knew all about that. He grilled me for at least a half hour trying to make me say something that wasn't true."

"It's a technique," Marshall said. "He's hoping you'll be inconsistent about your story and he can catch that. But you weren't."

"That's because I told him the truth. The argument was one lots of couples have. I wanted to get closer to Reese and he wasn't sharing with me. That was the beginning and the end of it."

"If others overheard," Daisy said, "then that's what they overheard. But if the detective kept questioning you about it, my guess is whoever overheard was too far away to catch exactly what the two of you were saying."

"Good deductive skills, Daisy," Marshall praised. "That's exactly what I told Tessa.

The police push even harder when they don't know the answers to the questions they're asking you. It's a good thing Tessa practices meditation because she did manage to keep her cool through the whole interview. I know that wasn't easy, especially when Rappaport started asking about Reese's vehicle."

"What about his vehicle?" Daisy asked.

"Detective Rappaport asked me how often I'd ridden in Reese's SUV," Tessa said.

"What did you tell him?"

"I told him I rode in it whenever we went out together. Then he asked me if I'd ever driven Reese's SUV."

"He found your fingerprints on the steering wheel," Daisy guessed.

"Apparently, though he didn't say that. I told him, yes, I'd driven it. I picked up boxes of frames for Reese at a public auction."

Now also setting his cup and saucer on the desk, Marshall frowned. "At that, I cut off the interview. I didn't like the way the questioning was going. If they want to charge Tessa, they're going to have to come up with more than her fingerprints in her boyfriend's SUV."

Apparently agitated again, Tessa stood up and paced Daisy's office, her flowery loose top wafting as she walked back and forth. "What if they arrest me, Daisy? What am I going to do?"

"They haven't arrested you yet, which means they don't have evidence — concrete evidence — to connect you to Reese's body."

Tessa went white. "But what if he was wearing clothes that he'd worn when we were together?"

That was a definite possibility, Daisy supposed. She was going to have to figure out sooner rather than later who murdered Reese Masemer, because Tessa couldn't live under this kind of stress.

After Marshall left, Tessa set to baking and Daisy let her. If Tessa went upstairs to her attic to paint, she'd be all alone with her thoughts. It was better if she stayed in the tea garden where they could all distract her. Daisy knew her friend was scared out of her wits, and she not only had her fear to deal with, but her grief, too. That was a powerful combination to combat.

Daisy was adding more scones to the case for the afterwork crowd when Foster came up to her. "I didn't want to bother you before . . . you know, when you were talking with Tessa."

"She needs all the support she can get," Daisy said. "She's afraid the police are going to charge her."

Foster's brow furrowed. "If there's any way I can help, let me know. I do have computer skills."

"If she needs that kind of help, we'll let you know. Is there something in particular you wanted to talk to me about?"

"Valentine's Day is coming up soon," he started.

"In less than five weeks."

"Vi's hoping to come home the weekend before, but she's not sure yet. I'd like to do more than send her flowers."

"Flowers are nice."

"I suppose," Foster said, "but I saw a heart locket in one of the jewelry stores. It's sterling silver." He spread his forefinger and his thumb apart about an inch. "It's that big. Do you think she'd like it?"

Should she caution Foster, as his mother might have, not to spend his hard-earned money on gifts? Or should she let him follow his heart and discover the consequences on his own? She went for the latter.

"I think Vi would like anything you give her. It doesn't have to be costly. Even if you make a Valentine's Day card out of construction paper, she'd appreciate it."

"She probably would," Foster agreed with a smile. "But I want to give her something special . . . something she'll have to remember me by when she's not here."

"Then the locket sounds perfect."

Foster nodded and grinned. "Thank you, Mrs. Swanson. You're the greatest."

"Daisy," she reminded him, as she had many times before.

He blushed. "That just seems informal for the mother of my girlfriend."

"But I'm your boss, too, and all the other employees call me Daisy."

He smiled at her. "All right . . . Daisy. Thanks again. I'll get back to work."

As she watched Foster walk away, she wondered if Vi was his first serious relationship. She knew he was Vi's. While Vi had dated in high school, none of it had been serious. She'd had her eye on grades and college and that's what had mattered. Now, Daisy hoped Vi still had her mind on grades and college. But thinking about that heart locket Foster wanted to give her daughter, Daisy knew she might be denying how serious Vi and Foster were becoming about each other.

On Thursday evening, Daisy and Jazzi walked up the pathway to a charming little

141

stone bungalow located in an older section of town on a street with mature trees, other bungalows, ranch houses, and modest two-story homes. A single-car garage was located on the west side. A gable with a tall Palladian window decorated the east side of the house. Probably one of her Aunt Iris's favorite parts of the house was the oval window with stained glass in the front door under the gabled overhang.

Jazzi strolled ahead of Daisy between the two white pillars onto the porch.

"I wonder what Aunt Iris is making for dinner?" Jazzi said. "Probably your favorite meal."

"And what *is* my favorite meal?" Daisy asked.

"It's between chicken pot pie and chicken with dumplings."

Daisy laughed as she rang the doorbell to alert her aunt that they were there. Then she opened the door.

The house was a little unusual in its floor plan. Standing on the ceramic tile floor in the foyer, when Daisy looked to the left she saw the doorway that led to the garage. The master bedroom was to her right and the living room was straight ahead. To her surprise it was dark. She couldn't even see the sofa cushions in their pretty green and yellow leaf pattern or all of the books that lined her aunt's bookshelf.

Daisy noticed Jazzi was hanging back. She stepped forward and called, "Aunt Iris?"

Suddenly the room lit up and at least twenty people yelled, "Surprise! Happy birthday!" The chorus of happy birthdays seemed to go on for five minutes.

Daisy turned to her daughter. "Did you know about this?"

"Of course I did," Jazzi answered her with a laugh. "I helped Aunt Iris plan it. Vi would have come home if she could have, but she has a test early tomorrow morning."

Daisy gave her daughter a hug. "That's okay. She texted me earlier and sent me an e-mail birthday card."

Now Daisy could peer into the small dining room and the table that was laden with food. The kitchen to the right was small, only about eight by ten feet, but the counters were filled with serving dishes.

To Daisy's surprise, her parents came forward to hug her. "Happy birthday, honey," her dad said.

"You're back from your vacation!"

"We couldn't miss your birthday. And look who else is here," her mother noted.

Just then Daisy spotted her sister, Camellia, who had driven in from New York.

Camellia was two years older than she was. Her brunette hair was cut in a chic bob hairstyle. She gave Daisy a huge hug too. They might have their differences, but they *were* sisters.

Tessa waved at Daisy from the kitchen and pointed to the two men, one on either side of the dining room — Jonas and Cade. All the staff from the tea garden was there, and Daisy felt the warm, loving glow of being back home in Willow Creek. Some days she didn't know if returning here and starting a business had been the right decision. But tonight she was sure it had been.

"First, we'll eat," her Aunt Iris called from the kitchen. "Then Daisy can open her presents. They're in the bedroom," her Aunt Iris told her. "I'll bring them out once everyone has been seated and finished eating."

Daisy didn't expect presents. Just having everyone here was the best gift she could receive.

Not only had her aunt prepared chicken pot pie, but there was chicken corn soup too along with sliced ham, rolls, cole slaw, chow-chow relish, and sweet and sour pickles. Desserts lined the other side of the table and included shoofly pie, apple cobbler, cherry crumb pie, and a teapot-shaped birthday cake.

Daisy went to her aunt and gave her a huge hug. "When did you have time to do all this?"

"I made the chicken pot pie tonight. But the soup I made yesterday in the slow cooker and the staff helped with desserts. Tessa made the shoofly pie. Eva made the cherry crumb, and Karina made the apple cobbler. And I did the cake. Go ahead and get in the buffet line. You eat first and then you can talk to all your guests."

Jazzi was at Daisy's elbow, probably because she knew her mom would get stuck talking to one person after another and wouldn't eat. Iris had probably enlisted Jazzi to make sure Daisy sampled everything. No problem. Daisy suddenly had an appetite.

She smiled at everyone, took food from around the table, then went to the sofa where she sat and started on her meal. Soon everyone else was sitting on the folding chairs and living room furniture and talking a mile a minute. Iris, Eva, and Tessa kept circulating, picking up dirty dishes, getting something for anyone who needed it. They were so used to working together that their movements were coordinated and they didn't duplicate each other's tasks. Foster helped too, but he was mostly on kitchen duty, washing up anything that needed it,

145

and loading the dishwasher.

There was hot tea for anyone who wanted it along with iced tea and soft drinks. After Daisy finished the piece of shoofly pie with whipped cream on top and the slice of chocolate marble birthday cake, she sipped her tea and set the cup and saucer on the coffee table.

"I'm going to circulate a bit," she told Jazzi, and got up to do that. She started in the living room saying a word or two or having a short conversation with each person who was there. When she crossed to the dining room, Cade was the first person she ran into. "I knew I'd be seeing you tonight," Cade said. "It was hard not to let anything slip."

"You did a good job. I can't believe everyone kept this a surprise."

"We knew your aunt Iris's wrath would come down upon us if we didn't," Cade joked. "And before someone steals you away, can you be free for lunch tomorrow?"

"I can," Daisy said with a smile, glad he remembered they were going to do that. But when she looked up, she saw Jonas was standing nearby and he might have overheard.

She groaned inwardly. But then she decided it shouldn't matter. Jonas had said his peace, hadn't he? Why should he care if she dated someone or not? But she wasn't sure if she was dating Cade. They were just going to have lunch.

Jonas was the last person she spoke with as she made the rounds of the kitchen and the dining room once again. He didn't have much to say. "Happy birthday," he congratulated her. "Why don't I sit beside you on the sofa? I think you might need some help with what's going to happen next."

As she turned a questioning gaze to him, her Aunt Iris and Jazzi carried in a card table from the bedroom. It was loaded with presents, many of them the same size. Daisy wasn't sure what to think about all of it.

As she sat beside Jonas on the sofa, she asked, "You knew about this too?"

"You mean the gifts? Yes, I did."

Daisy started with opening the present that was wrapped in pretty pink paper with fuchsia curly ribbon.

From somewhere Jonas produced a garbage bag.

"You're prepared," she said.

"I am. Iris asked me to help with the unwrapping."

Daisy glanced over at her aunt Iris. Was she matchmaking? She'd have to talk to her about that.

The first package held a birthday card from Eva. Daisy waved to her then lifted the lid. Inside, carefully wrapped in tissue paper, was a beautiful teacup and saucer painted with yellow roses. It was gorgeous.

"Thank you, Eva," Daisy said loud enough for her employee to hear. "It's beautiful."

To Daisy's delight, each box contained another teacup and saucer. Apparently, Iris had told everyone that would be the appropriate gift and the theme of the party. Before Daisy knew it, there were ten teacups on the card table. Jonas had somehow made all the wrappings disappear.

As she lifted another box, he said, "That one's from me."

Carefully she slid her fingers under the pale blue paper and released the ribbon. This box was larger than the others. Inside, she found a teapot and it was decorated with cats. One of them looked like Pepper and another resembled Marjoram.

"Variation on a theme," Jonas told her.

"I love it! I've wanted a teapot with cats for a long time and couldn't find one." She could tell immediately this one was bone china. "It's just right for me to take to my desk when I'm doing paperwork or working on the computer. Thank you."

"You're most welcome," Jonas said chivalrously.

Several of the women asked to see the teapot. After she passed it around, she leaned close to Jonas. "Now I really need shelves in my storage closet at the tea room."

"The one next to your pantry?"

"Yes, that's the one."

"I can put them in for you."

"That would be a lot of work."

"Shelves are easy. A few brackets and nails, two-by-fours. It wouldn't take much time."

"I'd be grateful, but you have to let me pay you."

"You can pay for the supplies. How about that?"

She felt a different vibe coming from Jonas tonight and wasn't sure what it meant. "All right. I'll pay for the supplies." And because everyone was talking at that time, she added, "Elijah showed Tessa and me the line of reclaimed furniture you want to put in. It really looks beautiful."

"Finding the reclaimed wood is the trick," Jonas admitted. "I'm waiting for the go-ahead from Aaron Zook. Once I get it, I'll be gathering wood from an old barn on his property that will soon be torn down. Maybe you'd like to go along and give me your opinion about it? I have to mark the sections I want. After all, you fashioned your house from an old barn, and you have some beautiful wood in your kitchen."

"I'd be glad to go along." With that out of her mouth before she even thought about it, she suddenly wondered if she was really that eager to spend time with Jonas.

"I'll text you when I find out how soon I can take a look around the barn," he told her.

She wondered if they'd just made a date, or if Jonas was simply making conversation to pass the time. He handed her another one of the presents and she began to unwrap it, putting the question aside for now. Time would tell if Jonas meant his offers or not.

The rest of the evening passed quickly in conversation and laughter. Soon, one by one the guests began to leave, including Cade and Jonas. Daisy's dad came up to her with a broad smile. He had a long face, kind blue eyes, and sandy brown hair gone to gray. Tonight he was wearing dress jeans and a plaid, snap-button shirt. He'd left his Phillies baseball cap at home, probably on the advice of her mother.

"I just want to wish you a happy birthday again. Did you enjoy the party?"

"The party was wonderful. Did you plan

on coming home for it all along?"

"We did."

Daisy's mom and her sister, Camellia, came over to her now too. Her dad leaned close to her and murmured, "They want to talk to you about something. I'll help your aunt clean up the kitchen."

Her father's words sounded ominous. Anytime her mom and her sister put their heads together, who knew what could happen? They had a habit of banding together. It had been like that when Daisy was growing up. Camellia was the older sister. According to her mother, Camellia had done everything right, from her performance in school to her job at a winery in New York. A marketing specialist, she knew how to sell and not only wine. She always looked perfect. Daisy, on the other hand, didn't much care how often her own hair was trimmed and styled. It waved where it wanted to. She braided it, pushed it behind her ears, or when it was long enough, tied it in a ponytail.

Her mother wore a smile when she approached Daisy. She usually wore bright pink lipstick. Her ash blond hair that was permed close around her head didn't move much when she walked. Daisy admired her mom, who'd always been a partner with her husband at Gallagher's Garden Corner. They both spent long hours at the nursery from spring to fall, and even over the holidays. Rose never ducked the work and had a hands-on approach to handling the nursery and the customers.

Daisy's mother said, "It was a lovely party. Your aunt knows how to pull a table together, though I think her chicken pot pie was just a little too thick. Don't you think?"

That was the aspect of her mother's character Daisy didn't appreciate — the critical side. She'd always felt that she'd gotten more of that than Camellia had.

"I liked Aunt Iris's pot pie just the way it was," Daisy protested automatically. "I think everyone else did too."

She wasn't even sure her mother had heard her as Rose stepped closer to her and lowered her voice. She glanced at Tessa, who was in the kitchen with Iris. "I wanted to talk to you about Tessa," she whispered.

"What about her?" Daisy asked.

"You need to stay clear of her situation, and maybe even clear of her."

"Mom's right," Camellia seconded. "You don't want any suspicion falling on you, and it's not good for business if the police are around the tea garden."

"First of all," Daisy said, "the police

haven't been around the tea garden much. And most important, Tessa is my friend and I won't desert her. She didn't do anything wrong, and I'm going to help her however I can."

Her father had stepped forward again so he was in the conversation too. She could feel her mother's disapproval emanating from her frown and her narrowed eyes.

Daisy's father patted her shoulder. "You should do what you think is right."

Her mother gave her dad a why-did-you-tell-her-that look, but then she launched from one touchy subject into another. "You really didn't tell me how Jazzi's weekend went with Portia Harding. Every time I asked you when we talked, you evaded it."

Daisy wasn't going to let her mother draw her into this conversation, either. Her own feelings about the matter didn't seem important compared to her daughter's.

She beckoned to Jazzi, who'd been folding the tablecloth from the dining room table.

Jazzi came over with a smile.

Daisy draped her arm around her daughter's shoulders. "I think Jazzi needs to tell you herself. Your grandmother wants to know how your weekend went with Portia."

As she expected, Daisy could see her mother also disapproved of her bringing

153

Jazzi into this conversation. Her sister, however, gave her an approving nod as if she understood why Daisy had done it.

As usual, Jazzi didn't hesitate to speak her mind. "I'm getting to know Portia a little at a time. I like her. The fact that I'm in her life is monumental for her, so we're both going to have to deal with that."

"Deal with it how?" Rose wanted to know.

Jazzi shrugged. "She hasn't told her family about me yet, and I won't push her to do that."

Rose looked stunned at that news, and Camellia appeared troubled.

From their expressions Aunt Iris must have guessed they weren't having the kind of conversation Daisy or Jazzi appreciated. She called, "Camellia. Rose. Would you like to take pot pie along with you? You can warm it up for lunch tomorrow. And Sean. How about helping me carry all those teacups of Daisy's out to her car."

"Sounds good to me," he called back.

Once again Daisy's aunt Iris, as well as her father, had saved her and Jazzi, too. She'd think of a special way to thank both of them.

When Tessa looked her way, Daisy could see that her friend appeared to be acting like her normal self. This party had been good for her, too. As far as Daisy knew, no one here had asked Tessa probing questions or put her on the spot. Daisy had meant what she'd told her mother. She would do anything she could to help Tessa.

She just had to figure out the best way to help.

CHAPTER EIGHT

Daisy's lunch with Cade at Sarah Jane's was thoroughly enjoyable. He didn't bring up one controversial topic and neither did she. When they drove back to the tea garden, he came around to Daisy's side of his car and opened the door for her.

Taking her hand, he held it as he walked her to the tea garden. "We'll have to do this again sometime," he said.

He was wearing a topcoat today over his suit. She thought she could read interest in his brown eyes, but not anything more. He touched the ends of her hair, then he said, "Have a good rest of the day. I'll see you soon."

So he didn't kiss her. Had this been a date? Was he interested in more than having lunch?

After a sigh, Daisy wondered if the world really could revolve without men. Maybe women could just take it over and run everything. Well, almost everything.

Daisy ran up the steps to the porch. She always enjoyed the look of the pale green Victorian with its yellow and white trim. As soon as she opened the door and stepped through the front entrance of the tea garden, she looked past the customers having cups or mugs of tea with the day's special of corn bread or the cinnamon scones that were selling so well. Immediately she saw Marshall standing near the kitchen talking to Tessa. *More bad news?* she wondered.

As soon as he spotted her, Marshall went into her office and beckoned to her and Tessa. She stepped inside with him, unzipped her jacket, and asked, "What's going on?"

Tessa sank down onto one of Daisy's chairs. "More bad news."

"It's not necessarily bad news," Marshall protested. "Some of the forensics is in."

"And?" Daisy asked, hanging her jacket on the clothes tree.

"We know for certain that Reese wasn't killed near the woods at the covered bridge. He was killed elsewhere and the body dumped there."

"Where was he killed?" Daisy wanted to know. That could certainly point to the murderer.

Marshall and Tessa both shook their heads at the same time, but Marshall answered. "They don't know. What are they going to do, scour the whole town looking for blood?"

At the mention of blood, Tessa paled.

Once more, Daisy turned questioning eyes to Marshall.

"The police also found blood in the back of Reese's SUV — *his* blood," Marshall explained. "Apparently, that was the vehicle that moved the body. Hence, all those questions to Tessa about whether she was in his SUV or not. And they did find Tessa's fingerprints on the steering wheel."

"They're going to arrest me," Tessa murmured.

"The same holds true today that held true the other times the police questioned you," Marshall scolded. "They don't have enough evidence to arrest you. You told them you drove Reese's SUV so, of course, your fingerprints are going to be in there. They're going to be in other places, too, because you rode in the vehicle. They might even be in the back because that's where you loaded the picture frames. You told the police that."

"But that doesn't mean they believe me," Tessa almost wailed.

"They don't have to believe you, but they

do need to find concrete evidence to dispute what you're saying. They haven't done that."

Daisy thought she heard a "yet" at the end of that sentence, but she was glad Marshall hadn't said it or Tessa might really jump off the deep end.

"So what do we do now?" Daisy asked.

"We wait. There's nothing else we can do. We can't disprove a negative. We can't prove Tessa *didn't* kill Reese. The police have to prove she did. And not only do they have to prove it, they have to find enough evidence that the DA will charge her. I'm sorry, Tessa, but you're just going to have to take one day at a time, one hour at a time. That's all you can do. Yell, scream, paint, walk, drive if you have to. But try to stay as centered as you can. That will help you with dealing with all of it."

"She already knows that," Daisy said. "She meditates."

"I don't think she's been meditating recently," Marshall said with a twinkle in his eye.

Tessa rose to her feet. "Right now I'm going to bake and then maybe I'll wash teapots. If I keep my hands busy, maybe my mind will follow." She went into the kitchen, her smock flowing out behind her, pulled out the flour bin, and started measuring

159

flour into a bowl.

"Is there anything I can do for her?" Daisy asked.

Marshall shook his head. "Not really. Try to keep her positive but realistic. I don't know if Detective Rappaport will come up with anything else. My guess is, he'd love to search her apartment. But he doesn't have grounds. I'd like to keep it that way. I'll say good-bye to Tessa on the way out. Hopefully, neither of you will need me anytime soon."

Marshall gave her a wave, stopped at the kitchen to do the same with Tessa, and then headed out the tea garden's front door.

Daisy had no sooner turned around, put on her apron, left her office, washed her hands, and gone to the counter where Tessa stood when Iris came into the kitchen and said, "There's somebody here to see you."

Daisy didn't recognize the man standing at the cashier's desk. He was about six foot tall and looked vaguely familiar. His hair was sandy brown, parted to one side. His nose was long, his jaw square. He was wearing jeans and his red down jacket was open over a plaid flannel shirt.

Daisy and Iris went to the sales counter.

"This is Daisy Swanson," Iris said.

Daisy studied the man. "And you are?"

He extended his hand to her. "I'm Gavin Cranshaw, Foster's father. Can I talk to you privately?"

He was a good-looking man with a bit of a rugged appearance. Apparently, they were going to talk about Foster but she didn't understand why. "How about hot tea and a scone? Chocolate or cinnamon scone?"

"Chocolate," he said, almost reluctantly.

"Do you like tea?"

"I drink it now and then. How about a nice black tea with plenty of caffeine?"

So he did know something about tea. He must have learned it from Foster's mom.

Daisy pointed to the yellow tea room, quiet for the moment. They could talk in there without being disturbed. She said, "Give me five minutes and I'll be there. Do you have the time?"

Gavin Cranshaw nodded. "I have the time."

His expression and his words portended a serious conversation. That made her nervous. Still, she brewed the tea expertly as she always did and used tongs to pick the scones out of the case and put them on a china plate. She carried it into the tea room and set it on the table.

After she was seated and poured both of them cups of tea, he looked down at the scones and then up at her. "I peeked into the tea garden over the weekend to find out just what Foster did here."

"He didn't tell you?" she asked.

"Tell me?" Gavin scoffed. "I just found out last week that Foster had this part-time job that was taking up a lot of his time."

Daisy was easily getting the feeling that Foster's father didn't approve of the job.

"I'm worried," he said. "Foster needs to keep his mind on his studies, not bussing tables."

So she'd been right about his not approving. This was one time she hadn't wanted to be right. "Foster does much more than bus tables."

Gavin stared down at his hand on the handle of the teacup. "I've worked with my hands all of my working years, as did my dad before me. I roof houses. I want more than that for my kids. My wife wanted more than that for her kids."

To make Gavin Cranshaw feel more at ease, Daisy said, "Foster told us about his mom and how much he misses her."

At that, Gavin looked surprised. He admitted gruffly, "Foster doesn't talk about her at home."

"I lost my husband three years ago," Daisy said. "My one daughter, Vi, talked about her grief and still talks about what she misses about her dad. My younger daughter, Jazzi, who's fifteen, kept it all in. It wasn't good for her or for us. Because of some other circumstances that happened, she's talking about it now. But don't you think it's good if Foster talks to someone about it?"

"You'd think he'd talk to his brother or sister or me."

"But you miss her as much as he does. That makes it harder for him."

His dad thought about that and then he nodded. "I suppose that could be true. I suppose I'm worried because Foster's the oldest and he sets the example. I don't want him veering off his path into a food services degree."

Daisy had heard many stories from friends and relatives whose kids went to college majoring in one thing then deciding they wanted a job in another. She asked, "What if Foster earns an MBA and still wants to be involved in food service? What if he manages or opens a restaurant?"

"Not my dream for him," Gavin grumbled.

"But what if it's *Foster's* dream?" Daisy asked.

Gavin Cranshaw's spine seemed to become straighter, his shoulders rigid and squared. "Restaurants hit the tubes more than they succeed. No offense to you," he added.

"I know how hard it is. After I lost Ryan, I had to take a risk. This tea garden was it. Moving back to Willow Creek was it. All together it meant a new life for me and Vi and Jazzi."

Gavin Cranshaw was silent.

"Mr. Cranshaw . . ." she started.

"Gavin, please," he said.

"All right. Gavin. Let me tell you what Foster does here. First of all he knows tea. He told me his mother taught him. He knows the different kinds, he can sense quality, and he knows how to blend and brew it. Besides that, he has people skills. He's great with my customers. Everybody loves him. On top of all that, he has computer skills. He's using them to help me market the tea garden on social media. I'm paying him extra for the time he spends on that."

Gavin looked shell-shocked. "I don't understand any of it. And there is something else." His face grew ruddier when he said it. And Daisy could only suspect what was coming next.

"I don't think Foster should be getting

involved seriously with a girl right now. From what I understand, Foster and your daughter are dating."

"They are. He's dating my older daughter, Violet. She's at Lehigh, so they're only seeing each other if she manages to come home on weekends."

"I thought she was local," Gavin said, looking a bit more relaxed.

Daisy wasn't sure how to get her point across, but she decided to try it anyway. "How old were you when you got married?"

Without even thinking about her question, he answered, "Too young to know better. But I don't regret a minute of it."

It was easy to see that Gavin had loved his wife.

"I was too young too," she said. "But I don't regret it either."

"Those were different times," he protested. "Dating seriously can keep Foster from achieving his goals."

"Or your goals for him," Daisy returned.

Leaning back in his chair, Gavin studied her. "You're not what I expected."

"What did you expect?"

"Not a young tea shop owner who got involved in solving a murder. I guess I expected somebody older."

She just smiled. "Life isn't always neat."

In the next few minutes, Gavin ate his scone while she sipped her tea. Then he drank down the rest of his tea all at one time. Afterward, he wiped his hands on his napkin and laid his hands on the table, ready to push himself up. "Thanks for talking to me."

"Anytime," she told him. "These are our children. We care more about them than anything else in our lives."

Someone walked past the window and when she turned to look, she saw Jonas passing by. He was looking in, by habit she guessed, and he saw her there with Gavin. She should tell him —

There was nothing to tell him. She had nothing to explain. Did she?

She stood to walk Gavin to the front tea room. At the counter he asked, "Does Foster bake scones too?"

"Sometimes," she said.

Again Gavin just shook his head. "I have to wrap my mind around all this. I was going to tell him he had to quit, but if what you say is true, it sounds as if he really enjoys what he's doing. I imagine being around the tea brings back memories of his mom. I don't want to take that from him if I don't have to. We'll just see how the dating plays out. Usually boys that age don't

166

stick to one girl very long."

"Unless it's the right girl," Daisy suggested.

But she could see that Gavin didn't want to entertain that possibility. He said, "Thanks for the information and the conversation. I'm sure we'll be talking again sometime." Then he turned and left.

"Did I hear right?" Aunt Iris asked. "That was Foster's dad?"

"It was."

"He's quite good-looking, don't you think, in a rugged man type of way?"

"Aunt Iris —"

"You can't fault your fairy godmother for trying, but you're not a very cooperative godchild."

"I see someone who needs her teacup filled. I'll take care of it," Daisy told her aunt. But she said it with a smile so her aunt knew she appreciated everything she did, even matchmaking. It showed how much Iris cared.

A few hours later, at almost closing, Daisy was putting dough for lemon tea cakes into the walk-in. Tessa had gone out to the counter to see what was left in the case.

When Daisy heard loud voices in the other room, she stepped away from the walk-in to peer into the tea room. It only took her a

167

second to recognize Chloie. She was pointing at Tessa. "You murdered Reese. I know you did."

Tessa's face was red and she was speechless, which was rare for Tessa.

Chloie went on, "Reese was going to break it off with you and date me. I told the police that too."

Daisy went to the counter to stand beside Tessa. She studied the too-blond blonde, who seemed to be in good shape. That reminded her that Tessa had said Chloie worked out at the gym. So it was feasible she could have killed Reese and disposed of his body.

Daisy spoke up since someone needed to defend her friend. "Chloie, I understand you're upset, and you're grief-stricken that Reese is gone. But if you can't be civil and speak in a normal tone when you come into the tea garden, then please don't come in."

"I can come in if I want to," Chloie said stubbornly, a defiant expression on her face, much like a small child's.

"No, you can't," Daisy insisted. "Customers are welcome here but only if they behave properly. You're not. I can call the police if you're disturbing the peace."

Chloie pointed her finger at Tessa again. "You'll be sorry." Then she turned and fled without a cup of tea or a scone.

Tessa started to apologize. "I'm so sorry she did that. Maybe I shouldn't even come to work."

"Don't be ridiculous," Daisy protested. "You work here. You have every right to be here."

The tea garden had emptied out with the commotion. After glancing around, Daisy said, "Aunt Iris, Eva, and Cora Sue can finish cleaning up and taking inventory. Just leave the clipboard on the counter. Why don't you help me hang these quilted wall hangings the customers can purchase. It will be a good advertisement for the Quilt Lovers Weekend. It will be here before we know it."

She kept talking and beckoned to Tessa, who followed her into the spillover tea room. A box lay on one of the tables with the wall hangings. White shelves ran across two walls, holding an assortment of teapots and teacups. The shelves sported pegs underneath where Daisy and her staff could hang decorative items like potholders or wall hangings.

Daisy stretched a wall hanging between her arms. "These are about two feet wide, so if we put the string in the back over three of the pegs, they should hang just right.

Don't you think?"

"I suppose," Tessa said, sounding disinterested.

"Do you want to be the one who crawls up on the chair or should I?" Daisy asked.

That seemed to take Tessa's attention. "We should really get the stepstool. Neither of us needs to fall right now."

"Good idea," Daisy agreed. "Why don't you pick out six wall hangings you like the best, and I'll get the stepstool from the pantry. Be right back."

Knowing that keeping Tessa busy doing something was the best way to keep her mind off of Chloie Laird, she hurried to fetch the stepstool. When she returned to the yellow room, Tessa had made her choices. All of the wall hangings could go anywhere, really. They had a multitude of colors that fit in with the painted teacups and teapots and the décor of the room.

Through the bay window, Daisy could see dusk falling. "We have a little more daylight than in December."

"You're an optimist. It's only about three minutes more a day," Tessa said acerbically.

"But each day gets a little longer. I look forward to that."

Tessa held up a wall hanging in a star pattern using shades of green, yellow, and orange. Then she headed up the stepstool.

Daisy held the back of the stool, steadying it as Tessa hung the wall hanging on the pegs.

Her friend said nonchalantly, "I went by Jonas's store earlier today."

"And?" Daisy asked.

"You should see the chairs he has on display. The backs and seats aren't upholstered with fabric but rather quilts. They're absolutely beautiful. You should stop in and see them."

"I imagine I'll see them sometime," Daisy said.

"You and Jonas seemed to be getting along well last night."

"I never know what to expect with Jonas, that's for sure."

"I love the teapot he gave you. I guess you're going to keep that one at home."

"I certainly am. I wouldn't want anything to happen to it."

"But you're going to use the teacups and saucers in here?"

"I might pick out a few of those to keep at home, too. That was such a sweet idea. I appreciate each one of them, whether it was from a flea market, an antique shop, or over-the-counter department store. They're all beautiful."

Tessa descended the stepstool and picked up the next wall hanging. "I know what your mom was probably telling you."

Daisy didn't comment as Tessa hung the next wall hanging.

Returning to the floor again, her friend said, "I'm sure your mother told you you should fire me."

"She didn't say that," Daisy protested. "She certainly knows better than to say anything like that."

"Then what did she say?"

Daisy and Tessa had been friends for so long that she knew only the truth would do. "She said I should stay far away from anything to do with the murder."

"And she's probably right."

"No, I don't think she is, Tessa. You're my friend, and you're in trouble."

"I know. I'm so scared the police are going to arrest me. What will I do?"

"You'll have Marshall by your side, and me and Aunt Iris, Jonas and Cade. You aren't alone."

"I certainly will be if I'm in jail."

"That's why I'd like to ask around and maybe find out more about Reese's background. There's no harm in that."

"I suppose not," Tessa agreed.

When Tessa was about to turn away, Daisy

caught her arm. "You should spend the night painting . . . to relax."

Tessa's caramel-colored braid fell over her shoulder as she shook her head. "Painting just reminds me of Reese. It's not good for me right now."

As Daisy picked up the last wall hanging, she studied it. It was a wedding ring pattern. "You know, maybe we should both take up quilting. Rachel is serious about having us join her quilting circle. What do you think?"

"I don't know if the other women would want me there."

"Then maybe you should ask Rachel what she thinks. Because in my experience with Rachel, she'll say you're welcome."

That brought a smile to Tessa's lips. Daisy was just hoping she could keep it there.

Chapter Nine

When Daisy looked out the window the following afternoon, she saw big, fat flakes of snow falling and collecting on the road. The tree branches were already frosted.

As Tessa peered out the window too, she said, "I have to pick up groceries. I hope the snow isn't going to mount up."

Even with current, more accurate weather predictions, they still varied. Daisy had forgotten to check the forecast for today. But the snow was coming down more heavily now. The cars on the main street were fewer and farther between.

"Go on and pick up your groceries," Daisy advised Tessa. "With this weather, we're only going to have a few customers in the hour or so that's left. I'll send Aunt Iris and Eva home soon and we'll close early. I've been jotting down ideas for new recipes. I'll pull them together, then I'll leave them in your apartment before I go. You can look them over and text me what you think. We might want to experiment now while we have a lighter customer stream." She checked the cell phone in her pocket. "No messages from Jazzi. She's spending the day with a friend. She's going to text when I have to pick her up."

In the next half hour, Eva and Iris were able to care for the kitchen and tea room because so few customers stopped in. Daisy sent them home early and sat at her desk, scribbling notes onto her legal pad. When she created recipes, she preferred to do it with a pen on paper rather than on the computer. Tessa knew that and wouldn't be surprised.

Daisy had five new recipes — two for baked goods, two for soups, and one for bread. When she glanced out the window, she noticed the snow had stopped and appeared to be melting. Reaching for her jacket, she took it from the clothes tree, shrugged into it, and zippered up. Then she found her keys in her purse and looked for Tessa's key on her ring. Ready to go, she picked up the recipes. Going out the back way, she set the alarm.

A brisk wind blew around the few flakes that hadn't melted or that were still floating from the sky. She hurried to the door that led up the steps to Tessa's apartment. Dusk was falling and the wind blew even stronger around her. She put the key in the doorknob but to her surprise the door wasn't locked. That didn't make any sense. Especially since Reese's death, Tessa locked up tight.

Opening the door, she called up the stairs. "Tessa? Are you there?"

No answer.

Maybe Tessa had been cold and in a hurry and didn't lock the door because she was expecting Daisy. She started up the stairs, listening as she went.

She'd climbed to the second step from the top when suddenly a looming shadow appeared. She was pushed . . . hard. Her feet went out from under her as she dropped her purse and recipes, tumbling down the stairs, banging her head on the baseboard and her shoulder on the wall. Whoever had been in the apartment rushed past her. All she could see were jean-clad legs and sneakers. The door banged behind the intruder, then swayed open again.

She wasn't sure how long she lay there seeing spots of light that resembled stars. Her chest felt tight and she realized her breath had been knocked out of her. After taking a few deep breaths, she wiggled her feet. No problem there. She carefully straightened her legs. Her shoulder hurt. But it was the bump on her head and the headache throbbing at her temples that made her groan when she pulled herself into a sitting position on the stairs.

The wind blew in the open door, banging it completely open until she saw a shadow there and then a hand on the door. She wanted to scream but the sound stuck in her throat.

Until Jonas peered in the open door and spotted her. "Daisy? Are you all right?"

She tried to get to her feet. She didn't want him seeing her sitting there like that, looking helpless.

She mustn't have done a very good job of it because he rushed to her, put his arm around her waist, and asked, "Are you sure you want to stand?" Without giving her time to answer, he followed up with, "What happened?"

At the same time, overriding his voice, she asked, "Why are you here?"

He responded, "I went to the tea garden and found it closed. When I checked the back lot, your car was still there. I saw Tessa's open door and I figured something was going on. I couldn't help but investigate."

With his arm around her waist, his

strength seeping into her, it wasn't so hard to arrange her feet under her.

"Can you climb the stairs?" he asked. "I'll help you up to Tessa's apartment."

"I can climb," she assured him almost breathlessly. She was not breathless from the fall, but because Jonas was so close . . . so sturdy . . . so warm.

In the shadows, she saw him glance at her. Maybe what he saw convinced him she could do it. Nevertheless, he didn't let go of her. "I'll get your purse and the papers after you reach the top," he told her.

She was ready to say that she'd stoop and get everything herself, but she didn't know if she'd be dizzy if she tried. That would be just too humiliating.

Once in Tessa's apartment, Jonas helped her to the couch, then switched on a floor lamp. Sitting beside her, he requested again, "Tell me what happened. Did you trip?"

"No, I didn't trip!" she protested. "I was pushed. Someone was in Tessa's apartment."

"Did you see who it was?"

"No. It's shadowy in the stairway, and I didn't expect anyone. I was almost at the top when suddenly I got this big push and I tumbled down the stairs. All I saw were jeans and sneakers as whoever it was ran by me. I couldn't even tell if it was a man or a woman."

"I'm calling nine-one-one," Jonas said grimly. "I don't like the sound of any of this. Do you need a paramedic?"

"No paramedic," she said vehemently. "I bumped my head and my shoulder. But I'm fine. Just make the call to the police. That's important."

Jonas didn't argue, but he didn't look happy, either.

Detective Rappaport himself arrived about fifteen minutes after Jonas called him. Daisy was explaining to the detective what had happened when Tessa came running up the stairs. All over again, Daisy related how she'd been pushed down the stairs. Rappaport took notes once more in his small notebook as if Daisy had left something out the first time. But she hadn't.

Detective Rappaport ordered Tessa, "Take a look around and see if anything's missing."

While Daisy stayed on the sofa with Jonas, Rappaport followed Tessa around the apartment.

"Nothing's missing," she told the detective as they returned from the bedroom to the living room. "Not that I can see at first glance, anyway."

"I don't know what to think," Detective Rappaport grumbled. "If someone broke in here, there was a good reason."

Detective Rappaport was making this seem like it was Tessa's fault in some way, and Tessa wasn't having any of that. Hands on her hips, she turned to him and asked, "Were Reese's keys found on his body?"

It was obvious that the detective didn't want to answer. She kept glaring at him.

Finally he admitted, "No. We didn't find his keys. Obviously, the murderer used them to drive Masemer's car."

"That explains it," Tessa said. "Daisy said the door was open when she arrived. No one had to break in. The keys to my apartment — the knob and the deadbolt — were on Reese's key ring."

"*You* could have that key ring," Detective Rappaport pointed out. "And you could have left the door open by mistake."

"I didn't leave the door open by mistake. But even if I had, that wouldn't explain someone pushing Daisy down the stairs."

The detective rubbed the back of his neck, then he focused on Daisy. "Should I call the paramedics for you?"

"No. Please don't. I'm fine."

"All right then. I'll be going. This is going to cause me a lot of paperwork that seems to be unnecessary, but I'll send somebody over to dust your door for fingerprints. Take care, folks." He warned Daisy, "Don't fall down any more stairs."

Jonas stood. "I think you should go to the urgent care center and be checked."

"I'm not going to go and have a lot of unnecessary tests."

"I don't think you should drive yourself home," he maintained.

She checked her watch. Then her phone that was in her jacket pocket sounded. "I have to pick up Jazzi."

"I'll take you to pick up Jazzi, and then I'll take you home."

Jonas was pulling his white knight act again, and Daisy wanted no part of it. She was about to refuse and not give in on principle when Tessa came over to her and touched the lump on her head. "This isn't *nothing,* Daisy. And I don't want to be responsible for you having an accident."

"You're not. Your intruder is the one who knocked me down."

"Maybe so. But this whole mess feels like my fault. I think you should let Jonas pick up Jazzi with you and take you home. Forget he's a guy and just think of him as a chauffeur."

Daisy really didn't want to give in, but her

shoulder and her head ached from the fall, so she agreed.

"I'll get my car," Jonas said. "I'll be back in five minutes." He gave Tessa a nod as if it were a thank-you.

Daisy felt as if they were conspiring against her.

"I'll walk you downstairs," Tessa said. "You're looking pale."

"I'm aching a bit. It will probably be worse tomorrow. I'll ice when I get home, and then take a hot shower."

They went down the stairs together and once they were at the bottom, they waited. They saw the patrol officer there. Rappaport had obviously left him there to guard the door.

Daisy said, "You have to think about what the intruder might have wanted."

"I can't imagine," Tessa said. "I don't have anything that's that valuable except a few pieces of jewelry and they weren't touched."

"Do you have anything of Reese's here?"

Almost immediately Tessa shook her head. "Nothing of value. Just an electronic cigarette he used. That's still lying on my dresser, the same place where he left it. I haven't touched it."

"That intruder wanted something, and we're going to have to figure out what it was. Maybe when my head stops throbbing, I'll be able to think more clearly."

Minutes later, Jonas pulled his SUV practically up to Tessa's door. Daisy climbed in and buckled her seat belt, gave Jonas the address of Jazzi's friend, then waved at Tessa.

Jonas let off the brake, made a K-turn, and headed to the parking lot's entrance. He didn't speak as he switched on the turn signal and made a right.

Uncomfortable, Daisy wasn't going to stand for silence the whole way home. "Why did you volunteer to help when you obviously don't want to be involved?"

"There's nothing obvious about this," he said tersely.

"I don't get it, Jonas. Either you want to be around me or you don't. All I'm feeling from you is ambivalence. It's not helping my headache."

After he sent her a sharp glance, he stared out the windshield again. "I heard you had lunch with Cade. What's that about?"

Of all the questions Jonas could ask, she didn't expect that one. She suddenly felt deflated as if any energy she still possessed just oozed out of her. All of her defensiveness went with it. "Cade and I are friends."

"And what about your tête-à-tête with

that man in the tea room yesterday?"

So he *had* seen her with Gavin. Patiently she explained, "That was Foster's father. He doesn't approve of Foster's job. He's a widower and trying to raise his kids the best he can. I understand how that's hard going. He doesn't seem to approve of Foster seeing Violet, either. At least he doesn't want them becoming serious."

"You don't want that either, do you?"

"No, I don't. Or let's just say, I don't want her dating to interfere with her college education. But I also know Violet's eighteen now, and I can't control what she does any more than Gavin can control what Foster does."

Her head still throbbing, she wanted to honestly know why Jonas was questioning her about Cade and Gavin. "So why do you care if I had lunch with Cade? Or if I was talking to Gavin?"

"Because I care about you."

She tried to let those words sink in, but they didn't make sense with everything else he'd said. "I don't understand."

"Look, I might not be ready to jump into a full-fledged family relationship, but I want to make the shelves for your pantry closet, and I'd like to go on seeing you."

"As what?" she asked, now feeling perturbed.

When he kept silent, she said again wearily, "You really *are* making my headache worse."

"I'm sorry. We'll have to have a long talk when you're feeling better. Just try to relax. We'll be at Jazzi's friend's in a couple of minutes. Your whole body got shaken up with that tumble. Don't be surprised if you can't get out of bed in the morning."

"Oh, I'll get out of bed," she vowed.

He shook his head and kept his focus on traffic.

Daisy suspected Jazzi was surprised when Jonas got out of the SUV and went to the door. Daisy saw him motion to his SUV.

A minute later, he opened the door for Jazzi and she climbed in the back. Jazzi studied her, and Daisy knew she didn't look normal.

"What happened, Mom? Is that a bump on your forehead?"

"I don't want you to be frightened or get upset," Daisy said.

"Then tell me what happened before I do," Jazzi returned, like the assertive teenager she was.

Daisy explained what had happened in as little detail as possible.

Jazzi got the gist. "So some bad guy or gal is running around, probably the one who murdered Mr. Masemer, and whoever it is pushed you down the steps."

"That about sums it up," Jonas said, as he pulled off of the side street and onto the main road. He headed for Daisy's house.

Daisy shot him a glare but she knew he couldn't see it in the dark. "We don't know who it was or what they wanted," Daisy conceded. "But whoever it was had to want something in Tessa's apartment. She just can't figure out what."

"Would this person have left a note or a message somehow?" Jazzi asked.

"I'm sure Tessa will be going through her place with a fine-tooth comb once she gets over the shock of what happened. I asked her if she had anything of Reese's there, but she said all she had was one of his electronic cigarettes."

"He smoked one of them?" Jazzi asked. "They're bad for you. I read a whole article about them, how they hurt the lining of your nose, and they cause sinus problems."

Daisy was glad her daughter kept up with the latest information, whatever it was. She just wondered what else she kept up with.

Less than ten minutes later, Jonas pulled up the driveway that led to the garage at

Daisy's house. "I'll come in with you," he said, driving practically up to the sidewalk.

"I have my key," Jazzi said. "I'll go open the door."

"You two are treating me like an invalid," Daisy grumbled.

"No, we're not. If you were an invalid, I'd carry you to the house."

He'd opened his door so she knew this time he'd caught her baleful glare under the dome light. She opened her door before he could come around and stepped out.

She wobbled a little on her feet, and if Jonas saw it, he didn't comment. He did nevertheless take her by the elbow to walk her to the door.

Jazzi had opened the door and punched in the code to turn off the alarm system. At the door, Jonas stepped inside with her. "I want to talk to Jazzi," he said.

Now what? Daisy wondered.

Jazzi had taken off her parka and dropped her backpack on the sofa. She'd also switched on a few lights. Jonas met her at the kitchen island as Daisy shrugged out of her jacket and took it to the closet under the stairs. She could feel his eyes on her. Making sure she didn't lose her balance again?

He asked Jazzi, "You still have my cell

number in your phone, right?"

"I do."

"I want you to watch your mom carefully. I know it's a lot to ask. But you really need to wake her every few hours and ask her questions."

"I've seen this on TV," Jazzi assured him. "You mean, like her address and her name, what year it is and who the president is."

"Exactly. If her thinking isn't clear, you call me. Any dizziness or nausea, you call me then, too."

"Jonas, you're worrying her unnecessarily," Daisy protested. "I'm going to put ice on my sore shoulder, maybe on the knot on my head, and go to bed."

"Mom, I'm going to sleep in your bed with you tonight," Jazzi insisted. "It's the best way. Don't worry, Jonas, I'll take care of her."

Crossing to Daisy, he took her gently by the shoulders. "If you have a concussion, it's nothing to mess around with."

She could see the worry in his eyes and she knew he meant well. "I understand, really I do. The least little symptom, Jazzi will call you or I'll call nine-one-one. I promise."

He gave her another long look, then he leaned forward and kissed her on the forehead. He glanced at Jazzi. "Don't forget to turn the alarm on after I leave."

She nodded.

When Jonas left her house and closed the door behind him, Daisy was almost relieved to see him go. On the other hand, she was disappointed he'd left. Absolutely crazy. Maybe that's what a bump on the head could do.

On Monday morning, Daisy was trying to function normally as Jazzi climbed on the school bus and Jonas came down the lane and up the driveway. Although she'd rested yesterday as Jazzi had continued to watch over her and Jonas texted to check in on her, her headache was still throbbing. She supposed that was normal after a bump on the head. Jonas had insisted on picking her up this morning if she wanted to go to work.

She'd just climbed into his SUV and wished him good morning when her phone buzzed. "It's Tessa," she murmured to Jonas. "It might be important."

Tessa didn't even give her a chance to say hello. "You've got to come over. You've got to come over *now.*"

Daisy tried to calm the pain in her temple so she could concentrate on Tessa's voice. "What happened?"

"You won't believe what I found in my apartment."

"You found something that doesn't belong there?"

"I'll say it doesn't belong here." Tessa's voice broke on the word and Daisy heard a small sob.

"What is it, Tessa? Something of Reese's?"

"No. It was behind one of my paintings up in the attic."

"What could be behind your paintings?"

"It's a bronze and fairly heavy. I think it's the murder weapon. It has blood on it. And I picked it up."

Tessa's voice was so loud that Daisy wondered if Jonas could hear it. At the look he gave her, she knew he could.

"Take it easy," she said, trying to stay calm because Tessa wasn't.

"You know what this means?" Tessa asked her. "My fingerprints are on it!"

"I'll be there in ten minutes. We're on our way."

After Jonas took a look at Daisy, he decided, "You look pale. I'm not sure you should even go to the tea garden . . . let alone to Tessa's."

"Did you hear what Tessa said?" she asked as she brushed his concern away. "She found what she thinks is the murder weapon behind a painting, and it has blood on it. Now it has her fingerprints on it too."

A grim expression stole over Jonas's face as he stepped on the gas and sped to the tea garden. They were both silent until they arrived in the back parking lot.

After he pulled up to Tessa's apartment entrance, Daisy opened her door.

"I'm going in with you," he said.

This time she didn't argue.

As Daisy ran up the steps, she felt a little lightheaded. She'd eaten a scone this morning before she'd left but she hadn't had her usual cup of tea.

Tessa met them in the living room. "I wrapped it in a towel."

"You have to call Rappaport," Jonas insisted.

"I did," she assured him.

At that moment, there was a knock on the door downstairs. Tessa called, "Come on up!"

Detective Rappaport took the steps at a fast clip. When he got to the living room, he saw the bundle in Tessa's hands. "You didn't rub anything off, did you?" he asked.

"No. As I told you, I found it behind one of my paintings in the attic. I picked it up the first time, then remembered I shouldn't touch it. So I just gently wrapped it in the towel." She held it out to him. "Here."

He took it and then glared at her. "It's awfully convenient that you found it. You used the whole intruder incident to find the murder weapon. It was probably in your car or somewhere else and you transferred it upstairs."

Daisy stepped forward then and pointed her finger at his chest. "You're crazy."

The detective turned on her and said in a loud voice, "Maybe there wasn't an intruder after all. Maybe you were covering for your friend, and *you* had it."

As Rappaport took out his phone, Daisy's head began to spin. Rappaport barked orders into the phone. Then he ended the call and said to Tessa, "You're going to have to come down to the station for more questioning. By afternoon, I'll have a search warrant to search this place and your car. This is just the excuse I was looking for."

Now Daisy was seeing floating black spots in front of her eyes.

Rappaport was still talking. "A patrol car will be here in a couple of minutes with an officer to watch your place to make sure you don't take anything in or out."

The black spots in front of Daisy's eyes became a gray veil spread out in front of her and seemed to fold her into its embrace.

She felt herself falling and knew someone caught her. But that was her last conscious thought.

Chapter Ten

Four hours later, Daisy lay on the gurney in her cubicle in the ER while Jonas sat in a blue vinyl chair by her bed. He was studying something on his phone as they waited for the results of her tests. The CT scan in particular. Her head still throbbed. But if she closed her eyes, the pain wasn't as bad. She wished she and Jonas could have a real conversation, but she knew he wouldn't do that when she was in this condition.

When Daisy heard footsteps, she opened her eyes and caught a glimpse of a scrubs-clad doctor with an electronic tablet in his hands coming into her cubicle. She sat up a little too quickly and put her hand on the bar of the bed to steady herself.

Jonas noticed. "Dizzy?" he asked.

"I'm fine," she said, looking up at the doctor whose ID badge said DR. SUTTON. "Aren't I fine, Doctor?" Her voice was almost daring him to tell her she wasn't.

He gave her a small smile. "I'm glad to say your CT scan didn't show anything troublesome. But you do have a concussion, and you need to keep that arm in a sling at least a few days. Ice your shoulder and give it time to heal. Your brain was bruised and it needs time to heal too. That's why you're having headaches and some dizziness. I can give you something for the headaches."

She shook her head. "No, I'd rather not."

"Daisy," Jonas said with a bit of exasperation.

"I'd rather not," she said again. "I won't know how I really feel."

"In the middle of the night when you have a raging headache," the doctor advised, "you might want something. Let me write the prescription. You have it filled, and if you don't use it, you don't use it."

"That sounds reasonable to me," Jonas added, in a tone that said if she wasn't reasonable, he might take measures to care for her himself.

No, that wouldn't do.

"I can't just stay home and rest. I own a tea garden. And then there's Tessa . . ."

Jonas cut in. "I just received a text from Marshall. He got her out of the police station without being charged and Tessa's back at work. She and Iris called in help to take

195

over for you for a few days. Cora Sue is going to work extra hours and so is Karina. Foster will add more time if you need him to. They're all pulling together for you."

"I can't stay away for three days," she said, almost with a groan.

Apparently, Jonas believed in negotiation because he suggested, "Promise me you'll give it today and tomorrow. Then you can assess how you're feeling and decide if you want to go in."

Daisy looked up at the doctor.

"You need time to heal," he repeated. "I'll write the prescription and it will be with your discharge papers."

Suddenly Daisy heard a voice in the hall she didn't want to hear.

"Daisy, I came as soon as Jonas called me. How much damage did that fall do?" her mother asked, rushing to Daisy's side, concern lacing her voice.

Daisy's first inclination was to be perturbed with Jonas for calling her mother. She took a quick glance at him and he just raised his brows, as if to say, *I did it for your own good.* Heaven spare her from a man who did things for her own good.

Her indignation faded away as her mother took her hand. He'd had her best interest at heart. But then she remembered he'd backed away from her for her own good too. Did he really know what her own good was? The doctor left the cubicle, and as her mother clucked over her and studied her, Jonas rose from his chair to give it to her mom.

Rose said, "I'm going to take you home and you're going to stay with me. Jazzi can come too. That's what spare rooms are for. I'll cook and you can eat and rest. Jazzi can do whatever she likes."

Daisy was about to protest but she realized she'd better obey doctor's orders. If she was at her mom's, she would be resting. The time spent overnight there, Jazzi spending time with her grandparents, would be good for both of them. Her mom had become somewhat removed from Jazzi, not really understanding a teenager's needs, wants, and pastimes. Maybe this would be a chance for them to catch up.

"All right," Daisy agreed, giving in to both Jonas and her mom.

However, as always, her mother pushed her concern too far. She warned her again, "You need to stay away from Tessa until the situation is resolved."

"No, I won't stay away from Tessa. Don't push it, Mom, or I'll just go home."

Her mother's face flushed and she looked

insulted. Daisy didn't want to hurt her mom, but she had to defend her boundaries. Her mother couldn't control her life, and now Daisy was more determined than ever to figure out who was trying to frame Tessa.

Maybe needing a minute to regroup, her mother said, "I'll find out how long it's going to take to spring you from here."

After her mother left the cubicle, Jonas came over to Daisy's bedside once more and took the chair. Then he reached for Daisy's hand and held it. "I know you don't especially want to go home with your mother, but it will be the best for you right now. I called her because I knew you wouldn't rest on your own. Jazzi's a great caretaker, but I don't think she'll tie you down. Your mother might."

He was smiling and she couldn't help but smile back. "Thank you," she said.

"For what?"

"For coming with me and waiting with me, and I guess for calling my mother. She's a force to be reckoned with, and I don't have the energy to argue with her right now."

"Except on Tessa's account."

"Yes. Jonas, I have to figure out what's going on and who's framing her."

"That's for the police to investigate," Jonas reminded her.

"You heard Rappaport. He thinks I might have even had something to do with hiding the murder weapon."

"No, I don't think he really believes that. He was trying to goad you and Tessa into telling him something he didn't already know. He went too far, and I think he knows it."

"How did Tessa hold up with the questioning?"

"She's okay. Marshall warned her before they went in to give the facts and only the facts. She did fine." He squeezed her hand. "When you're feeling better, you and I will have a talk."

She nodded and wished she hadn't. Nodding made the pounding in her head get worse.

Jonas must have figured that out. "I'm going to go. Call me if you need anything, but I don't think you will with your mom taking care of you." He leaned close to her, ran his thumb over her lips, and pushed her hair behind her ear. "You take care of yourself, Daisy Swanson. I don't want anything to happen to you."

After a last touch across her brow, he rose to his feet, picked up his jacket from the back of the chair, and left her cubicle. It was odd, but she felt as if her support had just been kicked out from under her. That was impossible. Jonas didn't want to be her support.

She lay back against the pillow once more because all of it was just too confusing right now.

Resting made Daisy tired and frustrated. Her mother expected her to stay in bed in the spare room and do absolutely nothing. That wasn't Daisy's nature. At first, any activity did seem to make her headache worse — especially if she used her eyes. So she tried to stay off her phone, electronic tablet, and to keep from jotting notes on a legal pad. Her mother had fed her chicken and dumplings, as much tea as she wanted, and blueberry cobbler. Daisy wondered how much weight a person could gain in just one day. Jazzi was being extra solicitous too. Her dad had waited at Daisy's house until Jazzi got home from school and then brought her over to her grandparents' house.

Before bed, she came into Daisy's room, gave her a kiss on the cheek, and actually had tears in her eyes when she said, "I don't want anything to happen to you, Mom. I called Violet and she's worried too."

Daisy hugged her daughter. "I don't want you to worry." She leaned away from Jazzi. "I'm feeling better, really I am. Tomorrow I'll get up for a bit and see how things go. I'll call Violet right now, and assure her she has nothing to worry about."

Jazzi looked reassured as she left Daisy's room. Daisy vowed to herself she would be careful but she was also determined to find answers. She was just picking up her phone to call Violet when her phone buzzed.

A text had come in from Jonas. How are you doing?

She texted back. I'm tired of being pampered.

Another day, he texted back. Promise.

So she gave him a thumbs-up emoji and texted, I promise.

He texted back, Sleep well.

The warm feeling in her heart wouldn't go away. She knew that was foolish.

Her call to Violet went in a similar fashion as her talk with Jazzi. When Violet asked if she should come home, Daisy answered, "Certainly not. Concentrate on your studies. I'll give you an update tomorrow. I'm feeling better already." She was.

In the morning Daisy insisted on going downstairs for breakfast. Both her father and mother looked her over carefully. "A little pale," her dad said.

"She's not squinting against the light like she was yesterday, though," her mother added.

"I'm in the room," Daisy told them both, resigned to their scrutiny. "I'm going to be up and around a little bit today to see how I really feel. I'd like to go back to the tea garden tomorrow."

Her parents exchanged a look. While her mother pursed her lips, her father said reasonably, "See how you feel by the end of the day."

He'd always given her reasonable advice.

When her mother insisted on making pancakes, scrambled eggs, and bacon, Daisy didn't argue. After all, she had to make concessions. She spent some of her time that morning creating more recipes on her legal pad. Writing on paper didn't bother her eyes like looking at her phone or tablet. She was sitting on the sofa going over them when her parents' doorbell rang.

"I'll get it," Rose called from the kitchen where she was baking cookies. Jazzi's favorite — chocolate chip.

When her mother opened the door, to Daisy's surprise, she heard Foster's voice. "Hello, Mrs. Gallagher," he said. "I came to check up on Daisy. Everybody at the tea garden wants a firsthand report."

"That makes sense, I guess," Rose said. "Come on in. But don't tire her out."

Daisy bit her tongue. She'd stand up for her rights against her mom another time. She smiled at Foster and patted the sofa next to her. "You don't have classes today?" she asked.

"Not this morning."

"How is everything at the tea garden?"

"Going smoothly. You have to trust us."

"I do."

He gave her a smile. "I know it's hard to let go of control, but Iris is good. With this cold weather, we're not swamped right now, either. Tourist buses have stopped for the moment. It's just too cold to stroll from shop to shop."

Foster might have stopped in to check up on her, but his hands balled into fists and at times he wasn't quite meeting her eyes. That wasn't like him.

"Foster, what's the matter? Why did you really come?"

He looked insulted. "I really came to see how you were."

"Besides that," she prompted.

He looked down at his sneakers then back up at her. "I'm sorry my dad bothered you.

Eva told me he stopped in at the tea garden."

Gavin's visit seemed like a long time ago, even though it wasn't. "Foster, it wasn't a bother. Your dad's concerned about you. He wants a better life for you than he had. Parents are like that. Really, it's okay. Your dad's a nice guy."

"Most of the time," Foster admitted. "But I'm old enough to know what I want, and he's going to have to respect that."

"Give him time to get used to the idea that you've grown up. Now tell me, how's Tessa?"

"Have you talked to her?" Foster asked.

"Her phone keeps going to voice mail. It's like someone is giving her orders not to talk to me."

"She probably just doesn't want to upset you."

"What would I be upset about?"

"The police searched her apartment and her car. They sprayed that luminol stuff that shows bloodstains, but they only found a trace in back of her painting."

"That makes sense. How's she handling it?"

"The truth is she's scared and jumpy and seems to be on the verge of tears all the time."

"I'm going to have to figure out who did this to her . . . to Reese. I'm just not sure who to talk to next," she murmured.

"Are you really serious about doing that after what happened?" He sounded amazed that she could keep at it.

"I'm serious about it. The police might be on this, but they're still focusing on Tessa. It wouldn't hurt to gather more information."

"I can give you an idea if you're serious."

"I'm serious. Someone gave me this lump on my forehead even if it was indirectly."

Foster nodded. "Now and then I stop in at the Smokey Palace with friends."

That isn't good, Daisy thought, concerned about Foster. The Smokey Palace was the electronic cigarette shop.

He must have seen her concern. "Don't worry. I don't smoke. I just talk with friends who do. It's set up like a lounge. Anyway, Reese Masemer was there sometimes when I stopped in. He does smoke, or did smoke. It's possible the manager of the place could give you names of Reese's cronies."

The Smokey Palace was only a few blocks from the tea garden. She'd never been inside, but now she had a reason to investigate it.

"I'm going to rest today and have my dad

take me home tomorrow. I'll putter around the house and I'll make sure I'm okay before coming back to work. But if there's a problem at the tea garden, any problem at all, I want to know about it."

"You have my word. Tessa's planning a service for Reese, though she still doesn't know when that will be. I know how hard it is to do that."

Because of his mother. Children shouldn't have to learn that so early. Foster looked grown up, but she knew he still missed his mom and always would.

"I'll talk to Tessa about it when I come back."

"Okay," Foster said, rising to his feet. "I'm going to leave so you can keep resting." He lowered his voice. "You're going to need all your strength if you're going to catch a killer."

The following day, against her mom's protests, her father took her home. Her mother had sent along a few days' worth of food. After her dad made sure she was settled on the sofa, he left.

Daisy had stayed put for an hour before she started to go stir-crazy. She couldn't just lie around and pet Pepper and Marjoram, though they'd be happy if she did. Her dad had stopped in to give them food and attention. On the sofa with Marjoram on her lap and Pepper beside her, she stroked them, considering the fact her headache was practically nonexistent. Practically.

Marjoram stood up on her lap.

Daisy studied the little split face, almost black on one side and golden tan on the other. The cat's golden eyes seemed to study her, and then Marjoram meowed. It was a little meow as if asking, *What's wrong now?*

"I can't just sit here," Daisy said. "I can't. I could bake something. I really should take Jonas cookies or muffins as a thank-you."

Pepper stretched out a paw, positioned it on Daisy's arm, and made a *mrr-wup* sound.

"I suppose you're agreeing with me," Daisy said, "because you like Jonas."

Both cats seemed to exchange a look. Then their attention was back on Daisy.

"I know Jazzi said you should take care of me, and you are. But I have things to do. I can't simply go into work tomorrow and spend a full day without testing myself first, can I?"

Marjoram sat back down on Daisy's lap as if this could be a long discussion. Or else she wanted to keep Daisy right where she was.

"How about this?" Daisy asked cheerily.

"I don't know for sure if I should drive, but I want to investigate while I have time off."

Both cats' eyes were trained on her as she talked. "So . . . I think Foster told me he doesn't have classes today until late afternoon. I'm going to give him a call and see if he'll drive me to the Smokey Palace."

This time Pepper patted Daisy's arm with her paw, and Daisy wasn't sure if that meant she approved or she didn't. But she was going to take the gesture as approval.

Both cats watched her as she picked up her phone and dialed Foster. "Are you busy?" she asked him.

"Daisy! How do you feel?"

"I'll feel a lot better if I can escape for an hour or so. Are you studying?"

"Just going over notes. What do you need?"

"I need a driver and someone who knows his way around the Smokey Palace."

"Are you supposed to be out and about?"

"I won't tell if you won't."

She heard him sigh before he said, "At least if I'm with you, you won't get into trouble . . . or do something you shouldn't."

"That's possibly true," she responded, being honest.

"Can you be ready in half an hour?" he asked. "That should give us plenty of time to drive there, ask a few questions, and drive back before I have to go to class."

"Sounds good. I can be ready."

And she was. Marjoram and Pepper weren't too happy about moving from their comfy spots using her as their pillow, but they adjusted. While she got dressed, they took their positions on the cushion on the deacon's bench at the living room window. Sunshine flitted through and they were happily washing when Foster came to her door. She was ready.

"It's called vaping," Foster told Daisy as they parked near the Smokey Palace ten minutes later.

"You mean instead of smoking."

"Yes. The object for some is to inhale pure nicotine instead of all the processed chemicals that are also in tobacco."

"That sounds just as bad."

"Could be. There's a condition called popcorn lung that's occurring in people who smoke e-cigs. Quality control is still a problem. Even teens are attracted to e-cigs because they can purchase their favorite e-juice flavor. The Smokey Palace is actually considered an e-juice bar where customers can have their vaping juices custom-made. So it's labeled a personal vaporizer shop."

"Do I need to know any of this?"

"I just thought you should know what you're walking into. I mean, at first glance, all of it can look inviting. The cigarettes come in all different colors and the juice for them — it comes in everything from traditional tobacco, to menthol, to peach, to peanut butter cup."

"Peanut butter cup?"

"The e-cigs themselves have rechargeable batteries. You can buy starter kits."

"How lovely! What about kids? Can they just walk in and buy?"

"Nope. You have to show ID and be over eighteen."

"That's something, at least."

"So are you ready?"

"As ready as I'm going to be. Do I have to act like I'm going to buy something?"

"That's why I told you a little bit about it. You could say you haven't made a decision yet to try it . . . that you want to stop smoking and you heard these are a great alternative."

"Okay."

"I know the manager. You'll be okay."

As they walked in the door, Daisy murmured to him, "But what if the manager isn't here and it's somebody else?"

"We'll deal," Foster said.

Inside, Daisy looked all around, amazed

by everything she saw in the cases, as well as the art on the walls. There were couches and chairs with customers sitting in them smoking, reading magazines, books, e-readers. So this wasn't only a place to buy the product, it was a place to *use* the product. She got it now. This place could be a small community in itself.

Foster waved to two young men seated on a couch, their focus on electronic tablets. Foster went to talk to them.

Daisy spent a few minutes perusing the cases — the juices, the cigarettes, the batteries — until Foster rejoined her.

When the man behind the counter saw Foster, he smiled and came over to Daisy. He looked to be in his fifties with thinning red-brown hair, a mustache, a soul patch, and black-rimmed glasses that sat on the middle of his nose.

Foster introduced Daisy to Harry Gilman.

He shook Daisy's hand. "First time here?" he asked.

"How can you tell?" Daisy asked.

"It's that wide-eyed, deer-in-the-headlights look. You have no idea what you're looking at . . . or what to look at first."

"Something like that," she said. "I have a friend who wants to quit smoking, so I thought I'd come in and scout out the place."

"Scout out all you want. Foster here knows his way around. But if you want me to explain anything, just give a holler."

"How about if you show me a basic set?"

Daisy thought she should be informed, just in case it ever came up again with Jazzi . . . or Violet, for that matter. Who knew what she was doing in college. Vi had been pretty open about what kids were doing in high school, but college could be a whole different story.

After Harry showed Daisy a beginner's pack, including a red case, she told him she was going to think about it and explain it all to her friend.

As he nodded and started putting it away, she said, "I did know Reese Masemer. He came in here a lot, didn't he?"

"Sure did," Harry said with a frown so deep his soul patch and mustache almost met. "What a shame. No one can believe what happened to him."

"My friend was dating him and she's really upset."

Harry looked at Foster as if to verify what Daisy was saying.

Foster gave him a nod. "Tessa Miller. I don't know if she ever came in with Reese."

"Pretty brown hair, clothes you notice? She met Reese here," Harry said, looking at Daisy. "So she's your friend, huh?"

"Actually, she works with me. She's my kitchen manager at Daisy's Tea Garden."

"I've heard of it. But I've never stopped in because tea isn't my thing."

"How about scones or apple bread or leek and potato soup? We have all those, too."

"Really?" he asked. "I thought it was just a bunch of little old ladies drinking tea."

"Nope," Daisy returned. "Reese was often a visitor. So are many of the other businessmen in Willow Creek . . . and from Lancaster. I don't think you'd feel out of place. Especially not during the tourist season. You ought to stop in during Quilt Lovers Weekend. I'm hoping we have a crowd."

"I don't think your quilt lovers are going to want to buy electronic cigarettes. That's why I didn't put money into the promotion."

"You never know. Their husbands might," Daisy commented.

"You think husbands are going to come along?"

"If it's a getaway weekend for couples. You just never know. Keep an open mind."

"Maybe I will run a special that weekend," Harry decided.

"Can you tell me if Reese was in here the days before he was killed?" Daisy asked.

The manager glanced at Foster.

Foster said, "She really is trying to help her friend. The police are looking at her."

Harry chewed on his lower lip, then gave a nod. "Yeah, he was here. He almost got into a yelling match with someone I've never seen in the store before. It got pretty hot. I had to ask them to take it outside."

"Does your shop have video surveillance?" she asked.

"Yeah, we do. But to get it, I'd have to see a warrant."

"That doesn't surprise me," Daisy said. Then she held out her hand. "Thank you very much for answering my questions. I'm sure someone will be in touch about your surveillance system."

After another smile, Daisy and Foster left the shop.

Foster said, "I think you could have asked Harry anything. Your blond hair and blue eyes —"

When Daisy gave him a sharp look, he held up his hand and surrendered. "It just sort of melts them."

"Oh, Foster. If only that were true! The one advantage of the blond hair and blue eyes is that men do underestimate me."

"How's your headache?"

"Not so bad," she said, though there was a little pounding in her temples.

"I'll take you home."

"I need to make another stop first —"

"Where to?"

"Jonas's shop. I want Detective Rappaport to know about the Smokey Palace and their surveillance system. But instead of going directly to him, because he might not listen to me, I want Jonas to contact him."

"I can take you to Woods, but I don't know if I should. Don't you think you should rest?"

"I will rest after I see Jonas. I promise."

At that, Foster gave her a nod of agreement and accepted her word for it.

Chapter Eleven

When Foster drove Daisy to Woods, Jonas was in his workshop behind the store. As soon as Daisy was inside and seated on a bench, Foster said, "I have to go to class. Will you be okay? Will your Aunt Iris or someone from the tea garden take you home?"

"I'll see that Daisy gets home," Jonas said. "Elijah is in the store all day today."

Daisy unzipped her jacket. She'd only had one arm in, and she let the jacket fall onto the unfinished bench where she was sitting.

Jonas sat beside her and they were quiet for a few seconds. She wondered if they were going to have their talk now.

Instead of that, however, Jonas looked down at his shoe boot and then back at her. "I have some news for you."

"Investigation news?"

He nodded. "Reese wasn't killed at the gallery, so that will be eliminated as a crime scene. There weren't any blood traces when the forensics team used the luminol there."

"I have news too," she said. "Foster took me to the Smokey Palace."

Jonas gave her one of his are-you-sure-you-should-have-done-that looks. She ignored it and told him what they'd found out about the argument Reese had had with someone. She ended with, "I thought Detective Rappaport might act on the information quicker if it comes from you."

"That *is* possible, but I'd like to cover more bases before I contact him."

"What kind of bases?"

"I think we should talk to Reese's assistant at the gallery. Whoever Reese had the argument with had to find him first. Maybe Chloie would know."

"She might not want to talk to me," Daisy admitted. "I had to ask her to leave the tea garden. She was really mean to Tessa. Tessa has been insecure about her affair with Reese and has suspicions that Chloie was sleeping with him. But she has no evidence of that. And there is something else. Chloie *could* be the killer."

"Let me ask you a few questions about who knocked you down the steps."

"I already answered all the detective's questions," Daisy protested.

"I know you did, but humor me, okay?"

She nodded, because she knew Jonas wouldn't ask without good reason.

"You went up the stairs and you told the detective you were on the second step from the top, correct?"

She nodded again.

"I want you to try to put yourself back there. The intruder mustn't have been that far away from you. Did you hear anything when you were on that step?"

In spite of her reluctance, Daisy tried to go back to that day in her mind. "No, I didn't hear anything. If I had, I might have moved to the side or stepped down a step."

"Good point. So you didn't even hear the floor creak?"

"No. When we bought the tea garden, we refinished the floors up there. But before we did, we made sure everything was nailed down really well. I didn't hear a sound."

"How about smell?"

"Smell?"

"Did you smell anything? Perfume, sweat, mouthwash, gum. Anything?"

This time Daisy closed her eyes and thought about it. When she'd opened the door to go up the steps, she'd only smelled one thing. "Very much like me, Tessa bakes when she's upset," she explained. "I caught the scent of brownies, but that's it. Again if I had smelled perfume, I would have thought it was odd. Tessa doesn't wear perfume. Essential oils once in a while, but I can tell the difference. The same way with mouthwash or gum or sweat. And it all happened so fast."

"Do you remember what the jeans looked like? Wide-leg or narrow-leg?"

"They were just ordinary," she said with a shrug. "And they came down over the sneakers."

"What brand of sneakers?"

"They were red and gray, and had that triangle on the side."

Jonas took out his phone, tapped the screen, and one of the icons. He tapped in something on the keyboard and then showed her a picture. "That triangle?"

"Yes, that's it."

"That's a Reebok, and at least a quarter of the population probably wears them. It's something, though."

"It's something," she repeated, not thinking it was very much. "I considered the size of whoever knocked me down the steps, but I still can't get a handle on that. I still believe it could have been a man or a woman."

Jonas stood. "Why don't I take you home,

then I'll visit Chloie."

"No," burst out of Daisy's mouth. "I want to go with you."

"But you said she might not talk to you."

"She might not, but she also might, and I can always goad her a little about Tessa. That might get her talking."

"Are you sure you feel up to it?"

"I do. All I've been doing is sitting in the car, and I asked the manager of the Smokey Palace a few questions. That's all."

"All right, let me go to the computer and find out where Chloie lives."

"You can do that?"

"I have skills," Jonas explained with a small smile. "Just as when I searched for Jazzi's mom, my detective skills come in handy."

Daisy stayed on the bench and waited.

A half hour later Jonas had driven to the edge of town where duplexes lined the road. They were small, one floor, with a one-car garage on either side of the structures.

"I wonder if these are for sale or rent," Daisy said.

"They're for rent, at least for now. I think the developer is thinking about building more of them."

"You found this out too?"

"I'm good," Jonas said with another smile, and Daisy had to smile back.

He came around to her side of the SUV and opened her door for her. Then he helped her out. "How's the arm feel?" he asked.

"Better each day. I'm going to try it without the sling tomorrow."

"I'm not going to ask if you think that's wise."

"Good, because if I'm moving around the tea garden, and the arm begins to give me trouble, I'll put the sling back on. I'm thinking of just spending a half day there."

"Good idea," Jonas said blandly.

Daisy rang the doorbell. When no one answered, she said, "Chloie could have found another job already."

"Or she could be home and not want to talk to anyone."

Daisy rang the bell again.

She and Jonas were almost ready to walk back to his SUV when the door suddenly opened. Chloie stood there glaring at them. "What do you want?"

"We'd like to talk to you," Jonas said.

"About Tessa?" Chloie asked with a sneer.

Jonas shook his head and extended his hand to her. "I'm Jonas Groft."

"I know who you are," Chloie said, a bite

still in her tone. "You own Woods."

"I do, but I'm a friend of Daisy's and Tessa's too, and I knew Reese."

As Daisy looked closer at Chloie, she could now see the young woman's eyes were red and puffy underneath. She'd been crying. Crying over Reese? Or crying over something else?

"I don't know how I can help," Chloie said.

Was that because she wanted to get closer to Reese but he wouldn't let her? Was Chloie angry about that? Angry enough to kill him?

"We found out something about Reese," Jonas started. "And it could lead to a suspect."

"Really?" Chloie asked wide-eyed. "The police asked me all kinds of questions but they wouldn't tell me anything."

"We don't have much to tell," Daisy said.

When Chloie frowned, she hurried on, "But we've gotten a clue. We'd like you to think about anyone who came to Revelations asking for Reese on the Wednesday before he was killed."

"Wednesday," Chloie repeated, closing her eyes for a moment as if she were trying to rewind the tapes in her head. Then she said, "Yeah, I do remember somebody. There was a guy in a hoodie with a buzz cut."

"How could you tell it was a buzz cut if he wore a hoodie?" Jonas asked.

Chloie gave him a glare. "The hoodie slipped to the side and I could see. His hair was brownish-gray, real close to his head."

"Could you estimate his age?" Jonas asked.

Again she thought about it. "Yeah. He was about my dad's age — fifty, fifty-five."

"Okay, good," Daisy said. "Did he look around the gallery?"

"No, he didn't want anything at the gallery. He just asked where he could find Reese. That's why I remember him."

"Did he say anything else?" Jonas asked.

Again Chloie thought about it, and then she snapped her fingers. "Yeah. He said they were friends from way back. I told him Reese was at the Smokey Palace taking a break."

"Was he wearing jeans?" Jonas asked.

"Yeah, jeans and sneakers."

"I guess you wouldn't recall what kind of sneakers," Jonas prompted.

"No. He was close to the counter when he was talking to me. And when he walked away, I just saw the backs. I think they were gray or maybe navy."

"One more thing," Jonas asked. "Was

there any printing on the hoodie?"

"No, just plain black with that pouch in front. He had his hand on something in there and I think it was his phone."

Daisy wondered if it was a phone or a gun. Then again, maybe she'd read too many mysteries lately.

Minutes later, after they had thanked Chloie, they were in Jonas's SUV again. "I'm going to drive you home," he said, once he'd started the engine and pulled away from the curb. "I'll go to the police station and talk to Rappaport face-to-face. But first I want to talk to you about something. Maybe we could make a cup of tea when we get to your house."

Daisy studied Jonas's profile. He obviously wanted to talk to her. About their relationship? She could see from the set of his jaw and the tight line of his mouth that he wasn't going to talk in the car. There was a reason he wanted to have a cup of tea.

As if he'd read her thoughts, Jonas added, "So we can sit down in an unhurried manner and hash things out."

She had the feeling she wasn't going to like whatever they hashed out.

As soon as Jonas and Daisy walked in the door to her house, Pepper and Marjoram trotted over to greet them. When Marjoram walked over the top of Jonas's boot, then in and out of his legs, he smiled and scooped her up. "So you want some attention?" he asked her.

She gave a sweet little meow.

"She doesn't talk much," Daisy said. "Just when she's playing with her toys and when she wants to eat. So you should feel honored."

"I do," he said. As he held the cat across his forearm near his chest, Daisy realized he'd apparently handled animals before or he wouldn't know to hold her that way. She really didn't know details about Jonas Groft.

So that Pepper didn't feel unloved, Daisy carefully scooped up the cat with her good arm, rubbed her cheek against Pepper's head, and carried her over to the deacon's bench to set her down.

Jonas did the same thing with Marjoram, who'd started to squirm. Both cats still had plenty of kitten in them.

After Daisy shrugged out of her jacket, she laid it on the bench. Marjoram proceeded to step on it, stretch out, and snuggle into the fleece.

Jonas followed Daisy into the kitchen, then took off his coat and hung it around the back of one of the stools at the island.

"Do you want me to make the tea?" he offered.

"I'm not an invalid," she protested, then glanced at her arm in its sling. "I'm trying *not* to be an invalid."

"How about if I fill the kettle. You choose the teapot and pull out the tea."

So that's how they handled it. "How about green tea with a hint of almond?" she asked him.

"Sounds good."

As Jonas reached for the teakettle on a back burner, he said, "I guess Chloie wasn't having an affair with Reese while he was dating Tessa."

"No, I don't think she was either. Tessa will be glad to hear that."

After he filled the kettle from the filtered spigot, he turned on the front burner and set the kettle on the stove. "Does it matter now whether Reese had or didn't have an affair?"

"It will matter to Tessa. She'll feel better knowing she wasn't betrayed."

"Something got him killed, Daisy. Something he was mixed up in."

As she spooned tea into the infuser in the bone china teapot decorated with cats that Jonas had given her, she knew he was right. Maybe Tessa hadn't really known Reese very well either.

Biding his time, Jonas asked about Portia's visit with Jazzi and listened to Daisy's feelings about the visit until they were sitting at the island, cups of tea before them.

Finally Jonas blew out a breath. "I want to tell you something about my partner when I was a detective in Philadelphia."

Daisy nodded. She knew it would probably be best not to interrupt him. The serious look in his eyes told her this wasn't going to be pleasant.

"Brenda and I were involved and I knew that was only going to lead to disaster. The flip side of that is that cops understand each other. Brenda and I had each other's backs. At least, we thought we did."

Daisy waited, intent on Jonas's story.

"One night before we went on duty, Brenda and I had an argument. She told me she was pregnant. I didn't know how that was possible since she had an IUD. But that night, she told me she'd had it removed without letting me know. She'd wanted to get pregnant, quit the force, and have a family. But that was everything I didn't want. Not because I didn't like kids, but because I didn't want to leave a child fatherless as my dad had left me."

Daisy sucked in her breath. She hadn't

known any of this.

Jonas looked down at the cup of tea as if that golden brown liquid was a reflection of the past. "My dad was a cop and he was killed in the line of duty. I knew better than to force that heartache on a woman or a child."

Daisy had to ask, "Did you and Brenda come to any agreement?"

"What kind of agreement could we come to? She was pregnant. We hadn't resolved anything when we went to work that night. I felt betrayed. The right thing to do was marry her. But at that time, marriage was everything I didn't want. There was tension between us when we went on duty. A lot of tension."

"Brenda was a detective too?"

"Yes, she was. She didn't have the experience I did, but she was a good detective."

Daisy kept quiet again because she suspected something terrible had happened.

"On our shift we received a notice that a witness in a murder investigation had been found. We left to question him, mostly silence between us. The man was holed up in a row house in a high-crime area of town. As soon as Brenda stepped out of the car, the witness shot her. When I ran to help, he got my shoulder. Brenda was dead and I was down. I called for backup and the paramedics, even though I suspected it was too late for that. Our witness holed up in the house with his girlfriend and our call turned into a hostage situation with SWAT. A negotiator finally talked the guy out, but Brenda was dead and I was hurt, maybe enough to end my career."

Daisy reached out and took his hand. "Jonas, I'm so sorry."

Not pulling away, he looked straight into Daisy's eyes. "I felt like I let Brenda down in so many ways. I should have done everything differently — from our relationship to our approach to that house that night. I blame myself on so many levels. If I had been pleased about her pregnancy, if we hadn't argued, if I'd asked her to marry me, if she hadn't moved so quickly out of the car, maybe the whole thing wouldn't have happened. Maybe I could have done something to save her."

Now Daisy understood where Jonas had been and what he'd come from. He'd lost his father and he'd become a cop. To continue his dad's work? To prove the same thing wouldn't happen to him? However, it had. He'd loved someone he shouldn't have loved. He'd had to absorb the news he was going to be a dad. As he was doing that, he'd lost his lover and a baby all in one night. She could only imagine his pain, despair, and grief.

Finally she said, "I know what it's like to have the world crashing down on you when someone you love dies."

She'd been holding his hand, but now he squeezed hers. "I guess you do," he said.

Although she ached for him and for what he'd gone through, she had to know where they stood now. "What do you want from me?"

After a moment, he admitted, "Maybe I want something you can't give."

"Tell me anyway."

He blew out a long breath and studied her. "I want to build the shelves in your storage closet and spend time with you without expectations. If you want to date other guys like Cade or Gavin, I'll have to deal with that."

She wasn't exactly sure what to say to that, but she decided to follow her heart. "I like you, Jonas. If you want to build my shelves, feel free. If I feel the need to have a swinging social life, I'll let you know. I also promise you that I'll be honest with you about everything."

They gazed into each other's eyes for several heartbeats. When he leaned toward her, she leaned toward him. His kiss was tender and sexy and everything she wanted the kiss to be.

When they came up for air, he brushed her hair over her brow. "Are you feeling okay?"

"Just a little dizzy," she said with a smile. "From the kiss, not from the bump on the head."

He gently ran his fingertips over the bump. "You scared me when you passed out."

"I scared me too. Believe me, I had to be in a weakened state to let my mom take care of me."

At that he chuckled. "Your mom means well."

"Sometime I'll tell you about me and Mom and Camellia, and why Aunt Iris and I get along so much better than I do with my mother."

"I'd like to hear about that. But for now I think you need to rest."

"I'd like to go with you to see Rappaport but I know it's not a good idea."

Jonas pushed back his stool and stood. "You're right. That's not a good idea. If you're going to take a nap, I'll wait and call you tonight."

"No. I won't be able to rest until I know

what he says. Call me after you talk to him, okay?"

"Okay." Jonas picked up his leather jacket from the back of the stool and she stood too to walk him to the door. At the door he kissed her again. But then he said, "I'm not being fair to you."

"Let me decide what's fair and what isn't."

After another long look at her, he nodded and left.

As Jonas walked toward his SUV, she watched him through the window, petting her cats to give her a small measure of comfort. She just hoped Jonas wouldn't pull away again, deciding *that* was for her own good.

Daisy had changed clothes into a pair of flowered leggings and a pullover tunic and was trying to rest on the sofa. Jazzi would be home soon, and she really should think about making supper. Maybe they could warm up something her mom had sent home with her. She was mentally ticking through the items in her refrigerator when her cell phone sounded. The tuba almost made her head hurt.

She answered the call quickly.

"I spoke with Detective Rappaport." Jonas relayed his news without preamble.

"And?"

"He's still focused on Tessa as the number one person of interest, but he said he'd look into the fight at the Smokey Palace and the video. He *will*, Daisy. He wouldn't want to be accused of not following every lead."

"You're sure of that?"

"I am. But you have to realize that he has to get a warrant first, and goodness knows how many loops of video he'll have to sit through. So this isn't going to be instantaneous. Don't get impatient."

"I'll be impatient, but I won't do anything about it," she agreed.

"How are you feeling after your day out?"

"I'm fine." As soon as she said it, she knew Jonas wouldn't accept that alone. "My head's throbbing a little and I'll rest till Jazzi gets home. I'm planning something easy for supper. Mom sent food home with me."

"I'm sure Jazzi will help you if she can."

"I know she will. She's happy with a peanut butter sandwich."

"What did your mother send home with you?"

"Chicken pot pie. She made it to prove hers was better than Aunt Iris's."

Jonas was silent at that assertion until he said, "One of these days, I'll look forward to you filling me in about your relationship

233

with your mom and your aunt Iris."

"One of these days," Daisy promised, thinking Jonas was talking as if they'd see each other for a while. Would they? Or would he back out again? Was that always going to be her fear?

"Are you still planning to go to the tea garden tomorrow?" he asked.

"Yes. I want to work. But I know I shouldn't drive. I'm going to call Aunt Iris and see if she'll pick me up. I'm sure Tessa will bring me home at lunchtime if I feel like I can't put in a full day."

"If you need a chauffeur, I'll be available," Jonas said. "Why don't I come over and take measurements for the shelves? Then if you feel you want to leave, you can."

"I don't want to put you out any more than I already have."

"Daisy, give up the fight and let me help you, okay?"

"And why do you want to help me?"

There was a beat of silence before he confessed, "Because I feel something with you I haven't felt before. And I *do* care."

She let out the breath she'd been holding. "I'll see you tomorrow."

After they said their good-byes, Daisy lay back on the sofa and closed her eyes. In no time at all she was asleep. But her dreams

were a mixture of Jonas's face along with
Tessa's and Reese's.

CHAPTER TWELVE

The following morning Daisy returned to the tea garden, her arm still in a sling. She didn't want to overdo and then have to put the sling back on. So she mostly worked on counter duty, being friendly, going table to table and serving tea refills. She realized how she took both arms for granted. Wasn't that the way it went? You weren't really grateful for something until you didn't have it anymore.

That was too philosophical for this morning. But she knew why she was thinking so hard. She was remembering her conversation with Jonas. She was also looking forward to seeing him again later. That made her feel like a foolish schoolgirl. Yet it was a nice feeling to have after all these years. Some nights she missed Ryan so much, she didn't know if she could ever love another man again. Yet when she was with Jonas, her years with Ryan seemed to fade into the background. Ryan didn't. But their life together did.

Daisy was in the kitchen with Tessa and Eva when Tessa's phone played an airy, meditative melody from her pocket. She pulled it out and checked the screen. "It's a lawyer's office," she murmured. "A lawyer in Lancaster."

"Go ahead and take it," Daisy suggested.

Tessa did and identified herself, but then she said, "I don't understand."

Daisy unabashedly listened to Tessa's side of the conversation.

"You want me to come to your office in Lancaster tomorrow? I see. Hold on a minute. I'll check to see if I can get someone to cover for me at work. I'm at work now."

She looked at Daisy. "It's Reese's lawyer. He wants me to come to his office tomorrow afternoon at two. Will you and Iris be able to serve tea without me?"

"Foster will be here in the afternoon, and so will Cora Sue. I can ask Karina to come in and handle the counter and whatever else has to be done. If it gets beyond all of us, Eva will lend a hand too. We'll manage."

Tessa said into the phone, "All right, Mr. Selinski. Can you text me your address? Yes, I'll see you tomorrow at two."

Almost as soon as Tessa ended the call, a

beep sounded from her phone that she'd received a text message.

"Did he have anything else to say?" Daisy asked.

"It has to do with Reese's will. He said I'd be receiving an official letter in the mail, but considering the circumstances, he'd like to see me tomorrow."

"I'll bet you're in the will," Daisy said.

"Why would I be in Reese's will?" Tessa sounded astounded. "We didn't know each other that long."

"If you're in his will, then he cared about you," Daisy assured her friend, knowing Tessa had been questioning that fact. Then she added, "But on the other hand, if you *are* in the will in any substantial way, Detective Rappaport will be focusing again on you."

"It just keeps getting worse and worse, doesn't it?" Tessa asked rhetorically.

An hour later, Daisy was refilling a cup of a customer's favorite tea when Rachel blew in the door with a gust of biting wind.

Daisy was glad to see her friend. They hadn't been in touch for a few days. "Earl Grey?" she asked as she went to meet her.

Rachel nodded. *"Ya."*

"Why don't you take a seat in the spill-

238

over room and we can talk for a few minutes."

"Are you *certain sure* you have time?" Rachel asked.

"I'm positive. How about a slice of apple bread to go with that?"

"Breakfast was a while back. *Danki,*" Rachel said with a shy smile.

"Wilkumm." When she was with Rachel, it was easy to slip into the Pennsylvania Dutch she'd used with her friend since she was a child.

Daisy motioned her again to the yellow room. "Take off your cape and warm up. I'll be there in five minutes."

Cora Sue was helping Daisy today when she tried to do something she shouldn't. "I'll carry the bread for you," she said now. "You prepare the cup of tea. We're a team today, remember?"

Cora Sue's bottle-red hair was pulled high on her head in a topknot. She was as bubbly today as ever.

Without giving Cora Sue an argument, Daisy nodded. "Thank you."

Seated, after she carried the tea to the table, Daisy asked after Rachel's family.

"We're all *gut,*" her friend said with a smile. She patted Daisy's hand. "But I came to see how you are. I heard what happened to you. I was worried and I spoke with Foster yesterday. He said the two of you went on a little outing."

"He was kind enough to take me on an errand," Daisy explained. "I was going stir-crazy sitting at home. I'm just not the type of patient who wants to sit and watch TV all day."

Rachel looked over her shoulder into the main serving room. "I came to ask about Tessa, too. How is she holding up? I have noticed she doesn't come out of the kitchen unless she has to."

"She's afraid everyone will ask her questions. I know the feeling. She's also worried that the police are going to charge her with Reese's murder."

Rachel looked aghast. "They would not."

"I don't know about that," Daisy said. "After finding what they think is the murder weapon in Tessa's apartment, anything can happen."

"The two of you need to come to the quilting circle."

"Are you sure about that?" Daisy asked. "Having us there could cause talk."

"The women who quilt in my circle won't pass judgment. We meet twice a week. You could come on your lunch break."

"Both of us couldn't come at the same

time because we'd leave Aunt Iris in the lurch. But we could alternate."

"However is best for you. What would you like to quilt?"

"Actually, I have been thinking about that. I'm going to look in my storage space for old outfits of Vi's and Jazzi's. I might even have a shirt of Ryan's. If I can use that material in a quilt, it will hold good memories."

"That is a *gut* idea. Memory quilts can be passed down for generations. We'll teach you how to make it right."

Daisy laughed. "Maybe I should practice on something else first."

"Oh, we can start you on piecing squares until you learn to even your stitches. We can also show you how to move around colors so they suit you."

"I have a feeling until I learn, and until I put the quilt together, this will be a year-long project."

"That is quite possible," Rachel agreed.

"You're serious, aren't you?"

"I am," Rachel admitted. "Especially if you want the quilt to last."

"Actually, I'd like to make one for both Violet and Jazzi."

"And one for yourself?" Rachel asked.

"We'll see how long the first one takes."

Rachel looked troubled for a moment. "What's wrong?"

"I have a question to ask you, but I do not want you to be upset."

"I won't get upset with you. You can ask me anything."

"You still miss Ryan, don't you?"

Rachel had met her husband when they'd come on visits to Willow Creek to see Daisy's parents and her aunt. "You must have read my mind. I was just thinking about Ryan this morning, and I do miss him. But the memories now are becoming sweeter rather than hurtful. After he died, I couldn't take a breath without hurting so much. I didn't think the pain would ever go away. I hid as much as I could from the girls. But the nights — the nights were awful."

"But your girls missed him too?"

"Yes, they did. Violet talked about how much she missed him; Jazzi not so much. And I realize now I should have prompted Jazzi more. I should have asked more questions about her feelings. Oh, we talked for months about selling our house in Florida and moving here. We spent many late nights going over the idea of Aunt Iris and I starting the tea garden. But their feelings about their dad — I let them slide into the shadows. I shouldn't have done that."

"You should know by now," Rachel said, "that *should* and *shouldn't* after the fact do no good when you're a mom. You just start from where you left off, and you try to do better."

Daisy squeezed her friend's hand. "You're always so wise."

"Maybe that comes from having family around me so much of the time. We all go through each other's lives moment by moment and learn."

"You're very fortunate to have that kind of support system."

"Not fortunate, Daisy, but blessed. We know it. You are blessed too. I know you and your mom and even your sister don't always see eye to eye, but they come through when you need them. Your dad is a great man."

"Yes, he is, and he always takes my side or figures out how to do it, and so does Aunt Iris. She's one of the reasons I recovered from Ryan's death as well as I have. She's helped the girls too."

"Do you think you're ready now?"

"Ready?"

"To keep company with a man again."

Daisy thought about Jonas coming over later to measure the storage closet for shelves. She felt her cheeks blush a little as she answered Rachel's question with, "We'll see."

Around noon Daisy realized she was slowing down. Serving tea one-handed seemed to be a good idea, but after a few hours of that, plus trying to do everything else one-handed, she felt as if her energy had drained. She was at the counter trying to layer chocolate chip cookies into a box with one gloved hand while trying not to hit her other elbow against the case.

Aunt Iris came up to her. "I'll do that. Why don't you take your lunch break? Or better yet, go home for the afternoon. Do you have a headache?"

"You sound like Jazzi now."

"Well, do you?"

"Just a small one," she admitted, though she really didn't want to. Her aunt was about to huff and puff more and tell her she should take care of herself when Daisy was rescued from a lecture by Jonas coming in the front door.

He came straight to the counter and looked from Daisy to Iris. "Have I interrupted something?"

Iris gave Daisy a glare. "My niece is not behaving or taking care of herself."

244

To Daisy's embarrassment, Jonas studied her. "You do look a little pale."

She scowled at him with her best fierce-mom scowl. "Another *good-for-me* voice heard from."

Jonas just arched his brows and she felt dismayed. She really didn't want to battle with everyone. Giving in to her aunt Iris and letting her fill the cookie box, Daisy said, "I think I'm well enough to show you what we want for the shelves in the closet."

Iris just shook her head. "She needs her lunch break," Iris whispered in an aside to Jonas before he started for the kitchen.

Daisy caught the thumbs-up he gave Iris before he followed her. "You and Aunt Iris aren't colluding, are you?"

"No collusion. A person has to eat."

"I can have a cup of soup here, and so can you."

"Yes, or I could follow your aunt Iris's wishes and whisk you away to Sarah Jane's for lunch. You'd get out of here for a while and soothe her concern. Win-win, wouldn't it be?"

"You make it sound so reasonable," Daisy said with a sigh.

Jonas laughed. "That's my middle name — *Reasonable*. Show me what you need here."

In a corner of the kitchen Daisy pointed to the white cupboards above the sink and the counters. "All of our teas are stored up there in those cupboards." She pointed to cupboards along the other wall. "In those we keep our dishes and glasses."

"Okay," Jonas said with a nod.

She pointed to the cupboards under the sink and the counter. "Our cooking pans, casseroles, and pots are all down there."

"Which leaves?" Jonas asked.

"That big closet over there across from our walk-in is our pantry. It holds our supplies of flour, sugar, cinnamon, dried fruit — everything we use to cook and bake. We knew exactly how we'd use the pantry when we renovated so the shelves were made to order then." She pointed to the closet nearest the door. "That's our storage closet." She opened it with a flourish. "Linens are stored on the shelves straight ahead." Then she gestured to an alcove on the left and one on the right. "That's just empty space. I thought if you could build shelves for these two spaces, I can line up my special teacups here, like the ones I received for my birthday. Then if I want to use one for someone special, I can just pull it right out."

"How would your servers know they're special?"

"My servers can tell bone china from porcelain, and they know the cups ringed with silver or gold need extra care."

"What *is* the difference between bone china and porcelain?"

"Porcelain is made from a type of clay called kaolin. When it's fired, the temperatures can reach twelve hundred degrees Celsius. The final result is fragile and translucent in a dinner plate. Bone china is similar to porcelain but was actually created in Europe. It's also translucent but it's fired at a lower temperature. It's usually a creamy off-white color."

"You have some other types of plates that don't look so . . . delicate."

"Those are stoneware. It's strong and heavier than porcelain, not as expensive either. When I serve a table family-style, maybe with a dozen scones, I might use a plate like that one." She pointed to the counter where Eva was preparing a plate to do just that. It was brown with a high glaze.

"And what about your teapots?" Jonas asked, obviously interested.

"Most of those are bone china, many made in England, like the one you gave me. Most of my teapots are James Sadler. They're some of my favorites."

"You have a lot invested in the tea garden,

don't you?"

"Iris and I both do. But we thought it was worth it, and so far, we're succeeding."

"You're trying to help clear Tessa so it doesn't hurt business," he said in a low voice.

In just as low a voice, Daisy responded, "I want to clear Tessa to clear Tessa. She's my best friend, Jonas."

He must have seen the determination in her eyes. Or else she was looking a bit peaked with her arm in a sling and the headache beating at her temples because he said, "Will you come with me to Sarah Jane's for lunch?"

"I will if you'll let me make a stop first."

"A stop where?" he asked suspiciously.

"I want to see if the man with the hoodie stopped at any other businesses before or after he argued with Reese. I think we should start with the convenience store at the edge of town because they would probably have video too."

"Start?"

"I have Sarah Jane's on my list. She doesn't have video but she does have hostesses and servers at the diner who might remember."

"So I'm playing into your plans."

"No, you'll be taking me to lunch and

helping me solve a murder."

After a long look in which Jonas didn't appear happy with that scenario, he took a tape measure from his pocket and started measuring.

A half hour later Daisy could tell by the expression on Jonas's face that he didn't approve of her mission. They'd stopped at the convenience store but it had been a dead end. The manager told them that Detective Rappaport had already checked their video from the Wednesday in question. So now they were going to Sarah Jane's for lunch and a little questioning.

After they got out of the car and strolled toward the diner with its huge hex sign of birds on the front wall and a hex sign with hearts on the other side of the door, Jonas looked as if he wanted to say something but he didn't. Daisy was sure whatever was on his mind would come out at lunch. One of the main things she liked about Jonas was his forthrightness.

Sarah Jane, who was hostessing as usual, her strawberry-blond curls falling over her forehead and around her ears to her jaw, smiled at them. Although she was a bit overweight, she had the energy of a youngster. She oversaw every dish on the menu and cooked some of them herself. She liked to hostess the lunch and dinner crowd so that she knew her customers. She often ran coupons for everyone over sixty, which helped some of the elderly population of Willow Creek buy a good hot meal. The town needed a service such as Meals-on-Wheels but they hadn't developed one yet. Daisy considered bringing it up at their next Chamber of Commerce meeting.

Sarah Jane's blue gingham apron and her fuchsia and green sneakers were always a homey welcoming sight. She studied Daisy and Jonas and then said, "It's nice to see you two here together."

Daisy felt herself blush a little.

Jonas cleared his throat. "How about that booth in the back?"

"So you need a bit of privacy?" Sarah Jane asked with a sly smile.

"Actually we do," Daisy answered. "Besides lunch, we'd like to talk to you if you have a few minutes."

Sarah Jane pointed to her chest. "You want to talk to *me*?"

"Whenever you have a few minutes," Daisy reiterated.

"I'll have Mary get you seated and give you menus and take your order. Then I'll leave my post and come and join you."

Sarah Jane's eyes were questioning but

Daisy didn't say any more and neither did Jonas. They walked back to the booth and greeted Evelyn when she came to them. They both ordered the shepherd's pie since that was the daily special. It must have been already prepared and ready to serve because their waitress brought them their servings along with cole slaw and applesauce. The shepherd's pie with its ground beef, carrots, and peas topped with mashed potatoes looked delicious.

"I should make this at home," Daisy concluded.

"It looks like a lot of work."

"It *is* a lot of work. But the end result . . ." She sighed.

"On the other hand," Jonas offered, "why go to the trouble of making it when you can buy it here and take it home."

Daisy laughed. "Do you do that often?"

"I've been told that fast food won't help me live a longer life," he said with almost a straight face.

"But I'm sure shepherd's pie will," Daisy joked with a grin.

Jonas's eyes lingered on her face. "You're looking better."

Jonas wasn't a flatterer and Daisy felt self-conscious, so she handled the compliment lightly. She ran her hand through her hair to fluff it. "Must be the new 'do.'"

"I mean it, Daisy. That day the killer knocked you down the steps, you had me worried."

"We don't know that's who it was," Daisy reminded him in a low voice.

Suddenly Sarah Jane was standing at their booth. "You two look intense."

Daisy leaned against the booth back and so did Jonas. They'd practically been nose to nose while they were talking. That close, Daisy thought of other things to do with Jonas instead of talking. She moved over to give Sarah Jane space to sit on the booth beside her.

The restaurant owner sat and asked, "So you have questions for me? How intriguing. What about?"

Jonas motioned to Daisy, letting her take the lead.

"I'm trying to help Tessa," Daisy explained.

"Help her how?" Sarah Jane inquired.

"By gathering information to give the police so they don't think she's a suspect."

"But she was dating Reese Masemer, wasn't she?" Sarah Jane asked.

"She *was* dating him. I believe she was falling in love with him or was already in love. She didn't have anything to do with what happened to him."

"I've known Tessa Miller for years. She's a good girl," Sarah Jane decided. "How can I help?"

"We have a description of someone who might be important to the case," Daisy explained. "So many customers come into your diner, out-of-towners as well as locals."

"They certainly do and I try to greet everyone. What's the description?"

"Do you remember anyone in a hoodie? If the hoodie dropped back he had a buzz cut."

"Hmmm," Sarah Jane said. "A couple of teenagers who come in here could fit that description. How old is this male?"

"Not a teenager," Jonas filled in. "I'd say in his early fifties."

"We don't have many tourists in January, though I'm hoping we do for the Quilt Lovers Weekend. I believe I'd remember a man who looked like that."

Daisy was disappointed and that disappointment must have shown on her face. Sarah Jane bumped her arm with her own. "Don't look so crestfallen. I'm not the only one who serves food in town. Think about it for a minute. If this man is connected to a crime, would he want to come in here and sit down and have dinner? Probably not."

"So you're suggesting he'd go to a fast-food restaurant?" Jonas asked.

"Possibly. Or he'd grab a sandwich and a bag of chips."

"At Dutch's Deli. That makes sense." Daisy squeezed Sarah Jane's arm. "Thank you." Then Daisy's gaze met Jonas's.

He gave a small, resigned shrug. "Next stop — Dutch's Deli."

Daisy was glad she and Dutch had spoken not so long ago. That made her feel more comfortable approaching him. Although Jonas might not be a hundred percent behind her on her quest, she could tell he felt no hesitation. But then he'd been a detective. He was used to questioning suspects and finding murderers. The ironic thing was he didn't want to do that anymore. Should she keep dragging him into this? On the other hand, this was Jonas. If he didn't want to do it, he wouldn't.

A half hour later, as they walked into the deli, Daisy nudged Jonas's arm. "Thank you for coming here with me."

"I wouldn't want you to get another conk on the head," he said acerbically, but then opened the door for her.

The inside of Dutch's looked like any deli. There was a counter across the back and a case beneath it filled with all sorts of meats and cheeses, a few salads, and a tray of sandwiches already made up to go. Tables with chrome bases and Formica tops were scattered all around the room. The metal chairs at each table were red. On the wall Dutch had hung a board with specials. The list showcased the sandwiches he could make and prices for catering trays that he would create. On the edge of the counter sat a carousel with several kinds of potato chips. Martin's and Utz seemed to be the most popular brands. Utz potato chips were made in Hanover and Martin's were made in Thomasville, near York.

Daisy realized that she and Jonas didn't need any food, but it didn't seem right to come in here asking questions without buying something. Dutch himself was at the counter and he looked up with recognition.

"Hi, Dutch," she said.

"I heard you were hurt," he said. "A concussion and a shoulder problem?"

Willow Creek was small, the community of merchants even smaller. News traveled fast.

"I'm on the mend. I put in a half day today and hopefully a whole day tomorrow. I want to take cheese home for Jazzi and me. We like it for snacks. How about a pound of sharp white American, a pound of Colby, and a half pound of sharp cheddar,

255

the orange one."

"Coming right up," Dutch responded, reaching into the case for the block of sharp white American.

As he was weighing the cheese, Jonas nodded to her. She might as well get started. "Dutch, do you mind if I ask you about something?"

He glanced up at her. "About . . . ?"

"You might have heard Tessa is under suspicion for Reese's murder. I'm gathering a bit of information."

He shrugged as if none of it mattered to him. "Go ahead and ask."

"You usually run the register yourself, don't you?"

"Yes, I do. I don't trust anybody else. Anybody can make a sandwich but not just anybody can handle the money. That's why I'm here three-quarters of my life. Why?"

"We're trying to find out the identity of someone. He's in his early fifties, wears a hoodie, and has a buzz cut. He had an argument with Reese and we'd like to find him. Can you tell me if he was in here?"

Dutch began wrapping the cheese as he thought about her question. "You know, I think he was."

"Do you remember anything more about him?"

"There's a reason I remember him. He placed an unusual order. He wanted a bologna and Swiss sandwich with dill pickles and hot peppers on a kaiser roll, along with potato salad to go. He asked for a double order of both. I told him that salad should be refrigerated. He said he had a cooler."

Daisy thought about the cooler idea. That meant maybe he'd driven a good distance. "Did he mention where he'd come from?"

"Yeah," Dutch responded. "He said he came from Pittsburgh and the traffic was terrible. I have his credit card charge receipt but that won't do you any good because now they just show the last four numbers of the account."

"No, it won't," Jonas agreed. "But the police might be able to find out more."

Daisy leaned close to Jonas. "I'm going to call Rappaport." Then she moved across the room and did just that.

CHAPTER THIRTEEN

"Would you like to come in?" Daisy asked Jonas as he walked her to the door.

"How about a rain check on that? I really need to get back to the store."

"Of course, you do. Stores don't run themselves. Thank you so much for going with me today."

"I'd say *anytime,*" he responded with a small smile, "but I don't want to encourage you. The police will figure this out. No matter what impression he gives us, Detective Rappaport is a good cop. I know he's looking at Tessa, but that doesn't mean he isn't looking elsewhere, too."

"Where else is there to look?" Daisy asked.

"Possibly the guy with the hoodie. Rappaport has more contacts than you do. He can also access any video cameras businesses use. He'll figure this out."

"But what if the murderer comes after Tessa for some reason, maybe because she knows something?"

"You're going to accuse me of being patronizing, I know you are. But let me ask you this question. Do you have anything to do when you go back into the house?"

"Do you mean besides think?"

"Exactly. I know only being able to use one arm is tough but isn't there a movie you'd like to watch, something you can stream on your iPad, recipes you'd like to create?"

"I'll consider all those after I'm inside and resting like everybody wants me to do. I know you're not being patronizing. You just want me to recover. So do I. I have beef cubes in there. I can put them in the slow cooker and make beef barley soup. Not much chopping involved."

"Do you need me to pick you up in the morning?"

"No, I'll let Aunt Iris do that. I'm going to try working without the sling tomorrow. If that goes well, then I can start driving myself."

"I should have known you always have a plan B."

"Not always," she admitted. If she came to care for Jonas seriously, there would be no plan B involved.

He gave her a hug. "Go on in. I want to

259

make sure you're safely inside before I leave."

She didn't argue with him. With a murderer on the loose and her one arm in a sling, feeling secure because Jonas was watching out for her was a good thing.

As soon as she stepped inside and turned off the alarm, Pepper jumped down off the bench under the window and wrapped around her ankles.

"I missed you, too." Daisy picked up her tuxedo feline in one arm, careful not to drop her. Marjoram, who stayed on the bench, stood, stretched, and yawned.

"Were you two listening to our conversation through the window?"

Pepper tilted her head and gave a soft meow.

Daisy laughed. "I'm glad one of you will admit it. How about a treat? After you enjoy that, you can keep me company in the kitchen while I put on supper."

The word "treat" made Marjoram's golden eyes sparkle even more. She jumped down from the bench and ran into the kitchen, fully expecting Daisy to follow.

Daisy put Pepper on the floor, then swung her jacket off and laid it over a chair. Going into the kitchen, she took the cats' treats from a cupboard and dropped a few into each of their dishes. When she thought about making soup in the slow cooker, she'd forgotten she'd have to lift the slow cooker from the bottom shelf of her cupboard. Not a great idea. She'd just wait a while and then start the soup on top of the stove.

Considering what Jonas had advised her to do, she decided to stream a movie on her laptop. It would be easier to watch on there than on her iPad.

After she changed into a comfy sweat suit and settled on the sofa, Marjoram jumped up on the back. Pepper stood at her stockinged feet, rubbed against them, rounded in a few circles, and then settled.

Daisy booted up the laptop. But before she decided on a movie to watch, she considered everything Dutch had told her. The man in the hoodie had come from Pittsburgh.

Taking a chance on a long shot, she decided to google "Reese Masemer" and "Pittsburgh." The requisite links for Pittsburgh attractions popped up. It was hard to search these days without somebody trying to sell you something. She skipped down below the ads and, to her surprise, she found several links.

What she discovered amazed her. Apparently, Reese had had a whole different life before he'd moved to Willow Creek.

At the tea garden the next morning, Daisy's shoulder hurt a little by eleven. However, she'd done well during the breakfast service and she'd insisted on baking the lemon tea cakes herself. The breakfast rush, as it was in January, was over. There was a sweet lull before the lunch crowd came in.

As if Jonas knew that, he came in the door ready to work on her shelves. He was wearing a tool belt and had his toolbox with him too. She couldn't help but gaze at him in a new light. She wondered if he knew how sexy he was.

He set down the toolbox at the closet door. "I have to bring in the brackets, then I can get started."

While Jonas did that, Daisy brought lemon tea cakes to one of the customers and Cora Sue poured the tea. Her staff was watching over her and she was grateful for that.

Jonas had been working for about a half hour when Daisy started for the closet, eager to tell him what she'd found out about Reese. But before she'd passed the sales counter, Gavin Cranshaw entered the tea garden and he didn't look happy. Foster was in the kitchen, watching the pot of soup they'd made for lunch. She'd decided her beef barley soup was worth a try on the customers.

But she didn't even have a chance to call to Foster because his father came right up to her. "Can I talk with you for a few minutes?"

Cora Sue and Iris gave a nod that they'd cover for her.

The spillover room was set up for afternoon tea, but she led Gavin in there anyway. It wasn't as if they'd mess up one of the tablecloths. He didn't even look as if he wanted to sit down.

She did, hoping he would. "Is something wrong?" She motioned to the seat across from her, inviting him to sit.

He didn't look as if he wanted to, but he pulled out a chair and lowered himself onto it. "I understand that you took my son to the Smokey Palace with you. I just found out from one of Foster's friends that he was there. I haven't talked to Foster yet because I wanted to talk to you first and give you fair warning. I think he should quit his job here because the tea garden is a bad influence."

Apparently, Iris or Cora Sue had told Foster his father was here because he appeared at the table looking as if smoke might come out of his ears. "I am *not* quit-

263

ting my job here."

"She had no right taking you to the Smokey Palace."

Foster looked dumbfounded. He glared at his dad and asked, "What do you think goes on at college? Believe me, there are more than electronic cigarettes there."

Gavin began to sputter and didn't look as if he knew what to say.

Foster went on, "And it wasn't the first time I was at the Smokey Palace. I'm the one who had a contact there who could help Daisy. So don't go blaming her. For your information, I don't smoke e-cigs, but I have friends who do and sometimes I meet them there."

"You don't tell your friends it's bad for them?" Gavin wanted to know.

"Do you tell *your* friends who still smoke that that's bad for them? They should know, don't you think? It's not like we live in the dark ages before the Internet."

"But if you go there with them, you're condoning what they're doing," his father protested.

"If I go there with them, and I don't smoke, I'm making a statement. Your way isn't always the *best* way."

Daisy really didn't want to interfere or get involved in a family squabble. She felt protective of Foster but she also understood where Gavin was coming from.

"Foster," she warned gently.

Not accepting her warning, he shook his head at her and addressed his dad again. "If you don't stop interfering in my life when I'm simply trying to make a life, I'll stop commuting, get more financial aid somehow, and move into the dorm or get an apartment with friends. Mom would be proud of my accomplishments, not constantly criticizing me. In fact tonight, I'll stay with a friend."

Gavin looked hurt, and Daisy didn't know what to do for father and son. She said, "Maybe you should talk about this when you both calm down a bit."

Not listening, Gavin spoke right over her. "If you feel that way then maybe you *should* think about moving into the dorm. If it's not too much trouble, text me tonight so I know you're safe." And with that, Gavin stood and without looking at either of them, left the tea garden.

Daisy stood too and put her hand on Foster's shoulder. "Foster, I'm sorry."

His brow was creased and his eyes were troubled. "I'm fine. This has been a long time coming."

"I understand your dad's side of it because

I'm a parent too. We spend ninety-nine percent of our lives worrying about our kids."

Foster wasn't listening any more than his dad had. "I'm old enough to make my own decisions. He can't control my life." Foster's voice had risen and he suddenly realized it. He shook his head. "I'm sorry, Daisy."

"There's nothing to be sorry about. Misunderstandings happen between parents and kids. But you need to have a serious discussion with your dad. Don't let a chasm form between you."

"It's already there," Foster confided morosely.

"Don't let that gap become deeper and wider, Foster. Stay with a friend tonight if you must, but then talk to your father soon. Promise me you will."

Foster stared out the window, then brought his gaze back to her. "All right. But I don't think it's going to make a difference. He doesn't understand me."

"Let me fill you in on a little secret. My guess is, since your mom died, he's tried to be both mother and father. I tried to do the same thing. It's really impossible. He probably feels like a failure at both. So cut him a little slack, Foster, okay?"

This time Foster seemed to pay attention.

"I'll remember what you said, but I still have to do what I think is right."

Oh, to be nineteen again, and to know exactly what to do or what was right, Daisy thought.

"I have to get back to that soup," Foster said. "It's my responsibility and I don't want anything to go wrong with it. The lunch crowd is already starting to come in."

He was right. They were. Maybe when Jonas finished what he wanted to do with the closet today, she could convince him to have a cup of soup and a few cookies.

An hour later Foster, Cora Sue, and Iris were getting ready to serve afternoon tea in the spillover room. It would only be about three-quarters full, but on an afternoon in January, that was still good. Apparently, residents of Willow Creek were looking for something to do on a cold day when they couldn't be out on the streets or enjoying gardening in their backyard. Jonas had just finished with the brackets for the shelves and Daisy's shoulder was hurting. She was afraid she'd spill or drop something. She had her sling hanging with her jacket, but she simply didn't want to put it on.

Before Jonas could pick up his toolbox, Daisy asked, "Would you like a cup of soup and lemon tea cakes?"

"That sounds good," he agreed.

She motioned to a table in the tea room that was still open. "Just have a seat in there and I'll bring it in."

"Your shoulder's hurting again, isn't it?"

"How can you tell?"

"Because it's a little lower than your other one, and remember, I had a shoulder injury too. I know what it feels like."

She had forgotten that. "It *is* hurting and I thought about putting the sling back on. But I just hate to do it."

"Because of the way it looks?"

"Not so much. I just don't want to be treated like an invalid. I don't want to think I still *am* an invalid."

"The way you've been moving around here, you're no invalid," he noted dryly. "How about if you dish out the soup and I'll carry it. You can bring the cookies."

"That sounds good. I might even have one with you."

Five minutes later they were seated at the table. She supposed the best thing to do with Jonas was just to plunge in. "I learned something yesterday after I got home."

"You were supposed to be resting."

"There's more than one way to rest," she shot back.

"I imagine there is. What form of resting

268

did you do?"

He picked up a spoon and was enjoying his soup when she said, "I found out something about Reese Masemer nobody knows."

"How do you know nobody knows? I imagine Detective Rappaport did a background check."

"Maybe. But he doesn't know where Reese was from, and we do."

"You mean Pittsburgh?"

Jonas seemed to have a photographic memory. Besides that, he remembered everything they talked about. "Yes, Pittsburgh. And I hit pay dirt."

"You googled him."

"Yes, I did. And on the second or third page of references I found a headline."

"What kind of headline?"

"A lawsuit headline. I'd like to get into the archives of the newspaper, but it requires a fee and I don't know what I'm doing. The headline revealed that Dr. Reese Masemer had a malpractice suit filed against him. If he was a doctor, he had a whole different life than what he pretended to be here."

"A doctor," Jonas mused. "That could open up another whole book of information. If he was sued, then someone had a bad outcome. You didn't get any more out of the article than that?"

"It didn't even give me a whole article. It was just the headline and about two sentences. Apparently, it happened at a private hospital in Pittsburgh. I took notes and I have the name if you need it."

"If *I* need it?" His jaw set.

"Don't you know your way around things like this?"

Jonas frowned and pushed his empty bowl of soup away from his place. He pulled over the dish with the lemon cookies. "I could look into it, but Rappaport might have already done it."

"If we look into it, and we gather all the information, and then we give it to him, maybe then he can do his job."

"You know he won't like it."

"Whether he likes it or not, it has to be done. How hard would it be? It's not illegal to access the Pittsburgh paper's archives. I know medical records are off the grid now with HIPAA laws, but that doesn't mean we couldn't go talk to someone there, get the layout, maybe pick up gossip on what happened."

"And how do you think this will help you find the killer?"

"You never know."

"Are you sure you don't just want to tell

Detective Rappaport?"

"That would be the wiser way to go, wouldn't it?" She didn't expect an answer. "I'm frustrated and restless. Tessa's not herself. She has our freezer filled with baked goods because baking seems to be all she wants to do right now. I understand that. I cook and bake when I'm stressed too."

His mysterious green eyes studied her for a very long moment. "Good to know."

"I'll give Detective Rappaport a call." She took her phone from her pocket, went to contacts, and tapped on his name. The phone provided his voice mail service. In as concise a manner as she could muster, she explained what she'd discovered. Then she ended the call.

"Does that make you feel better?" Jonas asked.

"If he pays attention to what I told him."

"He will. Unless he'd already discovered Reese's background."

Jonas took her hand in his and laced their fingers. "Now tell me if you did rest after you went home."

"After I finished with the laptop, I put ice on my shoulder and rested."

"Exactly what you should do now."

"The tea garden doesn't close until five. I have to take inventory and help clean up."

"Then take ten minutes to put ice on your shoulder and use your sling. The sling will force you not to do anything you shouldn't. Just think of it as a reminder."

"Is that what *you* did?"

"Not often enough, so healing took longer than it should have. Save yourself the aggravation, Daisy, and coddle your shoulder now or it will take twice as long to get better."

"You sound like a doctor."

"Experience talking, that's all." He picked up another lemon tea cake and ate it. "These are so good."

"I'll wrap up a few for you to take along."

After a nod, he said, "I primed the boards for the shelves before I left. I'll probably wait until tomorrow to paint them."

"You're painting the shelves? You don't have to do that. It's not as if they're open to the public."

"Whatever I make, Daisy, I want it to have my stamp on it. I want it to be a quality piece. So whether the world sees it or not doesn't matter. I just need to know that I did my best."

She nodded, totally in sync with that idea. "We're perfectionists."

"It's a hard habit to break. I'd better be going. Do you know if Foster has decided if he knows what he wants to do tonight?"

"No, but I haven't seen him on the phone. Maybe he'll chicken out and go back to his dad's."

"Not a chance after an argument like that. I'm going to talk to him for a few minutes. Is that okay?"

Inside the tea room, it looked as if everyone had been served, their tiered tray of goodies eaten and all the tea poured. She said to Jonas, "It's settled down in there. What are you going to talk to him about?"

Jonas gave her a look that maybe his conversation with Foster wasn't her business.

"I'm his employer," she reminded him. "What affects him affects me. Besides I'm worried about him. And another besides, he's dating my daughter."

At that, Jonas gave her a small smile. "I'm going to tell him if he needs a place to stay, he can crash at my place tonight. I have a duplex. I'll give him my number and he's welcome to call me. Are you okay with that, Miss Nosy?"

She wrinkled her nose at him. "I'm very okay with it. I think you're a kind man."

Jonas's cheeks grew a little ruddier. He just waved that comment away as he went to talk to Foster.

Late that afternoon, Tessa appeared to be shell-shocked when she returned from her appointment with Reese's lawyer. She was pale and drawn, and even her red-and-cream flowing blouse didn't make her look as young as she usually looked. She didn't even say hello to anyone as she came in. She went straight past Iris as if she didn't see her, past the counter where Cora Sue was ringing up an order, and walked straight into Daisy's office. Once there she closed the door and sat behind the desk in Daisy's desk chair. It was as if she needed a barrier between her and the outside world.

Checking the tea room where Foster and Karina had just served the last course of afternoon tea, Daisy caught Foster's eye. She pointed to her office and he nodded as if he understood.

Daisy opened the door to her office and then closed it behind her. She had a feeling this was going to be a private conversation. Just what had happened at that appointment?

Tessa was shaking her head before Daisy even had the chance to ask any questions. She pulled the chair that was positioned in front of the desk around to the back and sat near Tessa. "Tell me what happened."

Tessa's eyes brimmed with tears. "You won't believe what Reese did."

"What did he do?" Daisy asked softly, trying to keep her imagination from imagining.

"The lawyer called me into his office because I was named as executor of Reese's will. Not only that, but I received twenty-five percent of his estate!"

Daisy covered Tessa's hand with hers. "That means he cared for you a great deal. He trusted you."

"No, he didn't trust me," Tessa protested vehemently.

"How can you say that?"

"I can say that because the rest of it was bequeathed to Eric Masemer. Eric, the boy who was here over the holidays, isn't the son of a friend at all. Eric is Reese's *son.*"

The news was a blur to Daisy so she could only imagine how Tessa must have reacted. Tears were flowing down her friend's cheeks.

Daisy grabbed a tissue from the holder on her desk and handed it to Tessa. "I know how this must feel. I'm sure there's a reason he didn't tell you."

"Oh, there's a reason. He didn't trust me

to keep my mouth shut. He could have introduced me to the boy over the holidays. At the least, he could have told me about him."

"He wasn't still married, was he?" After this last revelation, Daisy didn't know what to expect.

"No, he wasn't still married. He was divorced."

"This whole situation could be a lot more complicated than we know. What if the divorce was truly rancorous? What if there was a custody battle? What if Eric wanted to go with Reese but had to stay with his mother? There are countless reasons Reese left his practice and Pittsburgh to go someplace absolutely new."

"Do you think it's possible Reese considered his ex-wife was a threat to him or to me?" Tessa asked.

"Anything is possible. Reese isn't here to explain himself. He obviously cared about you a lot. So maybe you should give him the benefit of the doubt."

"Is that what you'd do?" Tessa inquired, really wanting to know.

"You have to make up your own mind about this. I don't know how you feel. I don't know what your gut's telling you. There's no evidence Reese was seeing any other woman, not even Chloie Laird. I believe he was in the process of turning his heart over to you. But he had so many secrets. Maybe he couldn't do that just yet."

"I want to think the best of him," Tessa agreed. "And I do believe he loved me. The way we were when we were together —"

That could go under the subject of too much information, Daisy thought, but she was going to let Tessa vent however she needed to. "What happens next?"

Tessa gave a small, humorless laugh. "That depends on the investigation. If I'm not cleared, that twenty-five percent won't be mine. That's the way the law works."

"But you haven't been charged with anything. And if you are the executor, then there are things you're going to have to do."

"The lawyer addressed that. We're going to go ahead as if everything was normal. The first thing I'll have to do is inventory everything in the gallery. For the most part, lots of work will go back to the artists. It wasn't purchased outright by Reese. There's more on consignment."

"You're going to need a couple of weeks off."

"No, I'm not. I need to work here. And I can't be immersed in that gallery day and night. I have ninety days before the first tax form has to be filed. Mr. Selinski contacted the police after Reese died to tell them Reese's burial wishes included cremation. They contacted him a few days ago that the body was ready for release. I have to meet with the funeral director tomorrow to plan a memorial service possibly on Sunday. We can get the word out among the shopkeepers, don't you think?"

"Sure, we can. You just need to let me know as soon as you have everything planned. Aunt Iris has her contacts and I have mine. My mom and dad can get the word out too."

Tessa looked Daisy in the eyes. "Thank you for being my best friend."

"Always."

"You know, what Jonas said was true, though. I've inherited from Reese's estate, so the police are going to keep me in their sights."

"Then we'll just have to figure out who killed Reese, won't we?"

CHAPTER FOURTEEN

The next day, Daisy was feeling much better, as if she were pulling her weight again. It was almost one and Jonas might come in to check on her and have a cup of tea. She'd just taken a batch of cranberry bread from the oven and set it on the counter on cooling racks when her cell phone played its tuba sound. Pulling it from her pocket, she saw the call was coming in from Dutch's Deli.

"Hi, Dutch," she answered.

"Daisy," he said, his voice low and hoarse. "The man in the hoodie with the buzz cut is in the deli. If you want to talk to him yourself, come on over."

Daisy thought about calling Jonas but then decided against it. Did she have the courage to go to the deli alone? Sure, she did. It was a public place. She'd be fine. She hadn't taken her lunch break yet so she put her hand over the phone and said to

Eva, "Give the bread ten minutes, then dump it out of the pans, okay?"

Eva nodded as she emptied the dishwasher. Daisy told Dutch, "I'll be right there."

After she went to her office for her jacket, she told her aunt, "I'm going over to the deli and to buy a sandwich for lunch. Do you need anything?"

"No, I'm good. I'll just have some of our soup."

Daisy didn't linger to talk longer but hurried out the door of the tea garden and rushed down the street. When she came to the door of Dutch's Deli, she told herself to calm down and act natural.

Right. Act natural.

Going into the deli, she was glad to see there were two people ahead of her. She spotted the man with the hoodie at a table for two along the side of the deli at the window. When it was her turn, she ordered a turkey and Swiss sandwich on a kaiser roll. Dutch waited on her himself. He nodded toward the man.

Fortunately, most of the tables were taken. She went over to the window as if she were just wandering there, debating what she should do, when she stopped at the man's table.

"Hi," she said casually. "The place is a little full today and I'd like to get away from work for a while. Do you mind if I share your table?"

His hoodie was down now. He looked surprised but not threatening.

Sitting across from him, she unwrapped her sandwich and opened her bottle of water. She wasn't going to just sit here in silence.

Trying to start a normal conversation, she asked, "Are you a tourist?"

"Why do you want to know?"

She could play this two ways. She could act coy and see if she could inveigle information out of him, or she could just be honest with him. Acting wasn't her strong suit.

"My name is Daisy Swanson. I own the tea garden over there across the street. My best friend works with me."

His eyes were questioning as if he were wondering what the point of this conversation was.

"I know you had an argument with Reese Masemer and the police are looking into it. They have a video of you. My guess is they'll soon find you on their own. My best friend is a suspect in Reese's murder."

The man looked totally surprised and Daisy decided he couldn't fake that look.

Lowering his voice, he asked, "Are you sure you're not an undercover cop?"

She could have laughed at that but she didn't. Instead she pulled her driver's license from her purse and showed it to him.

The man shrugged. "The cops already know my background, databases and all that. Reese Masemer was my wife's surgeon. She died. So I sued Reese but he settled."

"If you settled, then why were you arguing with him?"

"We settled a while back. The thing is — I didn't settle for enough. I have two kids who lost their mom and who will need to go to college. I've been looking for Masemer for a long time and I finally traced him here."

"How did you find him?"

"There was an ad in the Pittsburgh paper about the Quilt Lovers Weekend. Masemer's name is listed as sponsoring the quilt show. My mother-in-law is into quilts and she saw it. So I came to town to make sure it was Masemer."

"And you told him you wanted more money."

"More money, or maybe a partnership in his gallery. Masemer said he'd think about it. I didn't murder the man but I sure thought about it often enough. The thing is, with him dead, I don't get any more money."

"So the police have talked to you?"

"Yeah. The guy's name was Detective Rappaport. He called me back here today to question me again. Like I need to lose another day of work."

"And you told them what you spoke to Reese about?"

"I did but I cut my answers short."

"Did the police ask you to stick around?"

"I told them I can't afford to do that. I have to work. Rappaport said something about the Pittsburgh PD keeping an eye on me."

Daisy really wasn't hungry. She wrapped up her sandwich once more and put it back in the bag. Then she capped her bottle of water. "Thank you for talking to me. I know what it's like to be grilled by the police and it's not easy."

As she stood to leave, the man stuck out his hand. "Bud Turner. And, you know, I'm sure the police will be keeping an eye on me until they have this thing solved. Are you sure your friend didn't do it?"

"I'm sure," Daisy said with certainty.

"Then good luck finding whoever did. Maybe Masemer made more than one mistake as a surgeon. Sometimes that kind of thing doesn't always hit the headlines."

As Daisy nodded and left Dutch's Deli, she thought about what Bud had said. And he was right. How many cases got settled before they went to court?

The police were probably following *that* lead too.

"I can't believe you didn't call me first, or call me to meet you there." Jonas scolded Daisy with an arched brow of disapproval.

"I had to get over there right away," she explained. "Bud might have left."

"If you had texted me, I would have met you there," Jonas repeated again, as if what he'd said hadn't sunk in.

Acting as sort of a referee, Tessa stepped close to both of them. They were inside Daisy's office, so no one outside of the office could overhear.

"So he actually said Reese killed his wife?" Tessa asked, getting to the point of the conversation.

Daisy switched her focus to her best friend. "He didn't go into details but I imagine any surgery can go bad for whatever reason. I don't know if the fact that Reese settled means that it was his fault or not."

"He would have felt guilty about it," Tessa decided. "I know he would have. Reese had a good heart. What I can't believe is that he used to be a doctor and he didn't tell me."

When Daisy glanced at Jonas, she knew what he was thinking. It was the same thing *she* was thinking. She put it into words. "Tessa, if he didn't tell you that, there are other things he didn't tell you too."

"You mean secrets?"

"I mean about the life he left. You have to ask yourself if you really knew him."

"I thought I did." Tessa's voice cracked and Daisy suspected how hard this was for her.

Jonas cleared his throat. "One good thing has come from this, Tessa."

"What could that possibly be?" she asked.

"The police will definitely be looking at Bud Turner as a suspect and that should take some of the pressure off of you."

"But as Bud said," Daisy mused, "if Reese was dead, Bud wouldn't be able to get any more money." She'd been running that fact around in her mind on her walk back to the tea garden.

Jonas's expression was grave. "Maybe he couldn't get any more money, but the revenge itself could have been what he needed. I've seen it before."

Daisy noticed that Jonas looked like a man who didn't want to see revenge at work again.

Daisy didn't like funeral homes. They brought back memories of pain and sadness that she'd rather forget. When she remembered Ryan, she wanted to remember him as they were when they were happy, when they went on vacation with their whole family, when they came back to Willow Creek for visits.

She tucked those memories away on Sunday as she walked into Parson's Funeral Home with its tall pillars and Colonial-style brick. In her mind Daisy knew that funeral services provided closure, at least the beginning of closure. But that still didn't make them any more palatable.

She was greeted by a representative of Parson's in a dark suit who waved her toward the guest book. After she signed her name, she walked on tastefully chosen carpet into the main room where funeral-goers were gathered. The room was filling up quickly with business professionals and store owners who had come to pay their respects.

Daisy walked up the main aisle toward the area where Tessa stood in front of a velvet rope that was a barrier to a pedestal which held the urn with Reese's ashes. That was surrounded by bouquets of flowers. Immediately, she spotted Chloie Laird seated among the assembled group. It was easy to see that Chloie's gaze was shooting daggers at Tessa. As if she could be a buffer, Aunt Iris was standing beside Tessa. In Daisy's experience, funerals and their counterpart — weddings — could bring out the best in people . . . or the worst.

When she reached Tessa, she gave her a long hard hug so her friend knew that she understood. Words in a situation like this could only be platitudes that were like a pat on the head. Her Aunt Iris gave her shoulder a squeeze as Daisy ended the hug. True to her nature, Tessa was wearing a pantsuit with black and teal wide-legged pants, a teal shell, and a black and teal jacket with flowy lapels and sleeves. Her long gold earrings and her loose hair made her look very different from the woman who ran the kitchen at the tea garden. This was the woman Reese had fallen in love with.

On the other hand, Aunt Iris wore a simple black sheath with long sleeves and a high neck. Daisy had also dressed conservatively in a deep violet skirt suit. Around her neck she wore the pearls Ryan had given her as a wedding present.

"I'm glad you're both here," Tessa said gratefully. "Chloie's been giving me the stink eye every chance she can ever since she arrived."

Iris harrumphed. "The Willow Creek gossip mill says that Chloie is furious that you're Reese's executor."

Tessa nodded. "I know. One of our regulars told me Chloie said that she should have been executor since she worked with Reese over a year, not a woman he had had a short affair with."

There was only one thing for Daisy to say. "I'm sure you were much more than a short affair to Reese, Tessa. In your heart, you have to know that too."

When Tessa nodded, Daisy could see her friend's eyes fill with tears. She was feeling a little misty herself and she fingered the pearls at her neck.

Tessa brushed a loose tear away from her cheek and nodded to a man who had just come in the room. "That's Abner Cogley. He owns the gallery property and he leased it to Reese."

Abner Cogley was a stocky man of medium height who looked uncomfortable in his suit. His tie was pulled a little loose around his neck. He wore his dark brown hair in a combover, and Daisy wondered if he dyed it. She wasn't sure what gave her that impression. Maybe because no strands of gray shone under the parlor lights. He had to be at least fifty-five. She sighed when she considered how petty that description sounded. Maybe she needed a distraction.

Tessa shifted a bit so she was behind Daisy instead of in Chloie's line of vision. "I'm going to need that week off. I have to have the gallery cleaned out sooner rather than later, or else I'll have to pay Cogley another month's rent."

Did all property owners act that way? Daisy didn't think *she* would. She'd be giving Tessa a little latitude. But she didn't lease property to renters. Well, except Tessa, of course, but that was different.

Several residents came up the aisle to speak with Tessa, so Iris and Daisy took their seats in the first row. Although Tessa was shedding a few tears, the condolences of clients and friends of Reese were likely to comfort her.

As Daisy sat beside her aunt Iris, she spotted Foster across the aisle. He gave her a wan smile. She imagined this service brought back memories for him, too.

Her aunt bumped her elbow. "There's George Beck and his wife," she whispered close to Daisy's ear.

289

George and his wife walked up the middle aisle. They waited while a couple in front of them gave Tessa their condolences and then they took their place. A few moments later, Daisy saw Tessa motioning to her. What was that about?

She stood and made her way up to Tessa and the Becks.

Before Tessa could say anything, the attractive brunette with George extended her hand to Daisy. "I'm Tanya Beck. We've just invited Tessa to dinner, and we'd like to invite you, too. I'm thinking of starting up my own business, a gift basket shop. I'd like to pick your brains about the startup. Do you think you'd be free to come?"

Out of the corner of her eye, Daisy glanced at Tessa. Tessa gave a little nod. "Sure, I should be able to come. I don't like to leave my daughter Jazzi at home alone too much since we live in a rural area. But she can always stay with a friend."

"Oh, I understand that," Tanya said.

With a smile, Daisy responded, "We have an alarm system but I still like to be there."

"That's understandable," George said.

Tanya asked, "How about tomorrow evening around seven o'clock?"

Again Daisy and Tessa exchanged a look. Tessa said, "That should be fine."

George glanced over his shoulder. There were a few more people behind him. "We'd better move on," he said to his wife.

The Becks moved away before Daisy could. The man who came up behind them was big and burly, and Daisy knew him. Jimmy Standish was one of the farmers who supplied her with produce.

He gave Tessa an uneasy hug and a pat on the back. "I'm so sorry for your loss," he said. When he'd straightened again, he lowered his voice to speak to them. "I just want you to know that Reese did some things that nobody knows about."

A look of fear passed over Tessa's face, and Daisy wondered what was coming.

Jimmy's voice shook a little as he revealed, "Reese helped me save my farm when I was having a tough year. If he hadn't loaned me the money, I would have had to sell to Abner Cogley, who was buying up farmland around here for a development. All he had to do was get the farmland rezoned. I'll always be grateful to Reese. I hear you're the executor of his estate. I still have a year on that loan. I just want you to know I'll be paying it. That is all right, isn't it? I don't have to come up with the money all at once?"

Tessa shook her head. "No, of course you

don't. We'll work something out. I'll speak with Reese's lawyer and then give you a call. We'll talk the next time you deliver produce to the tea garden."

Jimmy looked beyond grateful. "I guess folks aren't supposed to know the good works we do. I have a feeling Reese helped more folks than just me."

"Thanks for letting me know about the loan," Tessa said. "And thanks for telling me the rest."

Daisy was about to move with Jimmy back to the seats when she recognized the next man coming to pay his respects. It was Cade. She hadn't seen him since their lunch. She hadn't seen him since she and Jonas had talked. Not that they'd settled anything. But if she dated anyone, she wanted it to be Jonas.

Speaking of Jonas, when she looked down the aisle to the reception area, she saw him speaking with Dutch Pickel, who must have come in about the same time. If she was speaking with Cade and Jonas approached, this could be awkward.

However, Cade had just hugged Tessa and turned to Daisy when a strident woman's voice came from the lobby. When Daisy turned to look that way, she saw a woman whose chestnut hair was stylishly pulled back into a chignon at her nape. There was a teenager with her. She held the boy's elbow and pulled him along as she pushed in front of some of the other people in the aisle. Daisy thought her taupe coat and dress looked expensive, like cashmere.

Daisy asked Tessa, "Could that be Reese's son and his ex-wife?"

"The lawyer might have contacted them," Tessa answered. "I had no way to do that."

The woman practically pushed Cade aside as she and the boy stood in front of Daisy and Tessa. "Which one of you is Tessa Miller?" she asked with some authority in her voice.

Tessa didn't hesitate. "I'm Tessa Miller. And you are?"

"I'm Larissa Masemer, Reese's ex-wife. This is his son, Eric. Someone had to bring him to his father's service. I was elected."

Larissa's tone was acerbic. Although she was composed, she appeared angry. The teenager beside her, who looked to be about sixteen, was frowning and his eyes were sad.

Tessa extended her hand to Eric. "I'm so sorry for your loss."

"I'm glad you're not saying that to me," Larissa said in a low but vehement voice. "Reese was a coward and a deserter. He left our marriage and his son and I hated him for that."

If Daisy was making a suspect list, Larissa would be another suspect. With that much vitriol toward her ex-husband, it wasn't incomprehensible that she could have killed him. Daisy's common sense prevailed before she asked her, *And dumped his body?*

Larissa Masemer was slight but Eric Masemer wasn't. He had the height, over six foot, and the muscles that looked to be pumped up. How angry at his father was he?

Eric pointed to Tessa and then nodded to his mother. "She's the one Dad was sleeping with. She called when I was staying with Dad. I recognize her voice from the answering machine."

Tessa's cheeks had reddened and she looked embarrassed. She told Eric the truth. "I loved your dad, Eric. But when you stayed with him over the holidays, he told me you were his friend's son."

"Just like him," Larissa muttered.

Eric looked sullen, but he admitted, "My dad wanted a complete break from the past. He wanted to start over. If he claimed he had a son, that would lead to questions." He looked at his mom and said bitterly, "If Mom and Dad had been civil with each other, maybe my dad wouldn't have left

Pittsburgh."

His mother stepped in immediately. "Eric, you know that isn't true. Don't idealize your father now that he's dead. Everyone blamed Reese for that woman's death. He couldn't face his peers or country club members or his own family because he'd known he used poor judgment and her death was his fault."

"Can you tell me what happened?" Tessa asked.

"Why do you care?" Larissa asked.

"I do. Reese didn't share what had happened to him with me, and I'd like to know."

After a huff and a shrug of her shoulders, Larissa explained, "He didn't read the patient's chart correctly. He ordered an antibiotic that she was allergic to. It wasn't a mistake an intern should make let alone a respected surgeon. He'd had too many surgeries that day and not enough sleep."

"Then you divorced because of what happened to him?" Tessa asked quietly.

Larissa looked as if she might erupt, but after a brief hesitation, she explained, "We'd been having problems for a while. Doctors' schedules are the pits. Then with the lawsuit and stress, all of that ended our marriage."

This time it was Eric's turn to mutter, "But he was still my dad and he should have admitted it."

Daisy knew some men could walk away from their children, but she didn't know how. She felt sorry for Eric and she could see that Tessa did, too. Just what would Tessa do now that Eric and Reese's ex-wife were in town?

CHAPTER FIFTEEN

Daisy knew Tessa could be antagonistic toward Eric and Reese's ex-wife. Or she could take another road. Which would she choose?

Watching her friend, Daisy was proud of Tessa when she said to Eric, "I'm going to be emptying your dad's apartment, as well as the gallery. Would you like to stay here and do that with me?"

Immediately Larissa jumped in. "I can't stay. I have to get back to my job."

But Eric was looking at Tessa with questions in his eyes. "I can stay in a motel. I have my own money. If you don't let me, Mom, I'll hitchhike back here just like I did over Christmas."

So *that's* what had happened. Eric had probably turned up unexpectedly on Reese's doorstep. And the only explanation Reese could think of for Tessa was to say that he was the son of a friend . . . or else his secret wouldn't be a secret any longer.

No one wanted Eric to run away from his home or hitchhike back here. They were all looking at him, even Cade, with compassion in their eyes. The teenager was definitely grieving.

"I have a pull-out couch," Tessa offered. "You're welcome to stay on that."

Larissa was already shaking her head. "That would be totally inappropriate. No way will I agree to that."

Unexpectedly, Cade stepped forward and extended his hand to Eric. "I'm Cade Bankert," he said. "I went to high school with both Tessa and Daisy. We're all friends and they can vouch for me. I have a small house but I do have a spare room if you'd like to stay with me. I knew your dad and I liked him. I'm the one who found him the property to rent when he was looking for a space for his gallery. Reese used to tell me about his trips to museums. He went all over the country."

"I used to go with him," Eric piped up. He leaned a little closer to Cade. "Art isn't my mom's thing, but me and my dad, we both like it. If I stay with you, could you tell me some of his stories?"

"I'd be glad to," Cade said.

Because of their friendship, Daisy knew

Cade's parents divorced when he was around ten. He obviously had compassion for this boy, who was now truly fatherless.

Apparently still not convinced, Larissa said, "I can't just leave Eric with strangers."

"I'm old enough to take care of myself, Mom. I know tae kwan do."

"I can assure you, Mrs. Masemer," Daisy said, "Tessa and I will both make sure Eric is okay. He'll have three adults watching over him."

"I'll even videoconference with you, Mom, if you let me stay. We can do it every night."

His mother hesitated a few more moments. "All right. I can write a note for you for school. But there are conditions. You conference with me every night and tell me what's going on. You text me every morning. You have three days and then I'll be back for you."

Eric looked up at Tessa. "Can we do it in three days?"

"We can try. We'll start with your dad's apartment." Tessa asked Eric, "Would you like to say a few words about your dad later when we start the service?"

"Yes," Eric agreed, nodding.

Cade made a motion to Eric and his mom to sit in the grouping of chairs along the side of the room. "Why don't we go over here and talk for a few minutes."

As soon as the group moved over to the chairs, Jonas took Daisy's elbow and pulled her aside. "So you're going to help Cade with Eric?"

"I'll help both Tessa and Cade with Eric if either needs it. This isn't about me and Cade, Jonas. This is all about Reese's son. This is a slow time of the year for Cade. I imagine he'll take off and spend the time with Eric when Eric's not helping Tessa. I'll check in with both of them."

Jonas must have heard the resolution in her voice . . . or the truthfulness behind it. Leaning close to her he said, "I just want you to be careful. It's possible that Eric is hiding a lot of anger toward his father. Reese deserted him. Eric could have seen Reese as an out for living with his mother, and if Reese didn't agree to that, Eric might have gotten even angrier. A teenager that age can have a lot of strength."

Daisy's first inclination was to tell Jonas he was all wrong. Eric seemed like a normal teenager. But then what did she *really* know about teenage boys?

Cade inviting Eric to stay with him reminded her of Jonas helping out Foster. "How are you and Foster getting along?"

she asked.

"He's a good kid, Daisy. He's only at my place to crash at night. I'm an early riser but he's up before I am, studying, working on his laptop. We're good. I'm trying to convince him to talk to his father, though. I don't want to be a wedge between them."

That was exactly what *she'd* told Foster. Maybe she and Jonas were on the same page after all.

Early the next morning, before she went to the tea garden, Daisy drove to Willow Creek's police station. What Jonas had said about Eric had bothered her all night. She went to bed thinking about it and she woke up thinking about it. He'd said, *A teenager that age can have a lot of strength.*

She didn't want to believe a son could kill a father, but then she had lived in a pretty protected world and so had her girls. Jonas knew about another world where anything was possible, and not in a positive way.

The station had electronic front doors but the inside took Daisy back to earlier decades. A dispatcher sat near the front door at a scarred desk. Looking to be in her forties, she had short brown hair and was wearing earphones. Her focus was on her computer monitor. A wooden fence of sorts separated the reception area from the rest of the room. It had a swinging door in the middle. Inside the gate, there were six desks with computers. Officers occupied two of the desks. One of the officers came forward to meet her.

"Is Detective Rappaport in?"

The officer nodded and buzzed the detective. Rappaport appeared from a hallway and motioned to her. He took her into a conference room and shut the door. "If you want to talk about the case, you know I can't."

"I know you can if you want to."

"Not when it's an ongoing investigation, especially not now when your friend is one of my suspects."

"I didn't come here to talk about Tessa. I want to know if you knew about Reese's ex-wife and son."

"I can't share investigation information," he repeated with a scowl.

"Well, then, let's make this hypothetical. Hypothetically, can you tell me if they might have alibis for the time of the murder?"

Rappaport just shook his head.

"Look, Detective. Tessa, Cade, and I will be spending time with Eric. Cade has invited him into his spare room for the next couple of days. Tessa will be emptying

Reese's apartment and the gallery with Eric. They will both probably be alone with him. We all need to know if Eric is safe to be around."

Rappaport rubbed the back of his neck, studied Daisy, and crossed his arms over his chest. "Hypothetically speaking, Reese's kid has never been caught in any trouble. Hypothetically speaking, the boy and his mother are each other's alibis."

"And that means?"

"You're smart, Mrs. Swanson. You know what it means. If two people have the same alibi, that means they cancel each other out in my opinion."

"So you can't ease my concern about Eric."

"Take a look at the situation and tell me what you think," he directed.

"I think Reese's ex-wife is too slight to have dumped the body, or even gotten it into Reese's SUV. Eric, on the other hand, has the height and the muscles that he could have done it. Or they could have done it together."

"Hypothetically speaking again," Rappaport said, "the boy could have done it on his own. Hypothetically, if he borrowed a friend's car, he could have told his mother he was sleeping over at a friend's house,

303

driven here, and driven back the same night."

"Does he have a license?"

"He has a learner's permit but he doesn't have a car. In my experience, a learner's permit doesn't keep anybody from extending their curfew if they truly want to go somewhere."

"So you really don't have any answers for me."

"I don't really have any answers period." He looked disgusted and frustrated and like he'd spent all night at the station. She knew she shouldn't but she did feel a little sorry for him. "I have to ask you something."

"Your tone tells me I'm not going to like what you're going to ask me, am I?"

"I don't know, but I'll ask anyway. Do you really think I'd do something illegal to help a friend?"

Sighing, he rubbed his hand down his face. "Look, Mrs. Swanson. I realize you're usually an upright woman. You have values and I respect that. But you also have loyalty and determination. From what I've seen, you care deeply about family and friends. You got in my way several times when you were trying to help your aunt Iris."

She thought about protesting but she didn't.

"You thought I was on the wrong track, and you think that now. Do I believe you'd do something illegal to help a friend? I'm not sure. Why don't *you* tell *me*?"

Suddenly the question wasn't so easy for Daisy to answer either. What if Jazzi was in trouble, or Jonas, or Violet, or even Foster or one of her staff? Yes, she was loyal. Yes, she wanted to protect them. And if she believed in their innocence —

Rappaport crossed his arms over his chest again. "See? You're honest. Even *you* can't answer that question right now. But I will tell you this. I was trying to squeeze you for information that day. No, I don't believe you'd hide the murder weapon for Tessa Miller, but that doesn't mean I don't believe you wouldn't do something else. Bake some scones, Mrs. Swanson, and leave the rest to me."

Daisy picked up her purse that she'd set on the table, nodded to Detective Rappaport, and left the conference room. She couldn't leave it all up to him. She just couldn't. Maybe when she and Tessa had dinner with the Becks tonight they'd learn more about Reese's background.

Later that morning Daisy was thinking about everything Detective Rappaport had said. Could Eric and his mother really be each other's alibis? Could the boy and/or the mother be lying?

Daisy served tea but every time she served a cinnamon scone she thought about Reese. Had he been hiding more secrets than those that had been uncovered?

She was still mulling that over when Cade entered the tea garden. Her aunt Iris raised her brows as if asking if she should serve Cade or if Daisy wanted to do it.

"I'll take his order," Daisy said. She wanted to know if Cade and Eric had gotten along okay. Crossing to his table, she asked, "What can I get you today?"

"How about that new blend you told me about, black tea with blackberry, and three of those chocolate chip cookies, too."

"Tea and cookies coming up." She'd wait until she served him to ask him a few questions.

After she took him his tea and cookies, she poured tea into his cup from a white two-cup teapot trimmed in navy and black.

Cade motioned to the teapot. "Can you join me?"

It was midmorning and their service to customers had slowed down. The temperature was still bitter — in the teens. So there was little foot traffic. No buses today either.

Glancing around the tea room, she saw the two tables that were filled had been served and Cora Sue was standing guard in case they needed anything else. Aunt Iris was at the counter.

"Just a few minutes," Daisy told him. "The lunch crowd will soon be coming in, I hope."

"This weather isn't doing anybody any favors," he said. "Clients don't want to trek around looking at houses when it's this cold outside."

"Did your night with Eric go smoothly?" Daisy asked, trying for a nonchalance she didn't feel.

"It went fine. I took him to Sarah Jane's for a hearty breakfast. He insisted on paying for his own. He talked to his mother this morning too. He seems like a great kid. I don't understand how Reese just walked away from him."

"It sounds as if Reese needed to walk away from his life. Maybe he expected to keep up a relationship with Eric."

Cade shook his head. "You can't be a dad on a sometimes basis. You either are one or you aren't."

Daisy supposed that was certainly true. "Did Eric talk much about his dad?"

"A little. But he did want to know any

stories Reese told me about his gallery and museum hopping. We talked about sports. He did say he didn't start searching for his dad until last November. Then he found a renewal of his dad's driver's license online and the Willow Creek address."

"Was there a custody agreement?"

"His mom has full custody. They were both angry and bitter about Reese leaving."

So Eric had admitted he was angry. "Is Eric at the gallery now?" Daisy asked.

"I dropped him there after breakfast. Tessa was already boxing up paintings to return to artists."

After hesitating a moment, Daisy asked, "Do you think Tessa is safe with Eric?"

"What do you mean?"

"Eric and his mother are alibis for each other the night that Reese was killed. That's almost like not having an alibi at all. Eric is big enough and strong enough that he could have —"

"Daisy! You've got to be out of your mind. I told you, Eric's a good kid." Cade lowered his voice. "He would never have hurt his father."

"You spent one night with him, Cade. How can you be so sure?"

Cade just shook his head at her. "You're becoming jaded, do you know that? Maybe you've been hanging around cops or former cops too long."

She knew what that meant. He thought she was spending too much time with Jonas. She wasn't going to delve into that with Cade.

Rising to her feet, she placed her hands on the table and leaned down to him. "I'm not jaded, Cade. I've just become realistic and practical. In a case like this, anyone with a motive and opportunity could be the killer. I'm glad Eric will only be staying with you a couple of nights. Then I don't have to worry about *you*."

With that, she returned to the kitchen, her hands trembling a little. Of course, she didn't want to think Eric could kill his dad. Of course, she wanted to believe Tessa would be cleared. But wishes didn't become reality without hard work. She was just going to have to work harder to figure out who murdered Reese.

When business was incredibly slow mid-afternoon, Daisy said to Iris, "I'm going to take a snack down to Tessa and Eric at the gallery. I won't be long."

Aunt Iris, who was rearranging the baked goods in the case, just nodded. Daisy grabbed her jacket, scarf, and gloves and headed out. A few minutes later as she passed Woods, she saw a movement in the store. She didn't look in or stop. She kept going. She didn't want her aunt and her staff to be short another pair of hands if they did get busy.

Daisy found the gallery door locked, which made sense with what had happened. She pressed the buzzer. Tessa's voice came over the intercom. "Who is it?"

"It's Daisy."

"I'll be right down."

It wasn't long before Tessa opened the back door. "I'm surprised to see you."

"I brought you and Eric a snack." She handed Tessa the box of cookies. "I'm sure Eric will probably want to dig into them more than you will. He is here, right?"

"We've been up in Reese's apartment. That's why we had the doors locked. Come on up. Eric has been a big help, especially with stacking boxes."

Daisy undid her scarf, unzipped her jacket, and followed Tessa. As they climbed the stairs, she realized how difficult this had to be for Tessa and maybe Eric, too. When they reached the second floor and the door to Reese's apartment, Daisy saw that the space was set up like a studio apartment. The living room, bedroom, and kitchen were all open. She supposed the closed-off area was the bathroom. Eric was sitting on the black leather sofa paging through what looked like a sketchbook.

"Hi, Eric," she said.

The teenager looked up at her as if he'd come back from a long trip. "Hi, Mrs. Swanson."

She took off her jacket and laid it over a chair by a small round black enamel table. Then she went to sit on the sofa beside Eric. "What are these?"

"They're sketches my dad drew." Eric's voice was low and a bit husky.

Daisy saw why when she looked at the sketches. There were a few father-son drawings. The man was Reese and she suspected the boy was Eric when he was five or six. "You and your dad?" she asked.

Eric nodded. "I never knew he drew these."

"Did you know your dad painted?" Tessa asked him.

"He had a room upstairs that he kept closed. It smelled like turpentine and paint, but I never went in much. I knew he didn't want me messing with his stuff. But that was when I was little. I don't remember him painting much when I was in like fifth or sixth grade. I think he gave it up."

"Maybe this is one of his last ones," Tessa suggested, going to a painting in the bedroom area and pointing to it. She lifted it down off the wall and brought it to Daisy. It was a portrait of Eric and he looked to be around ten.

"I saw that hanging there when I was here over the holidays," Eric said. "I was surprised. I never knew he did portraits. He had a lot of stuff that you had to look at sideways to see what it was. He left it all behind. Mom has it stashed in a cubbyhole."

Daisy studied the frame on the painting. It was also black enamel like the side tables and the small dining table. The entertainment center was black also. But this frame on the portrait of Eric looked too stark to be surrounding a little boy. You could still see the little boy in the ten-year-old. That's what was so magical about the painting — the twinkle in the boy's eyes, the slight quirk of laughter on his lips, the bit of tousled hair. It was easy to see the boy who Eric had been.

But that frame — maybe Reese just liked black.

Eric took the painting from her and studied it. But as he did, Daisy saw something taped to the brown paper on the back of the frame. The wire for hanging the portrait disrupted her view. Her focus went again to Eric and the expression on his face as he studied the boy he'd been.

"Your father loved you," Tessa said. "That painting shows it. He wouldn't have been able to paint you like that if his heart wasn't full of you. Painting lets out what's inside. That's the beauty of it."

Eric's eyes glistened with unshed tears and Daisy felt so sorry for him. He handed the portrait back to Tessa.

Daisy asked, "Do you mind if I look at the back of that?"

Tessa gave her a puzzled look.

Daisy took it from her friend's hands and turned it around. She never expected what she saw there.

"What is it?" Tessa asked. Eric wasn't much interested. He still seemed lost in his thoughts or in his childhood.

Daisy didn't know if she should say what she'd found out loud. But then she decided they'd all had enough of dishonesty, including Eric. "It's a prescription for hydrocodone," she said in a monotone, not too loud and not too soft, but loud enough for Eric to hear.

His head jerked up. "It's what?"

"It's a prescription for pain medication."

"I know what hydrocodone is," Eric mumbled. "Why would Dad have that taped on the back?" He rose from the sofa and came to stare at it. He pointed to the date. "He never got it filled. That's dated a few days before Dad left."

"Did your father ever have any injuries?" Daisy asked.

Eric thought about it. "Yeah, he did. He used to jog. He always went running early in the morning. But one day he fell and he couldn't make it home. It was his knee. He called one of his doctor friends, who came with a brace and got him to the hospital. He had surgery. I remember seeing the hydrocodone pill bottle in Mom and Dad's bedroom."

Daisy had a feeling she knew why Reese had left his life behind, and what he'd done in between leaving and coming to Willow Creek. But she wanted to find out for sure. She told Eric, "I'd like to look into this prescription a little more. Could you text your mom and ask her to call me when she has a chance?"

"Sure. Give me your number and I'll text it to her."

Daisy did.

As he texted his mom with Daisy's message and her number, he returned to the sofa. "Why do you think Dad had that taped on the back of my painting?"

"That's what I want to talk to your mom about."

"You think he was using?"

This teenager probably knew more about drugs than she did. "I don't think he was using now. After I talk to your mom, I'll know more."

Eric nodded. "I wanted to check out my dad's computer. He had some great artwork on there, a list of the best galleries, and what museums his favorite paintings were in. You know, from the masters? But Tessa said the police took it. Not just his business one but his laptop, too."

"They're checking out everything to try to figure out who hurt him."

"He had a lot of stuff on those computers. It will take them weeks to go through it."

Tessa couldn't live in limbo for weeks, and that's even if the police found anything on the computers. Daisy hoped Eric's mother would call her soon. It was time to do more digging into what might have gotten Reese killed.

CHAPTER SIXTEEN

A few snow flurries swirled around Daisy and Tessa as George and Tanya Beck invited them into their home. The Becks' house was one story and sprawling. There was an open-concept great room, dining area, kitchen, and a hall that Daisy guessed led to the bedrooms. The kitchen's granite countertops and high-end stainless steel appliances told Daisy that everything in this house was high quality. It was decorated traditionally with lots of walnut furniture and Oriental rugs.

After greetings, Tanya took their coats.

George said, "How about a glass of wine to warm you up?"

Both Daisy and Tessa declined. Daisy said, "Thank you but I'm driving."

Tessa gave George a half-hearted smile. "I'm trying to keep my head as clear as possible. I never know when the detective is going to call with more questions."

"I was questioned too," George said. "But I don't know how much help I was. Men can be friends, but it's not the same way women can be friends."

Tanya returned from the coat closet in the foyer. "Isn't that the truth?" she asked rhetorically. "Women let everything spill out. Men just talk about sports."

"Reese and I — we talked art," George said.

Daisy took another glance around the great room. She guessed the paintings on these walls, from landscapes to still lifes, could be originals.

A buzzer dinged on the oven. "That's the twice-baked potatoes," Tanya explained with a smile. I made chicken in a garlic lemon sauce and steamed broccoli. I have cheese sauce for that, or if you're a purist, good old butter."

"All of it sounds delicious," Daisy said.

Tanya motioned to the dining area. "Good. Then go ahead and take a seat at the table."

"Can we do anything?" Tessa asked. "After all, we're both used to serving."

Tanya laughed. "I suppose you are. Consider this your night off. *I'll* be serving *you.*"

Seated at the table, conversation revolved around the Beck family, their son in college

317

at Notre Dame, and the ups and downs of running a small business.

After that, conversation turned to the Quilt Lovers Weekend. "I understand the Covered Bridge Bed-and-Breakfast will be having two raffles, both for quilts," George commented.

"They will," Daisy affirmed. "I'll announce who won at my tea on Saturday."

"That's terrific cross-promotion," Tanya acknowledged.

"I hear the bed-and-breakfast is almost completely booked," George noted. "And I understand tour buses will be coming from Philadelphia, Harrisburg, and Hagerstown. That should be good for all the businesses."

"I'm just hoping the tourists are coming for the quilts and our little stores rather than to gawk at the town where Reese was murdered," Tessa admitted.

George addressed Tessa. "The news cycle has died down. Follow-up even on the cable channels is hard to do these days with all of the news barraging us at one time."

Tessa took a sip of her water. "I've been spending time with Reese's son. He'll be in town until tomorrow. He insists he's going to call Detective Rappaport once a week for a progress report."

"That was a surprise when the boy and

his mother appeared at the funeral service. I can't believe Reese kept his past hidden so well." George looked a little hurt by that.

"It was a shock to meet them face-to-face," Tessa said.

"What do you think of Reese's son?" George asked.

This time Daisy responded. "While Tessa tells you about Eric, I need to make a phone call to my daughter to find out what time I should pick her up this evening. Is that okay?"

"Of course," Tanya said. "The powder room's right down that hall and George's office is the next door on the left. You're welcome to use it for some privacy."

As Daisy walked down the hall, she noticed a gallery of photos in frames depicting the Beck family — from vacations to their son's high school graduation. Daisy used the powder room to freshen up and then stopped at the first door on the left.

The door to the room was open. It was more of a library than an office though there was a computer monitor and a printer. Bookshelves lined two of the walls. Daisy couldn't help stepping close to them to take a peek. A leather-bound collection of classics caught her attention as well as volumes on architecture and travel. As she took her phone from her pocket to call Jazzi, she studied the folk art knickknacks on the shelves. Her gaze went to a collection of owls in all sizes from a white snowy owl to a big-eyed twelve-inch barn owl.

While tapping Jazzi's contact icon, Daisy noticed another landscape on the wall that was signed. She liked the tranquility of the painting. The Becks certainly had good taste.

After speaking with Jazzi, Daisy studied her watch. She and Tessa had about another hour before they should leave. Returning to the dining area, she rejoined everyone at the table, seeing a luscious-looking layer cake with mint green frosting in the center of the table.

With a broad smile, Tanya motioned to it. "I was just telling Tessa this is my first experiment with mint extract. It's in the icing and chocolate chips are in the white cake."

"If you ever need a job baking," Daisy teased, "come see me." She looked at George. "And if you ever want to sell those leather-bound classics, especially Treasure Island, give me a call."

George shook his head. "I hope to hand them down."

■ ■ ■ ■

An hour later after cake and coffee, as Daisy drove back to the tea garden to drop off Tessa before picking up Jazzi, Tessa said, "I guess accountants make a boatload of money. That house was really nice without being ostentatious."

"It was." Daisy's phone sounded its tuba message. She'd laid her phone on the console between the front seats. Glancing at it, she saw Larissa Masemer's name on the screen. "Finally. It's Reese's ex-wife." She'd been waiting for the call. Larissa mustn't have considered Eric's text asking her to contact Daisy as important.

The tuba ringtone played again.

"Want me to get it for you?" Tessa asked. "I can put it on speaker."

"Sure, go ahead."

"Larissa?" Tessa said when she answered. "This is Tessa Miller. I'm with Daisy and she's driving so I'm putting you on speaker."

"All right," Larissa said. "What do you want to talk to me about? When Eric texted me, he said this was about Reese's fall."

"Yes, it is," Daisy assured her. "Can you tell me what happened?"

"He went out for a jog, tripped on something, and fell. He wrenched his knee horribly. Thank goodness, he had his phone with him and he called an ortho friend. Stan brought a brace to him and helped him get home, then to the ER. That same week he had arthroscopic surgery but he had a hard time with recuperation. Even after physical therapy his leg would get fatigued and pain him on long surgery days."

"Do you know how long he was on pain medication?" Daisy inquired.

"I have no idea. By that time, we were growing apart. I know he stopped going to his doctor, but I still saw him taking pain medication. For some reason, I thought he'd switched to over-the-counter pills, but I'm not sure. I do remember seeing both around."

Daisy's shoulder still gave her a twinge of pain when she overused it. "Injuries can change a person. I had an injury and I've been much more impatient since then. Do you think Reese's personality changed from before his fall until after his fall?"

"It sure *did* change," Larissa said with certainty. "At first I thought it was the pain from surgery, and then the pain from PT. But even after he was on his feet and back performing operations again, he wasn't the same. It's one of the reasons we broke up.

He became short-tempered and overreacted at the littlest thing."

"Is it possible that was from the painkillers?" Tessa asked.

There was silence in the car as both women waited for Larissa's answer. Finally his ex-wife answered Tessa. "I never thought about it. Sure, you see on TV that people on drugs are like a different person after they start using. I didn't really think about that. After all, he had prescriptions."

"It's possible he was writing his own prescriptions," Daisy suggested.

"I never even considered that either!" Larissa seemed totally surprised. "Oh my gosh, what are you thinking? Are you thinking he left us because he was an addict?"

"It's possible he left because he didn't want to ruin your life or Eric's."

"But we could have helped him."

"Could you have?" Tessa inquired softly. "If he was an addict, could you *really* have helped him?"

"I'm going to give this information to the detective on the case," Daisy told Larissa. "I'm sure he'll get to the bottom of it."

"Do you think Reese was murdered because of drugs?"

"Not necessarily," Daisy answered. "There are a lot of loose ends. But the pain medication could have altered his judgment as far as surgeries went. That could be why the lawsuit happened."

"Because he was foggy or something?"

"Quite possibly. But I think he got clean. Did Eric tell you about his portrait?"

"No. I knew Reese had painted one and he took it with him when he left."

"On the back of it, Reese had taped a prescription for hydrocodone. It's possible that, every once in a while, he wanted to turn that painting around and remind himself of what he'd done or what his life had been. As I said, the detective will probably get to the bottom of this."

"Does Eric know all about this?" Larissa asked.

"He's smart," Tessa said. "He saw the prescription on the back of his portrait. I'm sure he's putting two and two together."

"Reese pulled out half of his savings and half of his retirement money. He left the rest of it and the house for me. It's why I didn't contest the divorce when I thought he'd deserted us. Everything went through our lawyers. We didn't even talk. That was a mistake. Maybe he didn't desert us. Maybe he left because he loved us."

Daisy intended to leave Larissa with that hope.

■ ■ ■ ■

When Daisy checked on Tessa and Eric at the gallery the next day, she found them packing up artists' work rather than finishing with Reese's apartment.

Tessa was bubble-wrapping a painting. "Memories were getting to us both."

Working in tandem, Eric unrolled some of the packing tape and went around the painting as Tessa held it. "I didn't realize I remembered so much. Just finding Dad's key ring with old keys on it made me remember coming home from Little League practice. He'd put me on his shoulders, open the door, and then say, 'Duck, we're going in.' " Eric shook his head.

"In a little while you're going to treasure those memories," Daisy assured him. "And they won't hurt so much."

After a glance around the room at what she still had to do, Tessa sighed. "I have to move at least half of this to a storage unit. In the long run, it will be more economical for the artists to pick up their work there than for me to package them to mail."

Eric picked up a smaller painting to wrap next and made eye contact with Daisy. "Do you think you can find out anything more about my dad and the pain medication? I talked to Mom last night after she spoke with you. She explained what you all felt was going on."

"I'm not sure who to contact, or how to find out if he went into rehab," Daisy admitted.

Eric looked pensive for a moment. "Do you know anybody who had contact with him when he first came to Willow Creek?"

Reese's son *was* smart. "That's a good idea."

Tessa propped a large painting against the wall. "What about Abner Cogley? That's who Reese rented the gallery from."

"You have an idea there," Daisy said.

"He has an office over on Maple Avenue," Tessa told her. "But do *you* mind talking with him? I have to deal with him about vacating the premises, and I lose my temper quickly these days. I know you'd be more tactful."

"Give me his exact address. I'll call Iris and see if the tea garden's busy, and if not, I'll just walk over there right now."

Twenty minutes later Daisy had briskly walked to the two hundred block of Maple Avenue. It was a side street with row houses that were three stories high. She easily found the one that said Cogley Enterprises.

She wasn't sure what enterprises he had, but that really didn't matter.

Opening the door, she walked into a reception area. A young man who looked to be in his early thirties with brown hair slicked back from his forehead was tapping keys on a keyboard. As soon as he heard Daisy's footsteps, he looked up. "Can I help you?"

Noticing his name — Ray Coolidge — on a nameplate at the front of the desk, she smiled. "My name is Daisy Swanson and I wondered if I could speak to Mr. Cogley for a few minutes. I don't have an appointment, but I'm hoping he's in."

"He's in, but he could be on a conference call. Let me check." Going to the door behind his desk, Ray listened at it and then rapped softly.

"Come in," a male voice called.

The receptionist opened the door. "Mr. Cogley, there's a woman here. Her name is Daisy Swanson. She would like to talk to you for a few minutes. Is that possible?"

"Mrs. Swanson, from the tea garden?"

The receptionist looked at her and she nodded. "Yes, sir."

"Send her in, Ray."

By the time Daisy stood in the doorway, Cogley was on his feet and rounding his

327

desk. He was wearing a red and black plaid shirt with a black tie and black pants. His stomach protruded over his belt. He had a short nose and close-set eyes. His brows almost met. His dark brown, combed-over hair still looked as if the color was fake.

He extended his hand to her. "I've been in your tea garden now and again, but I've never met you personally. It's a pleasure."

Ruthless in business but charming in public relations? Daisy wondered. She shook his hand, which was pudgy and a bit clammy. She pulled hers away quickly. "Thank you for seeing me."

He motioned to the utilitarian leather chair at the front side of his desk while he returned to his seat behind the desk. "What can I do to help you? Do you need to rent a property? Are you thinking about expanding the tea garden?"

"No, Mr. Cogley, neither of those. As you know, Tessa Miller works for me."

"The executor of Reese Masemer's will."

"Yes, but she's more than an executor. She loved Reese."

"Are you here to ask for an extension for her to vacate the gallery? Because I'm a businessman, Mrs. Swanson, and I can't just —"

"Oh, no. Tessa understands she needs to

be out. I'm here for another reason. We discovered some things about Reese that Tessa didn't know, and we have some questions."

Cogley sat back in his chair and folded his hands over his stomach. "I didn't know Masemer that well. I just rented him the property."

"That's what we have a question about. Eric, Reese's son, is helping Tessa pack things up. Apparently, Reese left his family suddenly, at least suddenly to them, and Eric is trying to figure out why. He needs some answers, just as Tessa does."

"I still don't understand how I can help you."

"Can I merely ask you about some of your observations?"

"Of Masemer?"

"Yes. Can you remember when Reese came to town and rented the property? Can you tell me how he appeared physically?"

Cogley's brow wrinkled. "You mean whether he looked well or not?"

"Exactly."

Cogley didn't even hesitate. "He looked wiped out and haggard. He was sweating, too, like he had a fever that was breaking. I told him we could sign the papers another time but he insisted he wanted to do it right away."

"How soon did you see him again?"

Putting his fingers to his brow, Cogley said, "Oh, let me think. He did move immediately into the apartment above the gallery, and he didn't come out for about a week." The man sat up straighter in his chair. "I know because I went by to check on renovations he said he wanted to make. No renovations had started and he wouldn't come out of his apartment. Through the door he said he had the flu or something contagious. He didn't want to give it to me. But standing outside the door, I heard a woman's voice in there. So I just figured he was having a rendezvous. It was about two weeks after that when he called me to tell me he'd hired a contractor to make some changes in the gallery. The work was going to start immediately. I asked him how he was feeling, and he said much better."

Two weeks to get clean from the hydrocodone?

Cogley went on, "Just to make sure exactly what was happening, I stopped by the property a few days later. A contractor was building a storage space and an office. I saw Masemer. He looked even thinner, maybe a little pale, but he wasn't sweating. He'd just had lunch delivered from Dutch's and he was eating. So I assumed he'd recuperated from whatever had ailed him. Does that help at all?"

"It might." Daisy stood to leave. "Thank you so much for talking to me. The next time you stop in at the tea garden, just ask for me. I'll make sure you receive a complimentary scone and tea."

"That's mighty kind of you, Mrs. Swanson." At the doorway he said to his receptionist, "Why don't you see Mrs. Swanson out?"

Ray nodded to his boss and then walked her to the door. "Thank you for fitting me into his schedule," she said.

"Mr. Cogley would take the time to meet a pretty woman any day of the week. So I was fairly certain he wouldn't mind being bothered."

Daisy wasn't sure what to do with his compliment. Ray had to be at least five to seven years younger than she was. She just smiled, thanked him again, and left. But she wondered who the woman was who'd been in Reese's apartment. She wondered if he'd been going through withdrawal . . . or if he *had* been sick with the flu.

When the oven timer buzzed that evening,

Daisy knew her chicken, noodle, and pea casserole was done. Just as she pulled it from the oven, the doorbell rang.

Jazzi called into the kitchen, "I'll get it." Checking the peephole, she called to Daisy, "It's Cade, Tessa, and some kid."

"That's probably Reese Masemer's son," Daisy explained. "He's working with Tessa to pack up the gallery during the day, then he's been staying with Cade at night."

"How old is he?" Jazzi asked, curious.

"He's sixteen."

Daisy set the casserole on the teapot trivet on the table and joined Jazzi at the door.

"Not bad," Jazzi muttered.

Daisy was absolutely *not* ready to have Jazzi thinking about dating, though she knew it was coming soon.

Jazzi went to the kitchen and opened a cupboard. "I'll set more places at the table. It's a good thing you made a big casserole, hoping to have leftovers. No leftovers now, but enough for everybody. The salad I put together is in the refrigerator. I'll get that too."

"Thank you," Daisy said as she opened the door. "This is a surprise."

"Sorry to barge in," Tessa said. "But Eric and I found something and we want to show it to you and talk to you about it. Is this an awful time?"

"No, it's a good time." Daisy smiled up at Cade. "I just took a casserole out of the oven. You can join us."

"We didn't mean to interrupt dinner." Cade looked embarrassed.

"It's no problem. Come on in." She motioned them inside. "Take off your coats and come join us at the table."

Marjoram, who had been sitting beside Jazzi on the sofa as she did homework, stood, did her cat stretch, then jumped over on the coffee table and down to the floor. Pepper, on the back of the sofa, just blinked at them.

Cade took Tessa's coat with his own and laid them over the deacon's bench. Daisy informed him, "If you put the coats there, cats will sit on them."

He chuckled. "Not a problem for me." He checked with Tessa and Eric and they just smiled. Eric laid his coat there too.

Marjoram, who was always curious about new people, came over to Eric, sat, and looked up at him.

Immediately Eric crouched down to her. "What's your name?"

"That's Marjoram," Daisy informed him.

"That's an odd name. What does it mean?"

"It's a spice," Tessa told him. "You use it like you would oregano or thyme."

"Sweet," Eric said. "That's different."

Daisy pointed to the black-and-white tuxedo cat on the back of the sofa. "And that's Pepper. We found them both in our herb garden."

Eric laughed.

It was good to see him laugh after so much sadness.

Jazzi said, "Come on over to the table, everyone. Dinner is served."

Daisy quickly introduced Eric to Jazzi. They awkwardly smiled at each other.

"Whatever it is, it smells good," Eric said. "Mom doesn't cook much. We mostly eat takeout. I'm going to soon look like a pepperoni pizza."

Jazzi laughed now, which is what Eric must have intended because he looked pleased.

After they all sat at the table and Daisy had dished out the casserole onto each plate, she asked Cade, "So how's it going with you and Eric?"

"I like the company," Cade said. "It's been awhile since I had a roommate."

"He likes the Steelers, too . . . and the Patriots," Eric said in an aside.

Cade nodded. "The sports channel is our

friend." He picked up his fork. "This looks really good, Daisy."

"It's my best use for leftover chicken. Nothing special, just easy to throw together and stick in the oven. That salad dressing is Sarah Jane's recipe for honey mustard."

"I thought she doesn't give that out to anyone," Tessa said.

"She must like me," Daisy joked.

"More like you give her free tea and scones when she comes in," Cade guessed.

Daisy didn't confirm or deny.

"If you're wondering why I tagged along," Cade said, "I stopped at the gallery to pick up Eric. He and Tessa were huddled over something and said they had to come see you. So I offered to drive."

"You're always welcome here, Cade, you know that," Daisy assured him. Whether they were romantically involved or not, they were friends.

"I didn't like the idea of Tessa driving out here all alone."

"She wouldn't have been alone," Eric mumbled.

Beside Eric, Cade placed his hand on the boy's shoulder. "No, she wouldn't have been alone. But there's still a murderer out there, and whoever it is could know you're both involved at the gallery. There's no point taking any chances. It's probably a good thing your mother's picking you up tomorrow."

"I'll have to go back to school," Eric bemoaned. "And then there's Mom. She doesn't listen as well as you all do."

"You can visit me," Cade said to Eric. "I told you that, and I'm not just being nice. I mean it."

"Okay," Eric mumbled.

Jazzi was the one to ask, "So what did you find?"

After a glance at Eric, Tessa took something out of her slacks pocket. She handed it over to Daisy. "It's a receipt that was stuck in a vase in Reese's apartment."

Examining the receipt, Daisy realized it confirmed her suspicions.

"I checked the date on it," Tessa said. "I've got lots of receipts that need to be sorted. That's for the week when Reese moved into the apartment over the gallery."

"What's it say, Mom?" Jazzi asked.

"It's a receipt for a private nurse for a week."

"What does that mean?" Jazzi asked.

"I think I know, but I'm sure I can't find out more information because I wasn't related to Reese." Daisy looked at Eric. "But your mom probably can."

"If *you* text her, she'll answer you," Eric

informed Daisy.

"Okay. I'll text her and give her the nursing agency's number, then we'll go from there. How about a whoopie pie? Aunt Iris made them today and I brought a bunch home because they're a favorite of Jazzi's."

"And yours," Jazzi retorted. "She sneaks one at midnight with a glass of milk."

"Your secret's out," Cade said with a smile.

Daisy rose to fetch the dessert. "Ice cream with those?"

But as she went to the freezer for the ice cream, she wasn't thinking about whoopie pies. She was thinking about texting Larissa to confirm the reason why Reese had left Pittsburgh.

CHAPTER SEVENTEEN

Daisy had already baked scones, cookies, and two types of bread with the help of her aunt Iris when Jonas arrived with the shelves for the storage closet the next morning. He brought them into the kitchen, two at a time. They were yellow, one of her favorite colors.

"If you can stand the noise, I'm going to tack them down," he explained. "I don't want them tipping if you happen to lean on the front of one."

"That sounds like a good idea," Daisy said.

Iris called to her from the sales counter. Apparently, this was going to be a busy morning. Quilt Lovers Weekend publicity paying off? She was glad she'd asked Foster to work this morning.

She glanced at Jonas before she left the kitchen. She wanted to tell him all about last night and what she'd learned this morning. She didn't want him to feel left out of the loop. Maybe when he'd finished with the shelves and morning traffic slowed.

The morning rush of patrons lasted almost until eleven. Some admitted they'd traveled to Willow Creek today to beat the crowd of tourists that would start on Friday.

As soon as Daisy could get free, she went to the closet where Jonas was putting the last shelf in place. When he stood, she said, "I want to tell you about last night and what I learned."

"What happened last night?" he asked.

She looked over her shoulder. Eva was washing teapots and Foster stood at the mixer ready to mix apple bread.

"How about a cup of tea? Or a bowl of soup? It's almost lunchtime. We can go to the spillover tea room."

He studied her carefully, obviously realizing this wasn't going to be a short conversation. "What kind of soup do you have today?"

"Beef barley and leek and potato."

"The beef barley sounds good, and a cup of tea."

"Any particular kind?"

"You choose. I'll just take my tools out to the car and meet you over there."

It wasn't long before Daisy brewed one of

her favorite black teas that came from Ceylon. She knew Jonas liked it. Instead of making up a tray because she knew that would be heavy to carry, and still reluctant to ask for help, she carried in the teapot first, then the soup, then came back for the mugs and a pot of honey. She had everything set up on the table when Jonas joined her.

"Is this *your* lunch?" he asked.

"Yes, it is."

"Does your shoulder still hurt?"

"Only if I lift something too heavy."

"If it keeps bothering you, you might want to think about physical therapy. It's not always pleasant but it helps."

"I'll think about it," she told him.

He took a spoonful of his soup and then looked up at her. "So tell me what happened last night. You didn't run into an intruder again, did you?"

"No, of course not. Jazzi and I were making supper when Tessa, Eric, and Cade showed up at the door."

"Cade did?" Jonas's eyebrows arched as they did when he was serious or questioning.

"He went to pick up Eric at the gallery, but Tessa and Eric had found something. She wanted to bring it to me so he said he'd drive them."

Jonas frowned but didn't comment.

Next, she filled him in on what Abner Cogley had said about Reese that first week he was in Willow Creek.

Jonas nodded, took the mug in his hand, and waited for Daisy to go on.

"Yesterday Tessa found a receipt for a private nursing service. The bill was for a week."

"And you believe Reese was going through withdrawal?"

"I do. So I texted Larissa. She called the nursing service this morning and got the number of the private duty nurse. I think she told them her husband had just died and she wanted to thank the nurse who took care of him."

"Even though that was years ago?"

"It apparently worked. She spoke with the nurse, acting as if she knew exactly what had happened. And it was what we thought. He was detoxing from the pain medication. That's why he left her and Eric. The nurse said his biggest worry was that he'd start taking hydrocodone again."

"Do you think he did?"

"Tessa isn't finding any evidence of it," Daisy said. "I think he stayed clean."

"You have a lot of information here that

could help Detective Rappaport if he hasn't looked into it already. Do you want to set up a meeting with him?"

"Yes, I do. At supper last night, Eric told me again he's going to call Detective Rappaport every week for a report."

"So everyone stayed for supper?" Jonas asked nonchalantly, as if her answer didn't matter.

"I was pulling it out of the oven when they came. The casserole was big enough for all of us. Jazzi had made a salad."

"And I'm sure you had some kind of dessert on hand." Jonas tried to say it in a joking manner, but it fell flat.

"Whoopie pies."

"Hmmm," he said. "How did Cade like those?"

Daisy reached across the table and laid her hand on Jonas's forearm. "Cade didn't think Tessa and Eric should drive out to my place alone. He's worried about her, like we all are if the murderer is still out there."

"He's worried about Tessa?"

Daisy looked straight into Jonas's eyes. "I told you I would be honest with you about everything. I don't intend to be a social butterfly or date two men at the same time."

"I suppose that means that we should go on an official date to make sure I'm the one who's dating you." His mouth curved in a small smile.

Daisy's heart fluttered a bit. They'd never called their time together "dating" before. "That would be nice," she said lightly.

He set down his mug and covered her hand with his. "I'll set up a meeting with Rappaport. After that, we'll decide where we want to go for a date. Think about it until then."

She definitely would.

After Jonas left, Daisy picked up her clipboard from her office and went to the tea cupboards to take inventory for her order this week. After she checked off several teas to discuss with her supplier — the green teas with infusions seemed to sell the most — she weighed some of the most popular ones into two-ounce bags. When they were busy, it was nice to be able to snatch a bag when a customer requested it. She was weighing out the green tea with lemon and almond tones when Foster came into the kitchen, his cheeks a little ruddy.

"My brother's here and he wants to talk to me. Is it okay if I take a few minutes to go outside with him?"

"Outside? It's twenty-five degrees out there, Foster," Daisy reminded him. "Why don't the two of you go into my office?"

"Are you sure you don't mind?"

"I wouldn't have suggested it if I did. I don't want either of you getting frostbite. Are you going to introduce me?"

Foster's eyes widened in surprise. "Sure, I can do that." He went back to the tea room and returned a moment later, a young man around twelve or thirteen in tow. He had the same cheekbone structure as Foster, the same color hair. No glasses, though.

"Mrs. Swanson, this is my brother, Benjamin. Ben, this is Mrs. Swanson."

Daisy extended her hand and Ben took it a little shyly. "No school today?" she asked. After all, Jazzi went to school, so Daisy was wondering.

Suddenly Ben's gaze was downcast, and he wouldn't meet hers.

"Ben," Foster said, a warning tone in his voice that said he was used to being the oldest and the big brother.

But Ben still didn't answer.

"Did you tell Dad you were sick and you stayed home?" Foster asked him.

"I had to," Ben blurted out as if he couldn't hold it in. "I wanted to come see you. I want you to move back home. We all do. Please."

Daisy could see that Foster was torn between loving his family and becoming an adult with more control over his life.

She motioned to her office. "Go inside and talk."

Foster and his brother were inside her office for a good fifteen minutes. Every once in a while she took a peek and could see them through the glass windows. She found herself watching as Foster gave his brother a hug that lasted awhile. Then she took a few steps back as they both came out of her office.

She asked Foster, "Do you want to run him home?"

"You're cutting me too many breaks," Foster said.

"I'm the boss so I'm allowed to do that," she told him with a smile. "It's too cold for him to walk home. I assume that's how he got here?"

Foster nodded. He glanced at his brother, who was standing in the hall looking uncomfortable. "I'm not sure what to do," he said.

"Have you talked to your dad?"

This time Foster shook his head.

"I'm just going to say one thing," Daisy said. "As an adult, you need to be practical. Even though I understand you want to stand on your own, you should take advantage of living at home to save money and not go deep into debt."

"How can I stand on my own with Dad paying all my expenses?"

"Then don't let him. What if you start paying your dad room and board? That way you can be more independent and show your dad how responsible you are. Maybe then he'll back off a little. It could be a win-win compromise."

Ben approached them then. "You told me you're going to think about coming home." His brother's voice was so hopeful, Daisy didn't know how Foster could disappoint him.

Foster blew out a resigned sigh. "Zip up your jacket. I promise I'll talk to Dad about it."

"When?" Ben wanted to know.

"This weekend. I promise."

Foster really was a responsible young man. Daisy was thankful that Vi had chosen someone honorable to spend her time with. She couldn't help but say to Foster, "After you put your coat on, you zip it up too. A scarf wouldn't be a bad idea either."

Foster gave her a smile that told her he knew she was half-kidding and half-serious.

It was late afternoon when Larissa, Tessa, and Eric came into the tea garden. Daisy was in her office and Aunt Iris sent them all to her.

When Larissa entered the room, she was smiling. She hung her arm around her son's shoulders. "I want to thank you for your hospitality to Eric. We both appreciate that. I already stopped in at the real estate office to thank Cade. I can see why Reese liked this town if you all help each other out like that. I just wish he had let us help *him*."

"Sometimes it's hard to accept help." Daisy knew from her own experience.

"I suppose so," Larissa said.

Eric looked up at her. "Mom, my guess is Dad was afraid he'd relapse. That's why he had that prescription taped to the back of my painting. He could turn it around and look at it and remember, and then become more determined that he wouldn't."

Although Tessa had been quiet until now, she stepped into the conversation. "Eric, I just want you to know that I never saw any signs of it. I know what addiction looks like. I was around it when I was growing up. And your dad knew too. If an artist came into the gallery with his work, and he had a glazed look in his eyes and he was rubbing his nose, your dad didn't take on his work because he insisted that artist wouldn't be dependable for either artistic or financial dealings. I never guessed he knew what he was talking about from personal experience."

"I didn't guess either," Larissa murmured.

"You can't blame yourself for not knowing the signs." Tessa's gaze was sympathetic to Reese's ex-wife.

Suddenly there was a commotion out in the tea garden. Daisy heard raised voices. Peering through the glass window, she saw Iris beckon to her. Now what?

By the time she'd reached the main tea room, her customers were gathered at the front windows and Jonas burst in the door without his coat. He was rubbing the arms of his chambray shirt and stood peering out the door.

"What's going on?" Daisy asked.

Jonas pointed down the street. "I saw the patrol car roll by. He actually had his lights flashing."

"No siren, though," Cora Sue noted.

"Do you think he had to kick somebody out of Dutch's Deli who got boisterous?" Iris asked.

"No," Jonas answered her. "I think something else is going on."

Jonas and Daisy stepped out onto the Victorian's porch to get a better look.

"What do you think is really happening?"

she asked him.

"If we give it a few minutes, we'll soon know."

It didn't take a few minutes. Two officers escorted Dutch from the deli and over to the patrol car.

"He's not handcuffed," Jonas noticed.

"But what does this mean? Do you think he's a suspect in Reese's murder?"

"My guess is Rappaport ordered the patrol officers to pick him up. He has something he wants to question him about. Any idea what that is?" Jonas asked.

"None at all."

"You mean Rappaport is a step ahead of you?"

Daisy lightly punched Jonas in the arm. He kept his gaze on the patrol car driving away.

"I'm going back inside," Daisy said. "It's too cold to be a busybody."

"You're not a busybody. You're an interested party and so am I. I'm going to go down to the station and find out what's happening. I'll tell Rappaport about Reese's addiction if I can get a minute with him."

"Do you think Rappaport will tell you anything?"

"If not, I can learn something just from standing around. But Rappaport might let me in on what's happening as a professional courtesy. Especially if I give him info about Reese that he doesn't have."

Daisy considered Jonas's history that had changed his path in life. "Does Rappaport know what happened to you back in Philadelphia?"

"He does. There's a cop network just like there's a tea garden network or a financial advisor network. Especially the bad stuff gets around."

"And do you know what happened to Rappaport? Why he came to Willow Creek?"

"No, I don't know. There was something about a hush-up investigation and then he left. But no one seems to know the details. I really have no right to poke into his career." Jonas gave Daisy's arm a squeeze. "I'll call you as soon as I know something and I'll see you at Quilts and Notions later."

Daisy smiled at him. They were going to work with Rachel and Levi to ready the store for Quilt Lovers Weekend, which began on Friday. "Thank you."

After a wave good-bye, he jogged down the street to his shop. She turned around to head inside. She knew she'd be facing questions from her staff and her customers. But she didn't have any answers.

Not yet.

Daisy had said good-bye to Eric and Larissa and was helping Aunt Iris and Tessa close up the tea garden when her cell phone played. She immediately took it from her pocket. It was Jonas.

"What did you learn?" She went into her office and closed the door.

"You're not going to believe this."

"What? Did they arrest Dutch for Reese's murder?"

"No. But it's possible he did it. Apparently, Reese's bank records showed a payout each month to Dutch."

"Does Rappaport think Dutch was blackmailing Reese?"

"Rappaport doesn't have concrete evidence yet. Dutch is telling him that Reese was paying for personalized deli service when he was too busy to leave the gallery or his apartment. They can't prove otherwise."

"I have a feeling that was a very expensive deli service."

"I'm sure you're right."

"Do you think Dutch found out about Reese's background and told him he'd spill the beans if Reese didn't pay him?"

"I'm sure that's what Rappaport is thinking."

"And Dutch killed him because Reese decided not to pay him any longer?"

"That's the scenario Rappaport is trying to put together. Dutch is still here. I have a feeling he'll be here for hours. Rappaport has a reputation for grilling long and hard."

Daisy and her aunt knew about some of that reputation firsthand.

"This could be all over," Daisy said.

"It could be. Now you can just concentrate on Quilt Lovers Weekend."

That she could . . . unless Dutch Pickel *wasn't* the murderer.

On a ladder at Quilts and Notions that evening, Daisy adjusted the quilt she'd hung near the ceiling. Quilts of all colors and patterns hung around the perimeter of the shop on the walls. Some had been made in Rachel's quilting circle. Others were for sale by Amish and English women alike. Daisy admired the center diamond quilt in dark purple, dark blue, and dark green. It had probably been crafted by an Amish woman who tended to use darker colors. The same could be said of the Sunshine and Shadow quilt. The Tumbling Blocks quilt, however, was possibly made by an Englisher in its pale blue, lilac, and flowered print. Daisy guessed it was fashioned by a resident of Willow Creek who just liked to quilt.

Jazzi said, "Come on down now, Mom, so

I can stop holding the ladder. You shouldn't be extending your arm for long."

When Daisy glanced down at her daughter, she spotted Jonas, who was watching her too. "My shoulder is much better. I'm steady on my feet and I'm not having any more headaches."

From his stance at one of the trestle tables he'd built for displaying quilts at the store, he reminded her, "Even people who haven't had concussions can fall from a ladder."

Daisy saw worry in both sets of eyes. Along with Tessa, Rachel, her husband, and her two oldest daughters, they were all at Quilts and Notions to ready the store for Friday.

Moving about, doing whatever she deemed necessary, Rachel stopped at the table Jonas had built. "That's a fine table. They all are."

Tessa brought a quilt to the table and folded it so that the pattern showed best. "I'm just grateful that the owners of the antique quilts are letting us display them here. We'll have to make sure they know that the quilts on the tables aren't for sale, that they're just for display. The Album quilts should probably go in the back in the safest corner. I'll print out a sign to put with them."

Daisy touched the fine stitching on the Baltimore Album quilt that was displayed beside Levi's grandmother's quilt. It was fashioned in a block design that was absolutely beautiful. As with the Fishers' quilt, it had a provenance back to the early nineteen hundreds.

She pointed to the daisies and to two horses who looked as if they were meeting for the first time under a tree, then to a wedding cake with a girl on one side of it and an Amish man on the other side. One of the later blocks depicted an older man and a woman and their reflection in an oval mirror. There were corner borders on two sides with colorful flowers.

"Can you imagine the time that went into embroidering and stitching this quilt?" Daisy asked. "The colors are beautiful and go together so well. A quilt like this could take a lifetime to make, and only the family knows what each of those blocks mean."

"Memoir keepsakes are important to you, aren't they?" Jonas asked.

"Yes, they are. I'm thinking about making a quilt if Rachel's quilting circle can teach me. I'd like to use bits of fabric from Violet's and Jazzi's childhood dresses and even maybe —" She stopped.

"Even maybe something of Ryan's?" Jonas

asked. He didn't look bothered by that.

"Yes, and something of my mom and dad's and Aunt Iris's, too."

"And you'll stitch the flowers that each of you are named for around the border," he suggested.

"I doubt if I'll be able to learn the skill for that."

"You will," Rachel encouraged her. "It just takes practice. You'll learn to take your quilting basket wherever you go so you can work on it."

Daisy knew that one of the tenets of Amish living was that hands should never be idle.

Rachel's oldest daughter, Hannah, who was twenty now, said, "It's so sad the gallery is closed. Mr. Masemer appreciated the history of these quilts."

"That's true," Tessa agreed. "He felt fortunate to display them."

Hannah said, "I heard Mr. Pickel was at the police station for hours."

Rachel frowned at her daughter. Daisy knew even though the family was New Order Amish that they didn't approve of gossip. But this wasn't gossip exactly. It was fact.

"I heard that too," Daisy said. "If you'd

355

like to know why, I can tell you. Jonas filled me in."

Rachel gave a little nod. After all, something that happened to Dutch could affect the rest of their businesses and the Quilt Lovers Weekend. So Daisy explained about the bank statements.

"How awful," Rachel responded. "Do you believe he really was providing a deli service?"

His brow furrowed, Jonas shook his head. "I doubt it very much. But the police won't arrest Dutch unless they have concrete evidence. Blackmail isn't the same as murder."

Rachel's younger daughter Sarah brought in bolts of material from the storeroom. With expertise she'd learned from being around her mom in her shop, she fitted the bolts of fabric into the shelves where the colors fit best.

"I know it's selfish," Daisy said, "but I hope they don't question Dutch again after the Quilt Lovers Weekend."

"Because of the bad publicity?" Tessa asked, straightening a corner of the quilt.

"Yes, and because I just don't see him as the murderer."

"Do you think his business is in trouble?" Rachel asked. "Otherwise, why would he blackmail Reese?"

Daisy exchanged a look with Jonas. They both knew the Amish way. The Amish didn't place much stock in possessions or how much was in a bank account. They lived *in* the world but not *of* the world. How could they ever understand a man like Dutch who might want to retire on an island in the Caribbean?

Jonas said, "Not everyone is like you and your family, Rachel. If Dutch was blackmailing Reese Masemer, we don't know why he did it. Some men want money for money's sake, or they're afraid of what they might need in the future."

"God will provide," Rachel assured them.

Daisy knew Rachel believed that with all of her heart. God did provide because she and her family worked hard to make that happen. In Daisy's mind, it was a joint effort.

Changing the subject, Jonas nodded out the window to the few snowflakes that could be seen hitting the window panes because of the store's front stoop light. "Hopefully, we'll just get a dusting of snow tonight."

Hannah peered out at the snowflakes. "We're making everything ready. It would be awful if the tourists didn't come."

"Don't worry," Jonas said. "According to

the forecast, the weather's clear for the weekend." Without preamble, he turned to Daisy. "Do you ski?"

She blinked, trying to adjust to his new thought path. "I went skiing a few times when I was in college, but it's been years."

"Maybe after the Quilt Lovers Weekend is over and done, we can take a day off to go skiing at Roundtop. It doesn't matter how well you can ski. We can just have fun."

Daisy realized going skiing with Jonas sounded like heaven. She could forget all about murder, suspects, and Quilt Lovers Weekend. They could just be together and enjoy each other . . . get to know each other even better.

Just how much more of his life would Jonas share with her? Maybe during a day of skiing, she could find out.

CHAPTER EIGHTEEN

With Tessa stressed out about the investigation into Reese's murder and Daisy fidgety about the Quilt Lovers Weekend, Daisy asked Tessa to meet her at the Covered Bridge Bed-and-Breakfast for breakfast on Thursday. The B&B opened at six AM.

As Daisy was getting dressed that morning, Tessa texted her that she'd be sketching at the covered bridge as long as she could stand the cold. She wanted to finish the *Morning Has Broken* series in memory of Reese. She'd meet Daisy at the B&B around seven-thirty.

When Daisy walked into the Covered Bridge Bed-and-Breakfast, she easily noted that they were ready for Quilt Lovers Weekend. Beautifully stitched quilts hung over the open banister that led upstairs. A raffle had already begun for two lucky people to win them. The first was a Log Cabin design in navy, burgundy, and cream. The other was a Double Wedding Ring quilt in gold, red, and purple. They were both stunning.

After Daisy turned right into the restaurant, Amelia Wiseman met her at the hostess's podium. Daisy smiled at her. "Are you overseeing everything yourself?"

"Are you as nervous as I am that this weekend will be a success?" Amelia asked her.

"I don't know if I'm nervous or excited," Daisy responded. "The bed-and-breakfast looks wonderful, not only the quilts but all the extra touches. You've changed the curtains." She'd noticed right away that the curtains at the double-paned windows were now green gingham with an off-white background. Their colors coordinated beautifully with the quilts and wall hangings. When Daisy glanced into the dining room, she noticed a quilted placemat at the center of every table under a vase of dried flowers including lavender and thyme.

"We're booked for the weekend, and even a few days beyond. New reservations came in last night. I guess when people realized the weather was going to be good this weekend, they wanted to get away. Cold but sunny is good for business."

"I'm concerned that the tea will go smoothly Saturday afternoon. We've never served afternoon tea in both rooms at the same time. Jazzi will even be helping to serve. I've called in Emma Zook's two daughters who sometimes help me in the summer during our busiest time. Tessa and I will be heading to the tea garden right after breakfast and prepping the rest of the day. But I thought we needed this break for breakfast before the madness starts."

"You have capable people working for you, Daisy, and so do I. We just have to trust them."

That was certainly true.

Amelia motioned to the dining room. "Sit wherever you'd like. I'll send a server out with coffee. She'll watch for Tessa and know when you want to order."

Daisy sat at the table covered with a cream linen, ready to order French toast. She was going to splurge this morning. A server, with the name tag of SUSAN, poured her a cup of coffee. However, twenty minutes later, Daisy had drained the cup of coffee and Tessa still hadn't showed. Had her friend lost track of time while sketching?

Daisy decided not to wait any longer but to go see for herself. Tessa had told her she'd be near the covered bridge. On the way out, she told Amelia, "Tessa's sketching at the bridge. When she does that, time passes her by. I'm going to go remind her we do have tons of work after breakfast."

"Do you want me to hold on to your purse?" Amelia asked.

Taking her phone from her cross-over bag, Daisy inserted it into her jacket pocket. "Thank you. I'm sure I'll be back in five minutes."

When Daisy exited the bed-and-breakfast, she turned left toward the back of the property and the path that led to the covered bridge. It was stamped concrete and resembled bricks. Everything about this bed-and-breakfast was tasteful and particular. Amelia and her husband had done a wonderful job with it. Its five-star rating brought tourists to the area.

The snow on the path had melted with the last two days of spotty sunshine though the lawn was still covered with at least four inches of snow. Maple and sweet gum trees, their branches bare now, dotted the lawn and grew heavier on both sides of the path as Daisy approached the covered bridge.

She spotted Tessa's multicolored wool poncho with the faux fur trim at the corner of the covered bridge. Before Daisy could shout to her, Tessa moved off the gravel road leading into the covered bridge and tramped around behind it. Daisy knew her friend often did several sketches for a painting, then she decided which angle she liked best.

Instead of trying to call to her, Daisy just hurried her pace. She'd rounded the corner of the covered bridge and was waving at Tessa when she realized her friend was totally engrossed with what she was doing. She was wearing an orange knit cap and her head was bowed over her sketchbook. Daisy called to her as she approached so as not to startle her.

Tessa looked up with an expression that said she'd been very far away, maybe sorting through memories of her and Reese. Daisy was about a foot from her friend when a shot rang out. Reflexively, Daisy tackled Tessa, taking them down to the ground to protect them from the line of fire. Another shot pierced the cold morning just as they went down, and Daisy felt a burning in her arm.

"You're too lucky for your own good." Detective Rappaport sat on the vinyl chair next to Daisy's gurney at the emergency room and he was squinting at her.

This time she was sitting up on the gurney for interrogation, totally aware of everything that was happening around her. On her arrival by ambulance, she'd learned Amelia had heard the shots, spotted Tessa and Daisy on the ground, and called 9-1-1. The paramedics had insisted on transporting her to the hospital, though she'd wanted to ride in Tessa's car. No dice. They said they didn't know how much blood she'd lost. So here she was . . . *again.*

This visit was very different from her last one. She was awake, conscious, and didn't have a headache, just stitches in her arm. It had been a flesh wound.

Facing the detective squarely as well as his comment about being lucky, she asked, "Just what is that supposed to mean?"

Suddenly Jonas was standing in the door to her cubicle, eyeing both her and the detective. "Tessa called me," he said. "She told me what happened."

Daisy motioned to the detective. "He's acting as if this is *my* fault."

Wisely, Jonas kept silent.

"Isn't it?" Rappaport shot back. "You were at the crime scene."

"It's not a crime scene any more. Tessa was sketching there."

"Detective, I don't mean to barge in," Jonas said quietly, "but I don't think the crime scene had anything to do with it. I think someone followed either Tessa or

Daisy to the bed-and-breakfast."

Rappaport brushed that idea away with his hand. After a glance at Jonas, he eyed Daisy. "It could be that a hunter got you."

Daisy's gaze met Jonas's and she knew he didn't believe that any more than she did.

"Someone tried to frame Tessa for the murder," she reminded Detective Rappaport. "And now for some reason, he or she thinks she's a threat. She's going to need a personal bodyguard. There are quite a few suspects — Dutch, Reese's ex-wife or son, even Reese's patient's husband."

"You think an out-of-towner did this?" Rappaport asked.

"Pittsburgh isn't that far," Jonas offered.

"Just where would a sixteen-year-old get a rifle?" Rappaport asked.

"I don't know," Daisy replied. "Do you know if Reese had guns before he left Pittsburgh? For all you know, there's a gun case in the basement with an assortment of weapons."

"I don't have probable cause to give the Pittsburgh PD for a search warrant."

After a sensitive pause, sorting through the thoughts in her head, Daisy said, "We might be asking the wrong questions."

"There's no *we* in this," Rappaport concluded hotly.

Daisy ignored him. "If Tessa was dead, who would benefit? Why shoot Tessa?"

If Tessa was dead, Eric would inherit the entire estate. Apparently, Jonas could easily see the path her thoughts were taking.

"If Tessa died, and she was the executor . . ." Daisy trailed off.

Jonas took her thought a step ahead. "Maybe as executor, Tessa might find a clue as to the murderer when looking through Reese's things. Let's say if a bank handled it, and I think the bank was the second option for executor if Tessa couldn't perform the duties, someone impersonal might not notice whatever clue might be there."

"That's far-fetched," Rappaport disagreed.

"Then how about this?" Jonas asked. "What if Tessa wasn't the target? What if *Daisy* was the target?"

Complete silence filled the room. Both men studied Daisy.

"What do you know that the killer doesn't want you to know?" Detective Rappaport asked.

After a sigh, Daisy shook her head. "I have no idea."

A few minutes later after Detective Rappaport left, Jonas sat on the gurney next to Daisy. "You're going to be sprung out of here in a few minutes. Tessa went to the tea garden to talk to Aunt Iris and the staff. She's going to tell them you had a little accident so they don't worry."

"Better they think I'm dopey than in danger."

Jonas took her hand and squeezed it.

"Everybody's going to be too busy today and the rest of the weekend to listen too carefully to a story I'm going to have to make up." She sighed. "What *is* going on, Jonas? Who do you think did this?"

"As you mentioned, there are a few suspects. But I'll tell you this. I'm going to stick close to you this weekend."

"I'm going to be at the tea garden most of the time, and so will Tessa."

"That's good. And Jazzi will be with you too?"

"Tomorrow after school and Saturday. She's spending Sunday with her grandparents. Do you think I should tell her what really happened?"

"Jazzi's a smart cookie. She'll know you're holding something back if you don't tell her."

"I suppose you're right. But I don't want her to be scared."

"And I don't want to scare *you,*" Jonas said.

"But?"

"I think the killer is getting desperate to cover his or her tracks. Between planting evidence in Tessa's apartment and the shooting today, somebody's fearful he or she is going to be discovered. Because of that, there's a good chance the murderer will make a mistake. We'll just have to be ready for it."

Daisy hopped off the gurney. "I'm going to go find my discharge papers." She had to get back to work.

Work was the only thing that was going to save her this weekend from thinking about catching a murderer.

Happy she was too busy to be nervous on Saturday afternoon, Daisy moved from table to table at the tea garden, making sure every guest who had bought a ticket to tea was satisfied with their service. Emma Zook's daughters had joined everyone on her regular staff to make the service less taxing. All of her tea drinkers had been given a special menu of tea blends, from Rosy Day, which was a green tea blended with rose petals, to Winterfest — a black tea mixed with cloves, cinnamon, and orange peel, to Daisy's Blend — a decaffeinated green tea infused with raspberry and vanilla. There were many more, but those were the most popular today.

They had begun the first course with cheddar bisque, a creamy, cheesy soup. The second course had been cinnamon scones accompanied by a nutmeg-infused butter. A ribbon salad with fresh strawberries and walnuts had been served next. Now with the fourth course, the guests were presented tiered plates that held crab puffs, egg salad sandwiches, and small triangle sandwiches with turkey and Swiss on rye. There was actually a lull as the tea room guests made their choices and ate the petite sandwiches while they sipped tea.

Daisy was checking on cleanup in the kitchen and the plating of the last course, which was desserts, when Foster joined her by the dishwasher.

His glasses sat high on the bridge of his nose and his eyes looked serious as he stood beside her and kept his voice low. "I have something to tell you."

At first Daisy wondered if Foster was going to quit because of Gavin's idea that she was a bad influence on him. But then he pointed to her arm. She'd worn a long-sleeved red sweater with black slacks, and of course her Daisy's Tea Garden apron on top. The gauze that laid over her stitches made a slight bump under the sweater. "I wanted to tell you how sorry I am that happened to you. I'm watching over you along with Tessa as Jonas asked me to."

Foster had known the truth about what happened because Jazzi had told Vi and Vi had confided her worry to Foster. "Nothing's going to happen here," Daisy assured him.

"I'll try to make sure of that." He looked down at his shoes for a moment, then back up at her. "I talked to my dad. You getting hurt reminded me that I'd lost one parent and I didn't want to lose the other one."

"How did it go?"

"All right, I guess." Foster's mouth quirked up in a small smile. "He must have missed me."

"Of course he missed you! I'm sure Ben and your sister did too."

"I told him I want to pay room and board, and I want to be treated like another adult living in the house. He said he'll figure out what I should pay him, and he'll try to treat me like an adult."

Daisy attempted to hide her smile. "I'm glad you settled it. Did you move back home?"

Foster nodded. "Jonas has been great about everything."

Iris called from the doorway. "Daisy, our guests are asking when you're going to announce the raffle winners."

Daisy motioned to the plates that Eva, Cora Sue, and Tessa were readying. "As soon as we serve dessert, I'll announce the winners."

"I'll spread the word," Iris told her.

Karina entered the kitchen, and she and Foster began putting dessert plates on trays to carry out to the tea rooms. On each plate sat a small shoofly tart, a peanut butter cookie, and a slice of hazelnut cake.

Daisy stood in the doorway of both tea rooms ready to announce the two raffle winners when the front door opened and Chloie Laird stepped inside. Daisy groaned inwardly. Tessa, who had come out to stand behind the sales counter for the announcement, stood stock-still in surprise as Chloie unsteadily made her way forward. Daisy suspected she had been drinking something *other* than tea.

Chloie pointed to Tessa and yelled, "You don't deserve a cent of Reese's money. *I* should have been executor. I'm the one who knows everything about the works in the gallery and Reese's clients."

Since Tessa seemed frozen on the spot, Daisy stepped toward Chloie. "You don't

371

want to do this here," she determined in a quiet, calm voice.

"Where else am I going to do it?" Chloie yelled. "Tessa was just the flavor of the month. I could have been executor. I could have had twenty-five percent of Reese's estate. I could have started my own business."

A few of the tea tasters were obviously put off by Chloie's behavior. They stood and headed for the door. Others seemed to be fascinated and were looking back and forth from Tessa to Chloie, maybe hoping for more fireworks.

Daisy knew she could be asking for trouble, but she was hoping Chloie's grief had just gotten the best of her.

Stepping close to Chloie, she kept her voice low. "I know you miss Reese. I know your heart hurts. But I don't think you want people to remember you or him like this." She circled Chloie's shoulders with her arm. "Come on, Chloie. I think you need fresh air."

Daisy beckoned to Karina, who she knew had an attitude as if she wasn't afraid of anything. She asked Karina, "Can you walk Chloie up and down the street so she can get her bearings?"

Karina nodded, took Chloie by the elbow,

and led her to the door.

Cora Sue rushed to Karina with her coat. Karina thanked her and led Chloie out.

To Daisy's dismay, however, she noticed several women had their cell phones out and had apparently recorded the whole scene. Just what she needed — someone uploading it to social media.

Quickly she raised her voice. "I'm going to announce the raffle winners now. I have their names right in my pocket."

Daisy reached into her pocket and pulled out the first winner. "Tara Watson from Camp Hill, PA."

Tara, a short woman in her thirties, raised her hand and yelled, "That's me. Which one did I win?"

"You won the Double Wedding Ring quilt."

The young woman jumped up and down and shouted, "Oh, I can't believe it. I never win anything."

Daisy pulled the second name out of her pocket. "Our second winner is Rena Jacobs from York, PA. Is Rena here?"

Rena waved both hands above her head. She was an older woman, probably in her fifties, with springy gray hair and bright red glasses. "That means I won the Log Cabin quilt. Oh, my goodness."

Raising her voice again above the chatter, Daisy explained, "As soon as you're finished here, you can pick up your quilts at the Covered Bridge Bed-and-Breakfast. Amelia will have them packaged for you and ready to go."

There were a lot of disappointed faces in the room. "I know many of you wish you had won the quilts. I wanted to spread the news that the Tumbling Blocks Inn on Hickory Avenue will be auctioning off two quilts to the highest bidders." Daisy checked her watch. It was almost three. "The auction will start at three-thirty, which will give you plenty of time to finish your desserts and sip the rest of your tea. Walk down this block and turn left at the intersection onto Hickory. The Tumbling Blocks Inn is one block down."

In spite of what had happened, Daisy said, "I hope you've enjoyed your afternoon tea with us. We'd be glad to serve you anytime. Please come back again."

After many good-byes, and "Everything was delicious," and "I'll be back for some of those shoofly tarts," the tea rooms emptied out fairly quickly. They'd been closed to customers while the afternoon tea had been served, but now Cora Sue turned the OPEN sign around in the window again.

The first one through the door wasn't a customer, though. It was Karina. She took off her coat and hung it on the clothes tree in Daisy's office.

Daisy went there to talk to her. "How did it go?"

"Chloie started crying, so I took her into Dutch's and sat her down and bought her a cup of coffee. She needs lots of coffee."

"She wasn't driving, was she?" Daisy asked.

"No. She called a friend who came to pick her up."

"Thank you so much for handling her. I didn't want a scene that would be worse than it already was."

Foster ran in from the tea room. "I don't know if this is good news or bad news, but you're on Twitter and other social media sites. The bad news is you don't want the tea room to be known for discontent. But, on the other hand, any publicity can be good publicity."

Daisy just groaned.

Tessa had come to join them and just as she was about to give her opinion, her cell phone played from her pocket. She closed her eyes for a moment and Daisy suspected her friend was worried Detective Rappaport was calling again. However, when she glanced at the screen, a puzzled look crossed her face. She took a step away and answered it.

Two minutes later, shaking her head, she came back to Daisy. "The alarm went off on my storage compartment. Someone cut the padlock. By the time security got there, whoever it was was gone. But now I have to go through the inventory list."

Tessa looked at Daisy. "After we close, can you go with me? I'll get it done a lot faster."

Aunt Iris butted in. "Go with her now, Daisy. You've both been here since five o'clock this morning. The rest of us will handle cleanup and any customers who wander in. I'll take Jazzi home with me when I leave."

Daisy's gaze went from her aunt Iris to Foster. "Are you sure?"

Foster was nodding too. "It's probably a good idea. Why don't you text Jonas where you're going to be. He'll be worried if he stops in here again and you're not here."

Jonas had stopped in several times during the day to check on her. Each time, she'd given him a thumbs-up sign and he'd left quietly, not wanting to distract from the tea service. She appreciated that thoughtfulness. She appreciated him.

Crossing to the clothes tree, she plucked off her jacket, then handed Tessa her poncho. "I'll meet you there. I'll text Jonas in the car before I leave."

After all, she'd be with Tessa. She didn't need more than one bodyguard. Did she?

CHAPTER NINETEEN

Just why had Tessa's storage locker been broken into? Obviously, there must be something there that the killer wanted. Daisy assumed it was the killer. Was it?

Tessa met her at the gate that had a key card lock and opened it for her. Anyone who rented a storage space received a key card. This was a small center with maybe fifty units. All of them were eight-by-ten and padlocked shut. Tessa had bought the padlock from the center itself. But bolt cutters could have released the lock.

Perhaps this break-in had nothing to do with the killer at all. Anyone could know Tessa had stored the contents of the gallery somewhere if they had watched and followed her when she and Eric were packing up.

Suddenly this puzzle seemed unsolvable.

As soon as the gate closed, Tessa jumped into Daisy's car and directed her to her storage locker. The gravel crunched under Daisy's wheels.

Tessa was staring out the windshield and appeared lost in thought.

"Did it look like anything is missing?" Daisy asked.

"Not at first glance. And I don't know what to think. Was this a thief who wanted art? Or was this the killer who tried to frame me?"

"I asked myself the same questions and didn't have an answer. How about you?"

Tessa shook her head. "All I know is that I'm weary of all of it, and there doesn't seem to be an end in sight."

Five minutes later, Tessa had pushed up the door to her rental locker and Daisy stepped inside. She was glad she'd worn her scarf and had her gloves. It was almost as cold inside the locker as outside of it. Tessa had switched on a high-powered lantern so she could see to do an inventory.

Before Daisy could ask the question that was in her mind, Tessa answered it. "There isn't anything in here that the cold will hurt. I sent all the watercolors back to the artists, or else they picked them up. The sculptures, bronzes, and oil paintings will be fine."

"Do you have your inventory list? I can check off the items as you call them out."

Tessa wore leather gloves that were skin-tight. She was also wearing a knit hat pulled down over her ears and a scarf around her neck. Her wool poncho almost draped to her ankles with the faux-fur trim. "The security guard said he'd check on us in a little while."

"Do you think you should call Rappaport?"

"What could he do? If I find anything was stolen, I'll call him. Let's get this over with so we both can go home and get warm."

Most art pieces were boxed so their owners could pick them up or Tessa could send them. As Tessa called out an ID number and a description, Daisy checked off a two-foot tall vase painted with cattails. As Tessa unboxed the next item, Daisy reboxed the one before it. The system worked well and they were soon halfway down the list.

Next they checked off a ceramic lamp, the base appearing to be an Amish hat. It was simple yet profound. It was kind of ironic, too, since Amish didn't use electricity. Even New Order Amish used gas lamps and battery-powered lanterns.

There were several painted and shellacked gourds. A few resembled cats, others resembled snowmen. Some were simply artistic in nature, painted with a pineapple or flowers.

There was a hand-carved and painted door topper depicting an Amish scene. Tessa also carefully unpacked blown glass vases and compotes. Swirled colors inside the glass made each piece unique.

Finally Tessa stood over the last three big boxes. "These contain items that were in Reese's storeroom," she said. "I had Eric pack them up and make a list for me. That way it won't be difficult to search through them if an artist wants to pick them up or if I have to send them. If Cogley had just given me another couple of weeks, this whole thing would have been much easier."

Tessa ran her gloved finger over the tape on the box. "This looks as if it might have been opened then resealed. But I can't be sure because I did that myself to a few boxes when I decided to add another piece." She sighed. "Do you think what Jimmy Standish said at the funeral home was true, and Cogley's trying to buy up land around here for development purposes?"

"I've always known Jimmy to be truthful," Daisy responded. "Maybe Cogley resented Reese losing him a piece of property by helping a farmer. What I wonder," Daisy mused, "is if Reese helped others. Maybe this was more than one farm deal gone bad."

Tessa ripped the packing tape off the

cardboard box. After she opened the flaps, she reached inside. "For the most part, these are bronzes." As she named each one, she set them atop another box. Among the statues was a farmer at a fence, several horses in a pasture, and a little boy reading a book.

"I like that one," Daisy said, pointing to the little boy.

"I'm sure the artist will accept an offer."

Daisy smiled. "I'm too cold to think about it now. Let's keep going."

Next Tessa unwrapped brown paper that had been wound around the replica of a barn. It too was bronze with an enamel bird-of-paradise hex sign painted on the front. As soon as Tessa saw it, the barn slipped through her fingers and Daisy caught it.

"That's like the murder weapon," Tessa exclaimed.

"What do you mean, it's like the murder weapon?" Daisy asked, realizing she hadn't seen the murder weapon. Tessa had always referred to it as a bronze.

"The bronze I found behind my painting looked just like this."

"Are you sure it's like the murder weapon?" Daisy persisted. "Because there are replicas of barns for sale in many of the gift shops in Willow Creek — all sizes and designs."

Tessa hesitated for a second. "Maybe it isn't exactly the same. I was in shock the day I found it. I wrapped it in that towel as fast as I could."

As Daisy examined the barn, something she couldn't quite figure out niggled at her thoughts. Hadn't *she* seen one somewhere else? Maybe in the gift shop at the Covered Bridge . . . maybe at the Tumbling Blocks Inn? In conjunction with the Quilt Lovers Weekend, she'd stopped in at many businesses. It could have even been a decoration or for sale in the flower shop.

But if she could remember specifically where she'd seen it, would that be another clue?

Tessa was looking at the barn in Daisy's hands as if it could bite her. She reached into the box again and pulled out another barn smaller than the first. After reaching into the box a third time, Tessa pulled out an even smaller version. "They must have come in a set of three."

The sad and lost expression on Tessa's face alerted Daisy that there might be something she could do to help. "Come on," she said to Tessa. "Let's finish the inventory. And I have a suggestion."

In spite of the cold and reddened cheeks, Tessa looked pale. "What?"

"I think you should come home with me and stay with me and Jazzi tonight. Wouldn't you feel more comfortable and safe with us than in your apartment above the empty tea garden?"

"I usually like the solitude. I usually like being alone."

"Tessa," Daisy said gently.

"But tonight coming home with you seems like a good idea."

Daisy had decided to keep the tea garden open until one o'clock on Sunday. There was a forecast for snow that evening. Any Amish businesses would be closed today. The Quilt Lovers Weekend was still going on for the English stores and shops. She didn't expect a large crowd because it was the end of the promotion and because of the possible snow. When she'd asked who on her staff wanted to work on Sunday morning, her whole staff agreed. It was easy to see, though, by midmorning she'd be sending some of them home early.

Spending the day with her grandparents, Jazzi had gone to church with them, out to brunch, and then would be helping her grandmother cook dinner tonight when

Daisy would join them.

Suddenly the door flew open and eight women chattering and laughing burst into the tea garden. "Are you still serving?" the tallest asked.

"We are," Daisy told her. "We're open until one."

"We're all staying at the Tumbling Blocks Inn. We were here yesterday and really loved your food. Can we have soup, scones, and tea?"

"Coming right up," Daisy assured the group. She and Tessa, Iris, and Eva were holding down the fort. The group of women were pleasant to serve. Daisy learned they were all from Chambersburg and had carpooled for the weekend.

"We want to get home before the snow starts," the tallest, whose name was Edna, said. "According to my Weather Channel app, we have two hours or more until that happens."

The women easily talked about their children, their jobs, and asked questions about the tea garden and Willow Creek. They sounded as if they might come back soon, and that was one thing this weekend was all about — drawing in tourists. The group didn't even mention Reese's murder, and Daisy was glad for that. On the other hand, that meant the news cycle wasn't mentioning it, either. If it didn't stay in the focus of the public eye, would Detective Rappaport push to solve it? Or would he rush to make Tessa the scapegoat?

Daisy was returning to the kitchen for a refill of green tea when her phone played.

Eva joked, "You can't mistake that sound for anything else."

Daisy smiled when she saw a text had come in. It was from Jonas. Closing the store at one. Going home to change. Meet me at the Zook barn at one-thirty?

Tessa had come into the kitchen. "I don't think they want to leave. They like our tea and scones, not to mention the soup."

Daisy frowned.

"What's wrong?"

"Jonas asked me to meet him at the Zook barn at one-thirty. I'd like to go home and change first. Maybe I should ask him to wait until two."

"Nonsense, get going. You have just enough time. The sky looks like it's going to release the snow at any moment. I'll close up with Iris. You've certainly covered for me the past couple of weeks."

"All right," Daisy agreed. "Why don't you give those women one of our coupons for a free scone? That might draw them back here sooner rather than later."

"Good idea," Tessa said. "Now get going. Maybe if you and Jonas are alone for a little while, you'll get back on a romantic footing."

"You think that's what I want?"

"Isn't it?"

"I think I do, but that depends on Jonas, too."

"Text him back before he thinks you're not coming."

Daisy did. Then she went to her office, shrugged into her jacket, said good-bye to Aunt Iris and her staff. The Zook barn was located about two miles down the road. She could easily arrive there by one-thirty.

At home, Pepper and Marjoram were awake and that meant that they wanted time and attention. But she didn't have either to give them right now if she wanted to be on time for Jonas. Both of the cats followed her to her bedroom where she changed into warm clothes — a color-blocked pullover in burgundy and navy along with navy wool slacks and fleece-lined shoe boots. She imagined the barn would be as cold inside as outside, especially if it was falling apart.

Instead of her cat-patterned fleece jacket, she exchanged it for her yellow down jacket with its white faux-fur-trimmed hood and sleeves. A yellow and navy scarf Violet had given her for Christmas was stuffed in one pocket while her navy leather gloves were in the other. Jazzi had given her those.

Pepper meowed at her. Marjoram, who had disappeared for a few minutes, came running in with her favorite toy that could be filled with catnip. It was a little green turtle.

"Okay, let's make a deal," Daisy told them.

They both sat back on their haunches and looked up at her, Pepper with round golden eyes, and Marjoram with slanted golden ones. They were waiting for her to negotiate.

"I'll fill your turtle with catnip," she told Marjoram. To Pepper she said, "And you can sleep on my bed, if you'd like. You know this is the brightest room when it's a dull day outside."

Both felines kept their gazes on her.

"Okay," she said in surrender, throwing up her hands. "I'll give you treats before I leave — three Greenies. How's that?"

Pepper meowed, turned, and headed toward the kitchen. Marjoram followed her, turtle in her teeth. If there was one word they understood above all, it was "treats."

After Daisy filled the turtle with catnip, she put an equal amount of treats in both of their dishes, ran her hand down both their backs, and threw them kisses on her way out. Feline babies could be as demanding as real ones if you understood them. She thought she did. She wasn't sure if that was good or bad.

Daisy was in her purple PT Cruiser, driving down her lane, when she realized she would be a few minutes late. But just a few minutes. As she stopped at the intersection of her lane and the rural road, snow began to fall. That had started a little earlier than the app had said it would. She and Jazzi joked about it all the time. Daisy checked the app. Jazzi said she'd just go outside and see what the weather was doing.

Right away Daisy could see that the snow was going to lay. Well, she was only driving two miles from her home, and certainly they wouldn't be collecting the wood today. The last time she talked with Jonas about it, he said he just wanted to mark the wood that he'd like to use. That shouldn't take too long. Maybe she'd ask him to join Jazzi and her parents for dinner. If he said "yes," then maybe she'd be sure he wanted more than a simple friendship.

When Daisy arrived at the barn, she didn't see Jonas's SUV. She parked on the gravel, already frosted with snow. She could sit outside in her car with the heater on. Then again, Jonas probably wouldn't be too long. She could just go inside and have a look around. One of the doors was completely missing from the dilapidated barn. She had Jonas's permission to be here, so she wasn't trespassing.

Once inside the barn, she took a good look around. Grayish light shone through the windows and through the separated timbers that looked as if they could fall apart. She could tell there had once been three horse stalls and a tack room.

Looking up at the hayloft, she could see wisps of hay lying across the boards, and she thought she glimpsed a bale or two. Could a barn like this be restored? She was sure there was history in its walls.

When she glanced to the left, she spotted a decorative star lodged against the wall. The barn and the star made her think about the barn that was wrapped up in Tessa's storage shed — the bronze barn with the hex sign that Tessa said was like the murder weapon. A flash of something intangible Daisy couldn't quite catch flickered in her mind.

When she concentrated on the two barns again, she had it. She remembered where she'd seen matching barns! On the bookshelves in George Beck's office. Hadn't Tessa said that they must have come in sets of three?

Only two had sat on those bookshelves — a small one and a medium-sized one. And the large one?

Shivers rippled up her spine. What if she was wrong? But what if she was right?

She took out her phone to call Detective Rappaport. As soon as she did, she heard footsteps behind her. She turned and found George Beck pointing a gun at her.

CHAPTER TWENTY

Daisy froze. Staring down the barrel of a gun emptied every thought from her head.

"Did you remember?" George Beck asked.

"Remember what?" For a moment, Daisy felt almost dizzy with fear. Panic squeezed her heart. Where was Jonas?

Beck was wearing jeans and shoe boots with leather soles. His jacket was open and she could see his sweatshirt underneath. Possibly the adrenaline running through him and whatever he'd planned was keeping him warm enough.

She was freezing.

"You went into my den to make your phone call. You talked about the classics that you saw there. But that wasn't all that was on that shelf."

Pulling her wits about her, Daisy attempted to compose herself. She had to stay sharp and focused if she was going to get out of here alive. "I saw owls there too, if that's what you mean."

"Not only owls," he insisted. "There were two bronze barns there. Apparently, you didn't associate them with the murder weapon."

"Murder weapon?" She knew she couldn't just keep parroting his questions, but it was all she could do for now.

"I know you saw that treasure I left in Tessa's attic. The two of you called Detective Rappaport to come get it."

"I didn't see the murder weapon that day. If I had, I might have connected it to you and called Detective Rappaport. Why come after me when the police didn't come after you?"

"Because you would have made the connection eventually. The description of the murder weapon would have come out sometime, even if Tessa didn't show you or tell you."

"Did you follow me to the bed-and-breakfast?"

"I have trackers on your car and your van. One on Tessa's car, too. All I have to do is check my app to know your whereabouts at any time. Sometimes I do the surveillance in person, like the day I hid the murder weapon up amongst Tessa's paintings. I wouldn't have wanted to miss out on all the fun."

"You're crazy!" She wished she had made the connection between the murder weapon and the barn and George Beck's shelves last night. "Why did you break into the storage shed?"

"Because I knew Reese had another set of those barns in his inventory. He told me that when I bought my set from him. If anyone found them and connected them to the murder weapon, they could have gone through his receipts and discovered I'd bought the other set before Christmas. If the security guard at the storage center hadn't been making his rounds and interrupted me, I would have found the other set."

She could see Beck had tried to cover all his bases. But she still didn't know the answer to the most important question. "Why did you kill Reese? I thought you were friends."

"I couldn't let him ruin my life."

That statement alerted Daisy that Beck had *his* secrets too.

Daisy dared to look around the barn again and up to the hayloft. If Beck didn't have Jonas tied up somewhere, maybe the text had been bogus. It hadn't been from Jonas.

It had been from George Beck. Had he stolen Jonas's phone?

But first things first. She slipped her hands into her pockets as if they were cold. She felt for her phone.

Beck waved the gun at her. "Give me your phone, and don't press anything. You're the type who would want to record this conversation and you're not going to do that. Do you think I'm stupid?"

She was so angry that she just had to goad him. As she passed the phone to him, she said, "Anyone who commits murder can't be very smart."

If he lunged at her, maybe she could get away.

But he didn't lunge. He stayed steady although his face did turn red. Blood pressure going up? It was too much to hope he'd have a stroke.

"You have to butt into everything, don't you?" he asked.

"Not everything," she murmured. Then raising her chin she asked, "Did you know about Reese's past as a doctor?"

"I did. We were baring our souls one night. His sorry story came out when he let it slip about taking painkillers and losing his profession. I should have held my tongue about what I was into. I guess I really didn't know what kind of man Reese was at that point."

"What kind of man was he?"

"He had scruples."

"I don't understand."

"You don't have to understand. You're going to be dead. You won't care."

When Daisy had reached into her pocket for her phone, she'd felt her keys there. There was a panic button on them. A teapot charm hung right beside the panic button. As she felt for the charm, she realized it wouldn't do any good to push the button if no one was around to hear it. It could be a distraction for Beck, but she had to do it at the right time. She'd only get one chance.

"If you're going to kill me, I want to know why. Sure I know you're the murderer, but I don't know what happened. Maybe I *am* a nosy busybody, so satisfy my curiosity before you get rid of me."

Beck eyed her as if she was playing some kind of game. But he must have decided there wasn't anything she could do in her situation. "Abner Cogley was a thorn in Reese's side. The man hated Reese because Reese was helping farmers in the area keep their farms. Cogley wanted to buy them cheap for development purposes. When a farmer hit hard times, Cogley swooped in."

"I heard that Reese helped out one of the farmers," she commented as if they were having a normal conversation.

"He'd been a doctor," Beck said. "He'd made good money even though he had to split it with his wife because of the divorce. He helped out more than *one* farmer. He'd lost his profession and his family and had to start over. Because of that, he didn't want to see it happen to others."

"So you had a connection to all of this?" She still wasn't seeing the motivation for Beck murdering Reese.

"I'm Cogley's accountant. That night Reese told me about the painkillers, I stupidly confided in him that there was a reason Cogley was rich. He'd cheated. Reese was too smart for his own good. He guessed that I was keeping two sets of books for the man, one for the IRS and one set with the true transactions."

"What were those transactions?"

"You mean other than compromised land deals? Cogley paid out bribes for rezoning. He inflated rents and only reported a portion of what he received."

"I still don't understand what Reese had to do with it."

Apparently, Daisy's playing devil's advocate didn't please Beck. His face reddened again. "I told you, Reese had scruples. He wanted me to report Cogley to the authorities. Talk about stupid. He kept telling me I could get immunity if *I* reported it."

Beck shook his head. "I was more afraid of Cogley than the authorities. The night I killed Reese, he'd threatened to go to the police himself about Cogley's dealings. Cogley was trying to buy up property that had been in a Lancaster County family for generations, and Reese insisted he couldn't let him do that. *I* couldn't let Reese turn Cogley in because then I'd be ruined too. Even if I wasn't prosecuted, my life as I knew it would be over. Tanya wouldn't stick by me. She only likes successful men. Starting over would have been too hard for her."

"Maybe you underestimated her. Maybe you're wrong. Maybe she would still stick by you if you go to the police and tell them Reese's death was an accident." She was reaching for straws but she had to do something. "Maybe you could tell them it was self-defense."

"What excuse would I have for rolling up the body in a rug, putting it in Reese's SUV, and then driving out to the covered bridge? That doesn't look like self-defense."

"You panicked. You were just trying to cover it up. If you murder me, too, you'll definitely go to prison for life."

"Yes, but if nobody knows you're murdered, I won't have to worry anymore. If only you hadn't gone into my den and noticed that barn."

"Doesn't Tanya know it's there?"

"Sure, she does. But she doesn't know a bronze barn was the murder weapon. The police kept that detail from the public. If they ever reveal it . . ." Looking sad, he stopped. "Then I might have to eliminate Tanya, too." His mind seemed to shift gears. "It's time to stop talking. It's time to get this over with."

Daisy was about ready to run and take her chances when George gestured toward the hayloft with his hand that wasn't holding the gun.

"Up to the hayloft, Mrs. Swanson."

"Why would I want to go up there?"

"Everybody knows you have a barn home. You were looking around this one to see if it could be restored instead of torn down, and you just happened to have a terrible accident. It was really lucky I stopped in at the tea garden last week and overheard Cora Sue and Karina talking. They were saying once the Quilt Lovers Weekend was over, you and Groft would start dating again. They were all atwitter because coming to the Zook barn could be romantic."

He motioned to the hayloft once again. "Go on, climb up that ladder."

Beck was too close. The gun was pointed at her heart or her midsection where it could do a lot of damage. But if she went up to the hayloft?

"Do it *now,*" he said in a rougher voice.

She was afraid if she didn't, he'd shoot her right there. There was a soulless look in his eyes, and she guessed she couldn't talk her way out of this. Maybe she could kick him after she started up the ladder.

But kicking wasn't an option. He kept that gun trained on her and he followed her up the ladder at a safe distance for him.

As she stepped onto the hayloft's floor, she considered swinging around and pushing him down the ladder. She couldn't just push the ladder away because it was bolted into the floor. That made it safer for anybody climbing up. But not for her.

Beck seemed to be particularly agile, though his foot slipped on the top rung of the ladder. She thought she had her opening and started toward him. He caught himself and waved the gun directly at her stomach again. "Get back. Get over there to the hayloft opening."

"Why over there?" She was wearing

rubber-soled boots and glad of it. The straw on the wood could be hazardous. The last thing she wanted to do was slip and end up prone.

"Stop asking questions!" he shouted.

She took a couple of steps toward the hayloft opening. The wood was crumbling away from the edge just as the rest of the barn was deteriorating from the weather. Taking a deep breath, she tamped down her fear. "I'm not going to jump."

"Then I guess I'll have to push you out. If the fall doesn't kill you, then I *will* have to shoot you and head south to bury you. Nobody will find you. I should have buried Reese, but I thought I could frame Tessa and not go to all that trouble."

Somehow she had to get that gun away from Beck. Somehow she had to use the slippery straw. Beck was wearing those leather-soled boots. She could make this happen. She could.

After reaching into her pocket to find the teapot charm, she centered her thumb on the panic button next to it. She'd only have an instant to react — an instant to move. She had to do this right or he would kill her. Her feet were planted as solidly as they could be.

"You don't want to do this. You really don't."

But Beck wasn't listening to her . . . rather he was listening to some instinct inside of him that said he *did* have to kill her.

She pressed the panic button.

It was loud and ear-splitting, and it was hard to tell exactly where the noise was coming from. Distracted for a moment, Beck looked around. She took the opportunity to move. She ducked but he stepped forward to grab her and push her out. She managed to tear away from him, almost falling out the hayloft opening. But she grabbed on to the wood along the side.

Beck pointed his gun at her, stepped forward to reach for her, but she tore away. His leather-soled boots slipped on the straw. She tried to grab him but it all happened so fast. He fell out of the hayloft into the falling snow, his arms flapping as his body dove to earth.

Daisy was scrambling down the ladder to check on Beck . . . to see if he was still alive, when she heard the wail of sirens. Someone had called the police. How? Why?

As she reached the door of the barn, three cars were pulling onto the gravel. The first was Detective Rappaport, who ran to George Beck. Two officers jumped out of the second car and hurried after him. And in the third car? It was Jonas's car and Tessa was with him.

While Jonas ran to Daisy, taking her into his arms and squeezing her tight, Tessa followed the detective.

Jonas murmured into her neck, "I was so afraid for you."

She just wanted to stay in his arms, but she had so many questions. She pushed away slightly. "How did you know to come?"

Jonas continued to hold her, looking down at her with something different in his eyes. She wasn't sure what. Clarity, maybe?

He cleared his throat. "I stopped at the tea garden to see if I could take you out for dinner. Tessa said you were headed here for a meeting with me. Immediately we knew it was bogus."

Tessa returned to them, shock on her face. "The murderer was George Beck!"

"Did George steal your phone?" Daisy asked Jonas.

After he absorbed the news of the identity of the killer, he answered. "He didn't have to. There are ways now, Daisy, to mask a real number and to fake another number. He probably messaged you from a burner phone but used my number. Since Tessa knew where you supposedly had gone, we took the chance, hopped in the car, and called Rappaport."

Speaking of the detective, the three of them looked over at him. He'd stood and was nodding his head. "We were closing in and he probably knew it. An ambulance is on its way."

Jonas brought Daisy tight into his body again and kissed her. Whatever their relationship was going to be, Daisy was glad to have Jonas Groft in her life.

Epilogue

Violet was back in town the following weekend. She'd come home on Saturday and they were all up very late that night talking about everything that had happened. At Vi's urging, Daisy had invited Foster and his family to dinner on Sunday. While he and his dad helped in the kitchen, Violet, Jazzi, and Foster's brother and sister played Cat-Opoly in the living room. Pepper and Marjoram looked on with curious interest. Every once in a while, Violet or Jazzi would throw the dice on the floor and both cats would race after them, pawing them like soccer balls until everyone was laughing.

Daisy had baked a ham this evening. Jazzi and Vi had asked for mashed potatoes and Foster was whipping those while Gavin carved the ham. Daisy was tending to the cauliflower made twice as good with cheese sauce. She'd baked loaves of yeast bread yesterday to go along with the meal.

After Foster switched off the mixer, Daisy pointed to the yellow ceramic bowl on the counter. "Just spoon them into that and then set it on the table. If you can, you can round up everybody."

"Is Jonas coming?" Foster asked.

"He's supposed to be here. But whenever he gets here, there will still be plenty of food to eat."

Foster nodded. "That's for sure. If we were at home and made mashed potatoes, we'd be eating out of the mixer bowl."

Daisy laughed as Foster spooned the whipped potatoes into the serving bowl and then took it to the table and set it on a trivet.

After Foster went into the living room, Gavin pointed to the ham. "All sliced."

"And I'll have a good bone for ham and bean soup, too."

"Is that hard to make?" Gavin asked.

"Not at all. You can even do it in a slow cooker if you use canned beans. I'll write down the recipe for you."

"I'd like that. I'm ready for the meat platter if you have one."

Daisy produced a white ironstone platter that matched her dishes.

Gavin forked the ham onto the plate. "I want to apologize for the things I said to you. I overreacted."

406

"I know how hard it is to be a single parent. I understand."

"That's still no excuse for my rudeness or for thinking I knew about Foster's life when I didn't."

"Our children can't tell us everything. And as they get older, they don't want to. I think they feel keeping things to themselves makes them more adult."

"I'm grateful for the solution you suggested. I don't want Foster to have to pay for living under my roof, but if it gives him more responsibility and makes him feel like an adult, that's what matters."

Daisy nodded. "He's really a terrific young man."

"That he is."

After Gavin had finished transferring the ham from the carving board to the serving plate, he shook his head. "I keep thinking about George Beck's son and the heartache his father's actions will cause him and his mother."

"I know. George was fortunate he didn't break more than his leg, arm, and collarbone when he fell."

"The snow probably cushioned his fall. What are the charges against him?"

Detective Rappaport had stopped by the tea garden on Friday to talk to her and

Tessa. Since the charges had been entered into the public record, he'd explained them. She related them to Gavin. George Beck would be charged with aggravated assault, criminal attempted homicide, and second-degree murder, to name the most serious.

"Foster told me about Reese being attacked at the gallery before he was murdered. Was that George Beck, too?" Gavin inquired.

"No. The police got to the bottom of that. Reese had a meeting with Dutch Pickel that night. Dutch was the one who assaulted him. Reese had decided to stop paying Dutch to keep his past a secret. Dutch was blackmailing him."

"I read in that newspaper article that fraud was involved too."

"I don't know much, but the detective told me they did find discrepancies in Cogley's books and there are charges of fraud and tax evasion pending against him."

"That was a good interview Tessa Miller did with Trevor Lundquist. If anyone *did* think she was involved in the murder, that should put those thoughts to rest."

"Trevor wrote about her and the situation in his online blog, too. All that has helped her to recover her standing in the community."

Foster had somehow managed to coax everyone to the table. They were all ready to take their seats when the doorbell rang.

"I'll get it," Daisy said, hurrying toward the door before anyone else could.

When she opened the door, she found Jonas there, holding a bouquet of pink roses. Daisy hadn't spoken to Jonas much all week. He'd stopped in at the tea garden a couple of times but they really hadn't talked, so she hadn't known exactly what he was thinking or feeling. Now, however, with him holding out the pink roses to her, she saw that look in his eyes that she'd noticed last Sunday at the Zook barn — clarity.

"I hope I'm not late." His mouth quirked up a bit.

"You're just in time. We're ready to sit down to dinner." But before she could move toward the dining area, he caught her arm.

"Daisy, I know this probably isn't the best time to say this, but almost losing you twice has shown me we have to live for today."

"What does that mean?" Her heart was beating so hopefully that she could hardly breathe.

"It means that I'd like to take you skiing and then to dinner and then for hot toddies or whatever else we'd like. What do you say?"

Daisy stood on tiptoe and placed a kiss on his lips. As she backed away, he surrounded her with his arms, roses and all.

She gazed into his eyes and answered his question. "I say *yes.*"

■ ■ ■ ■

ORIGINAL RECIPES

■ ■ ■ ■

DAISY'S CINNAMON SCONES

Preheat oven to 400 degrees.

2 cups all-purpose flour
1/3 cup granulated sugar plus 2
  tablespoons
1 teaspoon cinnamon (1/2 teaspoon in
  dough and 1/2 teaspoon mixed with 2
  tablespoons sugar)
1 teaspoon baking powder
1/4 teaspoon baking soda
1 teaspoon salt
8 tablespoons (1 stick) frozen unsalted butter, grated (I let it sit unrefrigerated 5–10
  minutes before grating.)
3/4 cup cinnamon chips
1/3 cup ground pecans
1 large egg
3/4 cup reduced-fat buttermilk

In a large mixer bowl, stir together flour,
1/3 cup sugar, 1/2 teaspoon cinnamon, bak-

413

ing powder, baking soda, and salt. Add grated butter to flour mixture and beat it in. Stir in cinnamon chips and pecans.

In a separate bowl whisk the egg with the buttermilk, then mix into flour dough with mixer. Scoop out eight large scones (I use a 1/4-cup scoop or measuring cup with handle) and place on a cookie sheet lined with parchment. Sprinkle with cinnamon/sugar mixture. Bake 17–19 minutes at 400 degrees until golden brown.

BEEF BARLEY SOUP

1 pound beef stewing cubes (cut in small
  pieces)
1/2 cup onion
3 tablespoons high heat sunflower oil
1 quart Swanson chicken broth
1 quart Swanson beef broth
1 cup water
1 bay leaf
1/8 teaspoon pepper
1 cup sliced carrots
1 cup sliced celery
1 cup zucchini, peeled and sliced
1/2 cup Quaker quick barley

In soup pot, brown stewing cubes and onion
in three tablespoons sunflower oil. Add
chicken and beef broth, water, bay leaf, and
pepper. Bring to a boil. Turn to simmer with
lid on pot for 1 hour. Add carrots and
celery. Simmer for 20 minutes. Bring soup
to a boil and add zucchini and barley. Cook

another 15 minutes at a low boil.

Serve with your favorite crusty bread . . . or scones!

Serves 6 to 8.

LEMON-PEPPER TOMATO MOZZARELLA SALAD

3–4 cups cherry tomatoes, halved (I like to use assorted colors.)
1/4 cup scallions, chopped (These can be omitted or just used as topping depending on your taste.) Use bulb and first inch of green.
4 ounces fresh mozzarella, cut into bite-size pieces (It comes in many forms — small or large balls and a log shape, sometimes sliced.)
1 1/2 tablespoons lemon pepper
1/4 teaspoon garlic powder
1/4 teaspoon onion powder
1/4 teaspoon sea salt
2 tablespoons sesame oil
4 tablespoons white wine vinegar

Mix cherry tomatoes, scallions, and mozzarella. Sprinkle with lemon pepper, garlic powder, onion powder, and sea salt. Stir gently to coat mixture. Drizzle with oil and then vinegar. Stir again. Refrigerate and serve when dinner is ready!

Serves 6.

ABOUT THE AUTHOR

Karen Rose Smith is the author of seven Caprice De Luca home-staging mysteries. Married to her college sweetheart, Karen has convinced her husband that felines can make purr-fect housemates. They share their home in the Susquehanna Valley of Pennsylvania with their three rescued cats. For more about Karen, please visit her website www.karenrosesmithmysteries.com.

The employees of Thorndike Press hope you have enjoyed this Large Print book. All our Thorndike, Wheeler, and Kennebec Large Print titles are designed for easy reading, and all our books are made to last. Other Thorndike Press Large Print books are available at your library, through selected bookstores, or directly from us.

For information about titles, please call:
  (800) 223-1244

or visit our website at:
  gale.com/thorndike

To share your comments, please write:
  Publisher
  Thorndike Press
  10 Water St., Suite 310
  Waterville, ME 04901